Snares without End

Snares without End

By Olympe Bhêly-Quénum

translated by Dorothy S. Blair

Introduction by Abioseh Michael Porter

CARAF BOOKS

University Press of Virginia

CHARLOTTESVILLE

This is a title in the CARAF BOOKS series

© Présence Africaine 1978
(original French version: *Un Piège sans fin*)
© Longman Group Limited (English version) 1981
This edition of *Snares without End* is published
by arrangement with Longman Group UK Limited, London.

UNIVERSITY PRESS OF VIRGINIA

Introduction to this volume
Copyright © 1988 by the Rector and Visitors
of the University of Virginia

First published 1988

Library of Congress Cataloging-in-Publication Data

Bhêly-Quénum, Olympe.
[Piège sans fin. English]
Snares without end / by Olympe Bhêly-Quénum ; translated by
Dorothy S. Blair ; introduction by Abioseh Michael Porter.
p.   cm. — (CARAF books)
Translation of: Un piège sans fin.
ISBN 0-8139-1188-5.   ISBN 0-8139-1189-3 (pbk.)
I. Title.   II. Series.
PQ3989.2.B5P513   1988
843—dc19   88-7301
                                        CIP

Printed in the
United States of America

I dedicate this book to Maryvonne
and Marie-Antoinette Quénum.
O.B.Q.

Know and believe firmly that your
life must be a continual death.

The Imitation of Christ

In certain almost supernatural
states of mind, the depth of life is
revealed in its entirety in the
spectacle that lies before our eyes,
however commonplace this may be.

Baudelaire

O Thou who didst with Pitfall and with Gin
Beset the Road I was to wander in,
Thou wilt not with Predestination round
Enmesh me, and impute my Fall to Sin?

The Rubáiyát of Omar Khayyám

Contents

Acknowledgment   viii

Glossary   ix

Introduction   xi

Snares without End   1

Acknowledgment

For the tale recounted by old Dâko in chapter 15 the author is indebted to M. Maximilien Possy-Berry-Quénum who revived interest in the traditional folklore of Dahomey with his book, *Au pays des Fons*.

Glossary

agouti: a species of large rodent, of the size and approximate appearance of a hare, living in the bush and hunted for its meat.

akassa: a stiff dough made from corn flour, wrapped in banana or cassava leaves; part of the basic diet in Benin (Dahomey).

asen: a sort of portable shrine or altar which can be deposited in a place where it can symbolize the presence of the dead, to whom offerings of water, alcohol, and sacrificial blood are made when required.

balafon (or *balafong*): a kind of xylophone.

boubou: a long, loose outer garment, worn by men and women in West Africa.

calalou (or *caloulou*): a rich, rather sticky, highly spiced sauce.

corporation: "with the beginning of a corporation" is a colloquial British expression meaning "slightly potbellied."

Dahomey: the former name of what is now the People's Republic of Benin, capital Porto-Novo. The name, according to legend, is derived from Dan-ho-mê, meaning "On-the-belly-of-Dan," from the story of the assassination of the king of that name by Aho, the founder of the kingdom of Dahomey.

dé-votchi: a malformed fruit of the palm, which develops no hard shell or kernel and so has no consistency; used metaphorically to refer to a futile undertaking.

Fon: the main ethnic and linguistic group of the southern region of Dahomey (Benin). The Fons are considered by the more primitive people of the north, particularly the peasants, as oversophisticated and shrewd.

fonio: a species of millet, part of the staple diet of the people of Benin.

griot: the professional musicians of West Africa; they are singers, poets, storytellers, chroniclers, acrobats, and general entertainers.

Jonu: a funeral wake which takes place two to three months after the burial.

kpété: a reed flute.

legbà: a protective, anthropomorphic spirit, modeled out of clay.

maize: corn, in British usage.

mâro: a market held after nightfall, as opposed to the normal daytime market.

naseberry (or *sapodilla*): large evergreen tree yielding edible fruit about the size of an apple and with the taste of a medlar (also called sapodilla plum).

pagne: an undergarment worn by men and women, usually draped around the waist.

sigi: a game of dice, played on a stool in which a certain number of little holes are pierced. The players move sticks along these holes as the game progresses.

tôba: a sort of small harp made of bamboo.

zogbodogbé: a fair-day on which certain fetishist sacrifices are also made.

Introduction

On the surface, Olympe Bhêly-Quénum seems to share some distinct affinities with Ahouna, the protagonist of his major work of fiction, *Snares without End*. Bhêly-Quénum, like Ahouna, became convinced of man's inhumanity to man quite early when, at about ten years of age, he saw an accused murderer who was not only shackled to a cross but also was paraded in front of a vengeful and bloodthirsty crowd calling for the accused man's immediate death. One can also surmise, based on the evidence of Bhêly-Quénum's other works, that the author, like his leading characters, believes in the overwhelming power of forces beyond human control as well as the need to blend the positive aspects of both traditional Africa and modern Europe. But this is where the resemblances between Bhêly-Quénum and Ahouna, Kofi-Marc (in *L'Initié*), and the other leading characters end.

In spite of Bhêly-Quénum's constant references to and fondness for the countryside and rural folk, he was born into a middle-class household in the city of Cotonou, Benin (then Dahomey) on September 26, 1928. His father was a schoolteacher. After graduating from elementary school in 1942, he traveled for quite a while within Dahomey itself before settling down for three years in Ghana, where he learned English while working for a British firm, John Walkden and Co.

Bhêly-Quénum went to France in 1948, and although he became ill and was bedridden for about a year, he was able to complete the various stages of the prestigious *baccalauréat* by 1954.

Introduction

A man of encyclopedic learning and very widely traveled, Bhêly-Quénum has been awarded several university degrees and diplomas, including one in literature from the University of Caen in 1957, and others in diplomacy, journalism, and sociology from the Institut des Hautes-études d'Outre-Mer and the Sorbonne.

In addition to writing for several journals and newspapers, Bhêly-Quénum served as an editor for two journals, *La Vie africaine* (1962–65) and *L'Afrique actuelle* (1965–68). In 1962 he also held administrative positions with the French foreign service and the Dahomeyan diplomatic service in Italy (Genoa, Milan, and Florence) before finally joining UNESCO, for which he still works in Paris.

To students of West African fiction, it may seem strange that Bhêly-Quénum's works—unlike those of his contemporaries such as Camara Laye of Guinea, Sembène Ousmane of Senegal, Chinua Achebe of Nigeria, Mongo Beti and Ferdinand Oyono of Cameroon—have received very little critical attention. What might make this lack of attention even more surprising is the fact that not only was Bhêly-Quénum among the pioneering writers of modern francophone African fiction, but he was also one of the few such writers whose works spanned the decade of the sixties through the late seventies.

On closer examination, however, it becomes obvious that, from the moment he started writing, Bhêly-Quénum's fiction did not fit into what might be called the dominant mold of francophone African fiction; and critics have consequently treated his works with benign neglect. But in order to understand the full implications of this statement it is necessary to look briefly at the sociohistorical environment from which Bhêly-Quénum and most of his francophone colleagues came and some of the major themes found in the works of these other authors.

Historically, the French began their colonial conquest of West Africa with the appointment of Louis Faideherbe as Governor of Senegal in 1854. From that time right on to 1910, the French overpowered other countries in the region such as the Ivory Coast (1886), Guinea (1887), and Dahomey (1894).

Introduction

Precolonial Dahomey was divided into three kingdoms—
Abomey or Dahomey and Porto Novo in the south and Bariba
in the north—which were peopled, in turn, by the country's
three major ethnic groups: the Fon, the Goum, and the Bariba. The north-south division of the country (which is quite
evident in *Snares without End*) came about as a result of mi-
gratory movements and settlements of the various inhabitants
of the country and its surrounding regions.

The north was settled by people of almost the same cultural
and ethnic background; the southern regions were populated
by members of different ethnic groups who nonetheless—
through conflict, subjugation, and interethnic marriage—became a cohesive group, even though ethnically heterogeneous.
Furthermore, the north-south division became even more
apparent with the introduction of French colonialism and
the French system of education. Because the north was pre-
dominantly Moslem—which meant that there were Koranic
schools already in place—and because the area was more
rural and conservative, it was more difficult to establish West-
ern-type schools and attitudes there than in the coastal south.

One other issue about precolonial Dahomey that is of significance to readers of *Snares without End* is that of political
administration. Because in traditional Dahomeyan society the
ruler of a clan, ethnic group, or even kingdom had to have ancestral ties with both the place and the people he was govern-
ing, he shared a certain sense of belonging and understanding
with his subjects.

But once Dahomey and other countries became colonies of
France, absolute power was vested in the hands of the colonial
administration headed by the governor and, to some extent,
his subordinates (the district commissioners, commandants,
and local chiefs). The latter, who often were chosen by the
French to represent French interests, were also at the mercy
of their overlords, as we see in Bhêly-Quénum's description of
the treatment meted out to Hourai'nda—the local chief of
Ahouna's village—by the local commandant. The introduction of forced labor, payment of poll taxes, and military con-
scription (all of which figure significantly in *Snares without*

Introduction

End and the sequel to that novel, *The Song of the Lake*), was a direct consequence of the absolute power the French and their allies held over the majority of the Africans.

Furthermore, French colonialism pursued the policy of *assimilation*, whereby an artificial and pernicious distinction as *l'indigénat* ("the natives") or as *les citoyens* ("the citizens" of France) was made among African inhabitants of these countries. According to this division, *l'indigénat* (who actually were the majority of Africans in the colonies) were uneducated, dispossessed, and hence unworthy of either representation in the French National Assembly or French citizenship. The citizens, also called the *assimilés* (who represented only a tiny fraction of the population), on the other hand, were the educated Africans who were trained for middle-level positions in teaching, administration, and other areas in their respective countries. As part of their training, however, this group of Africans was taught untruths, such as the absence of any history or culture in Africa. In brief, they were encouraged not only to exalt everything that was French but to look down on Africa and its culture.

But the years preceding and succeeding the Second World War (especially between the thirties and the fifties) brought a complete change in attitude among these formerly francophile colonials. Beginning in the 1930s, black African and West Indian intellectuals (such as Léopold Sédar Senghor of Senegal, Aimé Césaire of Martinique, and Léon-Gontran Damas of Guiana)—who, as we can expect, had been thoroughly schooled in their native countries about the virtues of French (and European) rationalism, common sense, and order—found themselves in a Europe where fascism and racism were on the rise and where evidence of man's inhumanity to his fellow man was manifesting itself in very frightening ways. Not surprisingly, these highly sensitive, educated, and articulate colonials started expressing views that not only negated the hitherto-accepted (even though false) notions of white supremacy but also praised quite highly the virtues of black cultural values through the philosophy of negritude.

Introduction

Parallel to this celebration of the beauty and value of Africa and its culture was a consistent denunciation of colonialism and its concomitant evils.

It should thus come as no surprise that most francophone African authors writing in the fifties and early sixties produced works that were particularly anticolonial (and, at times, anticlerical) in tone and that often stressed the vitality of black culture. For example, Camara Laye, in *The Dark Child* (1954), uses his early childhood experiences as a backdrop for the presentation of a very positive (some might even say idealized) picture of traditional life in Africa. Mongo Beti in both *The Poor Christ of Bomba* (1956) and *Mission to Kala* (1957) and Ferdinand Oyono in *The Old Man and the Medal* (1956) and *Houseboy* (1956) focus on such topical issues as the relationship between the colonizer and the colonized (which in this case means the relationship between European and African), the role of the church in a colonial society, and the irrelevance of the colonial type of education to Africans. Indeed, by 1960 Sembène Ousmane extended the anti-imperialist and anticlerical themes by adding a class dimension to them in his masterwork, *God's Bits of Wood*.

Because *Snares without End* (which was published originally in French in 1960, the year in which the greatest number of African countries become independent), deals only tangentially with the anticolonial and other political themes, it is perhaps understandable, if not wholly acceptable, that the majority of critics would have adopted an indifferent attitude toward the novel. Bhêly-Quénum shows a clearly anticolonial bias in scenes such as the one in which Bakari, the well-respected father of the novel's protagonist, is forced by the colonial administration to do unpaid and degrading hard labor or when, later on in the novel, Toupilly, the racist French prison official, subjects African suspects and prisoners to the worst forms of physical and verbal degradation; nevertheless, the author never handles this theme with as much gusto or passion as most of his contemporaries did during that period.

The decade of the sixties was, of course, one of great expec-

Introduction

tations for Africans. As subsequent history has shown, how-
ever, due to both internal and external forces, many of the as-
pirations and hopes of the African peoples were not realized.
Consequently, African novelists such as Chinua Achebe in
No Longer at Ease (1960) and *A Man of the People* (1964),
Sembène Ousmane in *The Money Order and White Genesis*
(1965), Wole Soyinka in *The Interpreters* (1968), Ayi Kwei
Armah in *The Beautyful Ones Are Not Yet Born* (1968),
Robert Serumaga in *Return to the Shadows* (1968), and Ahma-
dou Kourouma in *The Suns of Independence* (1968) all turned
their ironic focus on postindependence Africa. Through vary-
ing degrees of self-examination, these authors presented a
picture of the continent that was not pretty—indeed, they
showed Africa as a place where the "Beautyful Ones [Were]
Not Yet Born." But even a sketchy summary of *The Song of
the Lake* (1965)—Bhêly-Quénum's second novel—will show
that, there again, the Beninois author was not to subscribe to
the dominant thematic thrust of the time.

    The Song of the Lake is set years after the conclusion of
events in *Snares without End*. In the introductory section of
the novel, we meet Houngbé who, as one of the conspirators
in the burning death of Ahouna in the earlier novel, had been
"punished" by being sent to fight for the French during World
War II. Just before Houngbé dies on board a boat that is
taking him back to Dahomey from France, he expresses to
a dozen young Dahomeyan students going home on holidays
his desire to liberate his people from the superstitious knots
that have tied them to the lakeside gods that have not only
been occupying the peoples' lake but have actually been intimidating them. Although the students vow to end this form
of religious enslavement (thereby fulfilling the wishes of their
newfound hero), and although a local politician, Cocou Ouhénou, also attempts to bring about a politically independent
and superstition-free world for the people, it is the politician's
wife, Noussi Ouhénou who, with her children and a boatman,
is finally able to expose the "gods" of the lake as nothing more
than water snakes.

Introduction

What is particularly impressive about this story is the way Bhêly-Quénum has skillfully developed a Fon myth into a modern novel dealing with the conflict between the traditional, at times superstitious, world of a people and the outside world of strictly rational, scientific thought. He also introduces a dilemma that will not be foreign to most educated Africans, when, at the end of the story, he leaves the clear impression that even though the forces of modernity have won and the people can no longer fear the "gods" of the lake, there is still some lingering doubt about tampering with time-honored traditions or beliefs in such a manner.

The conflict between the forces of good and evil is given an additional twist in Bhêly-Quénum's most recent novel, *L'Initié*, published in 1979. In this work, the struggle is between Kofi-Marc Tiongo, who—as a French-educated medical doctor and a locally trained expert in parapsychology and traditional African medicine—represents the true forces of progress, and an old villager who also claims to be practicing traditional medicine and parapsychology, but who is actually a charlatan.

Kofi-Marc who, when quite young, had demonstrated some extraordinary qualities as an *abiku* (i.e., a spirit-child who is born to die but who is reincarnated several times in the womb of his mother), is endowed with some supernatural powers by his uncle, Atché—a man whose name means power. From the outset, the old man makes it strictly clear to his nephew that a major criterion for the favorable use of such powers would be the need to use them only for serious purposes (in other words they should be used as life-giving or life-preserving instruments and not as mechanisms for intimidating or exploiting people).

After his return from studying in France, Kofi-Marc and his French wife, Corinne (who is also a medical doctor), set up a clinic where they offer genuine medical assistance to the local people. In fact, Kofi-Marc (whose name is, no doubt, symbolic of the cultural synthesis he is trying to achieve) combines his knowledge of both traditional African medicine and para-

Introduction

psychology with Western medicine to cure the sick. It is because of this, however, that he comes into direct conflict with Djessou (whose name means death), a religious fraud, who has been using his pseudoparapsychology to exploit the people.

The clash between Kofi-Marc and Djessou comes to a head not too long after a local religious ceremony, when Djessou realizes that his fraudulent conduct will soon be exposed by the more sincere Kofi-Marc. In several scenes involving the use of fabulous and inexplicable powers, the charlatan seems to be winning this classic battle (for example, in one episode Djessou apparently deprives Kofi-Marc of all flesh, leaving him only as a skeleton), but in the end it is the forces of good (represented by Kofi-Marc) that win. Bhêly-Quénum obviously makes the point in this novel that a sincere blend of good traditional African culture and beliefs and Western science can produce only good results.

As we can see from these examples taken from his major novels, Bhêly-Quénum has often refrained from dealing with purely topical (or even the most popular) themes. Thus, even when he decided to use a theme that has remained quite popular among African authors—tradition versus modernity—as the main subject of *The Song of the Lake,* he did it at a time when most of the other writers were increasingly turning their attention to the more overtly political themes of African literature: political and economic corruption, inequality in the distribution of wealth, social and class stratification, neocolonialism, and so forth.

The point is not that critics of African literature merely follow the fashion of the moment and ignore works that do not conform to the dominant or most popular thematic pattern. Indeed, criticism has served African literature very well. Consequently, some scholars might be quick to maintain that there are now so many different "schools" of critical thought that it is absurd to suggest (as I have done) that a writer like Bhêly-Quénum has not received his due share of critical attention because he has refused to jump on any thematic bandwagon.

Introduction

The point, however, is that critics of the African novel have developed a tendency to focus almost exclusively on only a few, well-established authors. In addition, and perhaps more significantly, even though one publishing house (and it is still just one publisher among many) has published more than a hundred and twenty novels by Africans, scholars still have the inclination either to treat only a few masterpieces as "the African novel" or to regard all African works of fiction as having uniform characteristics. In other words, because most critics of African literature have continued to look at this literature only in terms of the major divisions into fiction, poetry, and drama, they seem to forget the contributory role the gamut of genres and subgenres can play in the creation of uniquely African literary types. Thus, a critic like Eustace Palmer, in his two volumes *introducing* and discussing the *growth* of the African novel, does not give even one example of the existential novel—a category that certainly would have taken into account at least one of the following: *Snares without End,* Malick Fall's *The Wound* (1968), and Peter Palangyo's *Dying in the Sun* (1967).

It is necessary to stress this dearth of genre criticism properly adapted to written African literature because it helps to explain not only why so little has been written on Bhêly-Quénum but also why even some of the few critics who have written on *Snares without End* have at times been only lukewarm in their praise of the novel. One suspects that because some of these critics have not given enough consideration to the subject of genre in their interpretations of the work they have not been able to appreciate it in its entire perspective. Thus, Dorothy Blair, in an otherwise fine and detailed discussion of the original French edition of the novel, states that "the incoherence, the unconvincing nature of some of the episodes, the lack of focus on the main character might be attributed to a deliberate attempt to propound the theme of the absurd, which has no consistency."[1] Similarly, Willfried F. Feuser

[1] Dorothy Blair, *African Literature in French* (Cambridge: Cambridge University Press, 1976), p. 255.

Introduction

(who, like Blair, recognizes affinities between Bhêly-Quénum's work and those of European existentialist writers such as Dostoevsky, Kafka, Camus, and Sartre), suggests that "despite certain deficiencies in psychology, style and structure, . . . this first novel is powerful evidence of human anguish suffered by homo africanus."[2] Still another critic, François Salien, goes even one step farther than Feuser, who does not bother to give *Snares without End* much discussion. Writing in a French-language dictionary of African literature, Salien maintains that this Bhêly-Quénum work—despite its existentialist leanings—is not really a novel. Deploring the lack of proper character development and an inordinately long and incoherent second half of the text, Salien sees this book as an essay focusing on the emptiness of human existence.[3]

This is not the place to enter into a discussion of what constitutes a novel. It is my opinion, however, that *Snares without End* is Bhêly-Quénum's attempt to wrestle in fictional form with the problem of existentialism—a peculiarly twentieth-century phenomenon—in an African context. In order to see why I think this work succeeds best as an existentialist novel, we should perhaps look at some of the more fundamental traits of existentialism as a philosophical concept.

Reduced to its bare minimum, existentialist philosophy has the following general characteristics: (*a*) it emphasizes *existence* rather than *essence;* (*b*) it rejects the certainty of an external universe; (*c*) it views life as something meaningless, since it leads only to death; (*d*) it does not accept human reason as being capable of explaining the puzzle of the universe; (*e*) there is also a feeling of complete meaninglessness in a world that only breeds loneliness, anguish, and despair; (*f*) finally, existentialists try to objectify or externalize nothingness, i.e., they attempt to reify the state of nonbeing.

[2] Willfried F. Feuser, "The Works of Olympe Bhêly-Quénum: From Black Anguish to the Mastering of Dark Forces," *Présence africaine* 125 (1983): 187 (my English translation).

[3] François Salien, *Un Piège sans fin,* in *Dictionnaire des oeuvres littéraires négro-africaines de langue française,* ed. Ambroise Kom (Sherbrooke: Naaman, 1983), pp. 601–4.

Introduction

Even a brief consideration of *Snares without End* in the context of these basic characteristics of the existentialist novel would show why this Bhêly-Quénum work succeeds as an example of the genre. In addition to specific events and statements in the text, Bhêly-Quénum gives us some cues right at the beginning of the novel to the kind of fictional universe he has created.

It is no coincidence that the three epigraphs he uses are from authors who stress existential themes. They appear throughout the writings of Thomas à Kempis and Omar Khayyám. In the specific passages quoted from *The Imitation of Christ* and *The Rubáiyát* (with their emphasis on the rejection of determinism), as well as the quotation from Baudelaire, one finds a good number of themes characteristic of modern literary existentialism: the futility of life and the tenuousness of hope among them. In *The Imitation of Christ*, Thomas à Kempis lists, among other things, several virtues that any true Christian should practice: modesty, humility, selflessness, prudence, obedience, mutual love, and so on. He also suggests that in order to receive divine love, humans must be prepared to accept God as the only source of real consolation in this otherwise perilous world. If one has the understanding that earthly pain and injustice are just fractions of Christ's suffering for all humankind, it becomes easy to see why one's "life must be a continual death." It is this kind of selfless devotion, shown by Abraham in the Old Testament or Christ in the New Testament (and suggested by the epigraphs), that is often stressed in the writings of Christian existentialist philosophers such as Søren Kierkegaard and Gabriel Marcel.

Because Bhêly-Quénum is a devout Catholic and is thoroughly familiar with European culture, it should not surprise readers of *Snares without End* that he uses the Thomas à Kempis and Baudelaire quotations to hint at an essentially religious, especially Christian, form of existentialism. We should remember, however, that Ahouna is a northern Moslem (who, in the midst of his tribulations, even exhibits some agnostic tendencies). Thus, to forestall any potential objec-

Introduction

tions Bhêly-Quénum also quotes from *The Rubáiyát*, a piece of devotional literature from the Moslem world that, like *The Imitation*, emphasizes religious existentialism. But it is the events that take place in the novel, coupled with Ahouna's behavior, that provide and sustain the work's existential bent. Critics have uniformly praised Bhêly-Quénum for his depiction of both characters and events in the first half of the novel. Reflecting what is perhaps the majority view among critics of this work, Dorothy Blair says: "The first part [of *Snares*] has more unity of action and of tone than the second part, where the interest that should be intensified with the tragedy closing in on Ahouna is dispersed over a number of incidents, with secondary characters taking the centre of the stage."[4]

It is views such as these that convince me that critics have misinterpreted *Snares without End* because they have failed to give consideration to its genre. If the assumption were true that this is just another tragic novel written in the realist tradition of eighteenth- and nineteenth-century European fiction and dealing with a heroic individual who is either overwhelmed by ill luck or (in the manner of Thomas Hardy's heroes) destroyed by hostile forces inherent in a society that he cannot understand, then such criticism might be valid. Bhêly-Quénum makes it obvious from the outset, however, that we are not merely going to be dealing with a protagonist whose life in an almost idyllic, pastoral setting is brought to a premature end through a series of vicious setbacks. The novelist shows that the question of existence is going to be the central concern for Ahouna when, at quite a young age and in the bucolic and peaceful surroundings of his hometown, Kiniba, the boy evokes existence in a song he learned from his Fon playmate. In it he makes this comparison between himself and the elephant:

> It's just the same with the elephant: He is happy just to exist and is unconcerned with the little creatures round him. He asks no more than to live with his father to a

[4] Blair, *African Literature*, p. 254.

Introduction

certain age. What can others do with me or against me?
Men who are by nature bad, what can they do against me
in this world I live in? Nothing! They too are mortal
creatures like me. (p. 8)

Indeed, this preoccupation with what constitutes existence
and with other issues such as the meaninglessness of human
activity, the failure of reason to explain human behavior, the
attempts to codify nothingness (all existential themes) per-
meates the novel.

When, at the beginning of the novel (but much later in
the story's chronology), Ahouna is providing information
about his family background to Monsieur Houénou, Ahouna
launches quite unexpectedly into a short philosophical dis-
course: "How I envy those people whose existence is uneventful, even and transparent as the panes of glass in your
window, set between two rows of metal bars; a life devoid of
misery and misfortune such as they say the abode of Allah to
be. I also admire those people who deny that evil exists at all,
and think themselves clever enough to convince others that
this is so" (p. 15). It was probably passages such as this one
that led Salien to conclude that *Snares without End* is merely
a philosophical essay. But unless we want to restrict ourselves
to the traditional and rather narrow definition of the novel as
an extended piece of realistic prose fiction that has a coherent
beginning, middle, and end and in which the problems regard-
ing the central characters are all resolved at the end, we should
have no problems accepting Bhêly-Quénum's work as a very
good existential novel.

Whether it is Mariatou, Ahouna's mother, consoling the
young boy after his father's suicide by describing life as a "series of nameless absurdities" or as a "wasteland of rotting refuse, in which men devote their energies to futile, vain things"
(p. 38) and Mariatou again affirming that "everything in life
is cruel, inhuman and unreasonable" (p. 44); or Camara
making comments such as "life is quite ridiculously absurd"
(p. 40); or Ahouna himself speaking of "the vanity of man's
existence, of the futility of all the reasons we give for our exis-

Introduction

tence, of the meaninglessness of everything in human life"
(p. 108), Bhêly-Quénum constantly has the characters articulate the existential themes of the work.

Furthermore, we notice that, like other existentialist authors such as Sartre in *Roads to Freedom* and Camus in *The
Stranger,* Bhêly-Quénum views the determination of human
destiny as something irrational; and like his fellow novelists
also, he allows his protagonist to conquer absurdity itself by
gradually gaining knowledge of the absurd fate that plagues
all human life.

Now, if we accept that a work of existentialist fiction is
one in which (among other things) human reason does not explain everything and the irrational side of human nature and
the meaninglessness of human activity are emphasized, then
Snares without End is indeed a fine African example of that
type of fiction. Numerous references are made to characters
questioning the very nature of existence; moreover, we also
see how many actions and events that take place within the
text cannot simply be explained away by logic and common
sense. There are, of course, the natural disasters, including the
deaths of the livestock by anthrax disease and the destruction
of the plants by locusts, but events start taking a more bizarre
and inexplicable dimension soon after Bakari is driven by his
tormentors to commit suicide.

It is ironic that, in an almost perverse way, Bakari's death
temporarily brings harmony and bliss into his household:
Séitou, Ahouna's long-departed sister, rejoins the family fold
with a husband and children who are loving, caring, and
understanding. Ahouna himself gets married to Anatou, a
belle from a neighboring village, and they soon begin raising
what looks like an ideal family. But a few years after Ahouna's
marriage to Anatou, he discovers that (to use his own meta-
phor) the "orange" known as Anatou (pp. 60, 64) is a very
bitter one. Quite suddenly and inexplicably she wrongfully ac-
cuses Ahouna of infidelity, becomes extremely hostile toward
him, and harangues him until he finally has to abandon his
home and family.

Introduction

These series of unmotivated actions continue to manifest themselves in an ever graver manner after Ahouna's departure from Kiniba. First, he notices how "a veritable army of tiger-beetles" (p. 109) senselessly devour a dead man; then, in a state of utter confusion and irrationality, he murders Kinhou, the woman from Zounmin, whose cry he mistakes for his wife's. From this point on, Bhêly-Quénum's protagonist confronts a world that becomes more and more devoid of inherent meaning to him (and perhaps the reader). The novelist uses incidents such as the weird dream of the archaeologist, Monsieur Houénou, about excavating in Ahouna's native Kiniba, Ahouna's strange (even if modern) journey to Calvary, the insensate behavior of some of the jailers (Toupilly especially) and prisoners (Boulin and Affognon), as well as the behavior of some of Kinhou's survivors, to stress the lack of logic that pervades Ahouna's universe.

In Bhêly-Quénum's hands, the young, sensitive, and artistic Ahouna becomes a convenient instrument for examining (as he has Ahouna say) "the futility of [one's] existence, the vanity and vacuity of all the actions [one] had ever performed and [is] still performing" (p. 85). In truth, Ahouna seems to be calling attention to at least one major theme (if not the major theme) when he says: "Emptiness, the only thing that really exists, for the very reason that it is all around us, had become palpable. I could touch it with my finger" (p. 85).

It should be understood, however, that in stressing the novel's existentialist qualities, one is not somehow overlooking its weaknesses or the possibility of reading it as a work belonging to another subgenre, such as the domestic novel. Even if one is not prepared to go so far as to suggest that sensitive, intelligent, but illiterate African farmers cannot philosophize, it is obvious that *Snares without End* has some serious flaws.

Some of the characters' statements and actions strain credulity. Let us, for example, look at M. Houénou's appeal (translated from the Fon language) to Ahouna to come back after the latter has fled from Houénou's house in the dead of night:

"I was telling Ahouna to come back. We are all strangers on earth, seeking everywhere for true happiness. Where is it? How can one recognize it and grasp it? No one knows! But come back Ahouna, my brother, come back. You must make a fresh start, and it is here in Zado, that the path to happiness opens up for you, maybe" (p. 117). One also finds it difficult to grasp the significance of the "acute knowledge" that Houénou claims to use in apprehending some local thieves (p. 119). In addition, Dorothy Blair rightly points out that the "digressions into ethnic lore, as with the descriptions of different funeral rites and the introduction of the moral fable told by Dako to his family to warn them not to play with danger also detract from the desired atmosphere of terror and tension in a world dominated by invisible, inimical powers." [5]

But, while it is true that *Snares without End* is not a flawless novel, it is also no exaggeration to say that Bhêly-Quénum has attempted to create a world in which the very nature of the African's existence (on both the literal and the philosophical level) becomes the primary subject of discussion, and that, to a large extent, he has been successful. This makes the novel, even for now and certainly for the time it was written, worthy of more consideration. Dorothy Blair deserves our highest commendation for an excellent translation.

Abioseh Michael Porter
Drexel University

[5] Ibid., p. 256.

Snares without End

Chapter I

He was of medium height. Poverty and hardship had shrivelled his skin, robbed it of its lustre and reduced his frame to a skeleton. His face was like that of a child wizened by malnutrition, and his beard was grimy with dust, damp with sweat and spittle. I met him one day in the course of my long journeyings through Dahomey and was so struck by his appearance that I went up to him. In the dark gleam of his eyes I read the story of a fugitive in fear of pursuit and intimations of an uneasy conscience. I smiled at him and to my great surprise he started, about to take to his heels, but I reassured him, speaking instinctively in the Fon language, 'I'm not from the police, you can take my word for it. Don't be afraid; come with me. I can see that you're hungry.'

He nodded and followed me to my farm at Zado, where I offered him our traditional hospitality. He washed and ate with uncommon appetite the food I set before him. Only then did my guest volunteer his name and, fetching a deep sigh, lowered his eyes as if the tale he was about to begin was a tissue of lies. But as he launched into his story and felt himself relive his life, his gaze met my eyes steadily and unflinchingly.

'I am a child of Founkilla,' he began. 'I no longer have a father; my mother is still alive. My father's name was Bakari. He was big and sturdy. Like all men from the northern areas he wore his hair close-cropped revealing a clean and glossy head; his beard was always neatly trimmed – not unkempt like mine is now. He owned cattle and flocks of sheep and goats which he herded himself, like most of the people from his tribe. He also owned a large field which Tertullien later estimated to be about fifty-five acres in extent.

He sowed our land with maize, millet, *fonio*, beans and groundnuts; we planted cassava, sweet potatoes, yams.

We also had – oh, we still have – a little vegetable garden and an orange grove.

My mother – poor old Mariatou – also comes from the north. She is tall and supple with muscles rippling under her black skin like carved ebony, and she has a small round head on which her hair is always neatly braided in the fashion of the local women. Her eyes are fine and black with clear, shining whites. I am said to take more after her than my father, which makes me very proud as she is really beautiful. How I loved to sit and feast my eyes on her.

Bakari and Mariatou had two other children: my brother Bouraïma and Séitou, my sister. Bouraïma died when he was seventeen, just after the end of the 1914–1918 war. He caught a terrible sickness brought by people from the southern areas when they fled to the north in search of peace and to build up their fortunes again, after they had lost everything in the disasters which had overtaken them. As for Séitou, her story is like that of many of our pretty, hot-blooded local girls.

One day, eight or nine years after Bouraïma's death, when I was about ten and Séitou was going on for nineteen, a white man arrived in Kiniba from the south. His name was Monsieur Tertullien. I never knew what his job was ... He saw Séitou and took a fancy to her. He made advances to her, which she fell for. Then Tertullien asked the local chief to arrange with my father for Séitou to accompany him when he went back to the southern areas, to work for him and be his mistress. The necessary arrangements were made and Tertullien returned to Cotonou with my sister. For some time he continued to send my parents presents and even occasionally money. From Cotonou the couple went on to Cameroon. Fifteen months after they left Kiniba I heard that my sister had given birth to a son. We were all very pleased, and as for me, I walked on air for a whole year, so delighted was I to be an uncle. Two years after the birth of my' nephew, whom they called Rémy, my sister had twins: Jean-Claude and Mireille. Six months after this happy event father went to see the children and their parents in the south.

There he learnt from Séitou that her 'husband' had gone back to France leaving her and his children. He was furious that his love-making had resulted in a brood of half-caste kids, and made it clear that they brought shame and humiliation on him. According to him, in his country it was a disgrace for a white man to set up family life with a black woman. In spite of father's insistence my sister refused to come back and live with us in the north, where we were prepared to lavish on her and the three children all the care and affection we were capable of – as indeed we did in due course.

Tertullien stopped writing and sent nothing to support his children, so Séitou was forced to take on the most menial work, even to prostitute herself, to bring them up. Then one day a young man from Conakry came to Cameroon, saw Séitou and fell in love with her. Camara took her and the children back to his own country where they were married. I shall return to this episode which had a very great influence on my adolescence.

So, when I was ten years old I lived with my parents as if I was an only child. I hated this as I saw how selfish other only children became though some of my friends envied them. Camara also told me about youngsters like this that he knew, and even now I can't help hating all older brothers and sisters who act as if they were only children just because they are the eldest. This made me regret that my parents had not had more children or that my father was not polygamous. But rivers cannot run backwards; what can't be cured must be endured; and so my childhood was spent sharing the farmwork with my parents, helping with the sowing and harvesting the crops and taking the animals out to graze.

We would set off for the field at daybreak with our hoes on our shoulders and our machetes in our hands, the wet grass sprinkling our feet and our half-naked bodies with dew, so that we were fully awake by the time we reached the field.

There, we weeded and cut down the undergrowth. I can still see the tall grass and scrub falling under the furious blows of our machetes. All useless growth gave way before us as we cut our way into the thick bush that overgrew the land.

When father invited friends to help us, the work was much more fun. The machetes rose and fell, cutting deep gashes into the thick green jungle; the steel blades clashed, glinting in the sun, as in a war dance. Sometimes the women joined in, working with as much determination as the men. They set about the undergrowth as if it were a personal enemy, with a vindictiveness that they would only equal if they grew into embittered, neurotic old maids or jealous wives, taking offence at imaginary slights. I found their onslaughts quite terrifying to watch. Any youngsters of seven or eight who were around would have the job of singing and beating time with a stick on the blade of an old hoe, or often just using two sticks. Their music cheered us up and made the work go surprisingly fast.

So we kept just ahead of the sun which rose from a corner of the field in front of us, behind a huge baobab or an enormous bombax or a gigantic kapok-tree – according to which part of the field we were clearing. The sky would now be flooded with golden light, and the birds who in the early hours of the morning had greeted our departure without enthusiasm now filled the whole universe with their joyful chorus. By now the sun's rays beat down on our bowed backs and heads were bent towards the ground.

We straightened up for our midday meal: boiled yams, grilled cassava and fried sweet potatoes brought out to us by mother, who had been busy with her accustomed domestic tasks while we worked in the field. We also ate coconuts, or groundnuts roasted in hot ashes or cooked in the sand, and there was always plenty of fruit.

When we heard mother calling we dropped our tools where we stood and rushed towards her, dripping with sweat, with beating hearts and empty bellies. She served us, joking and laughing, while everyone congratulated her on her husband's rich land.

'I'll bet that Bakari loves his land as much as his wife,' said Assanni.

Snares without End

'His fields make up for all the women he loves but keeps away from, as he's decided against polygamy,' said Anoutcha, Boubakar's wife.

'That's what you think! Bakari is the worst polygamist in Kiniba,' Mouctar would retort. 'He's married to his herd of twenty cows and his thirty goats.'

Everyone laughed and chattered, gobbled and drank and then we went back to work with renewed zest. The sun took its relentless course across the sky. Beads of sweat stood out on our foreheads; sweat dripped from our bodies on to the reddish-grey soil from which arose wisps of steam as we cut our way through the bush.

At the end of the day mother had again prepared a meal for us: calabashes of couscous, maize porridge, millet, cassava, dishes of *calalou*. As we waited to be served, we feasted our eyes on the abundance of chicken and goat's meat, floating in these highly-seasoned sauces. Mother also brought us grilled *agouti* with *akassa* balls, seasoned with ground pimento and served with slices of tomato and onion, salt and lemon ... When we had eaten our fill, the surrounding fields echoed with our laughter and our shouts of satisfaction.

Life was good, existence easy. We worked till nightfall, then father and I returned home with the other men who worked for us and who had shared our evening meal.

Six or seven days spent working in this way were sufficient to clear our fifty-five acres. Then the ground was left exposed to the heat of the sun for a week, after which father and I went back and lit an enormous bush fire. What a sight that was! We raked the dried grass, branches and weeds into huge heaps with forked sticks, then we set fire to one of the heaps, from which we kindled all the other heaps with a bunch of burning twigs.

In an instant the brushwood began to snap and spark; the dry wood crackled; the green wood hissed and spluttered; the fire spread, scorching mounds of grass, igniting piles of branches, burning up everything in its path. It roared, heaved, rumbled, boomed like thunder, rending the air with each detonation. The wildfire raced on in a blaze of sparks. Panic-stricken birds and insects rose up from the ground and took flight. Other birds, less timorous, wheeled above the flames, snapping up the insects in flight.

Naturally we were helped by the wind. When it died down for a few moments, where our field had been we could see only a wilderness of dense, blood-red flames moving between an invisible earth and a vast canopy of opaque black smoke.

We watched the fire till it burned itself out on the boundary of our land where ditches acted as firebreaks.

A week later we returned to the field with the same workers to help us. We were armed with machetes, and with hoes which were more use for the job we now had to do.

Often we set out very early in the morning when the sun, as the saying goes in my country, 'was still asleep in the jaws of the crocodile under the horizon' and had not yet tinged one corner of the sky with red. Grasping the handles of our large-bladed hoes, we stooped down and the work began. The blades dug deep, turning the fertile soil. Bending down, legs apart, we crept forward like caterpillars, breaking up the whole field into deep furrows between high parallel ridges. As we advanced resolutely, a diaphanous haze rose from the ground and mingled with the sweet, indefinable smell of the newly turned earth.

How long did this work last? A week? Two weeks? I cannot remember. I only recall women following us like our shadows, some armed with stakes, some carrying calabashes full of seeds. And this is how it was to be much later when I was a grown man and married with a family of my own, and working on my father's lands which I inherited. Some of the women made little holes with their sticks in the tops of the ridges while the others dropped a few seeds into each hole and covered them with a light tap of their heel; that is how they did the sowing.

In a few days the first delicate green shoots broke through the earth. My parents and I then proceeded to plant slips of manioc, yams and sweet potatoes between these, each in their own patch. Further on we sowed a few rows of beans and groundnuts.

Sometimes, during the sowing season, the weather was pleasantly cool. We used to start out before sunrise in order to get as much work as possible done during daylight. Sometimes the sun never shone at all; a fine, steady, cool drizzle would fall; however the birds would still sing in the trees while we happily went on planting. The gay, green carpet of the cereals spread as far as the eye could see, lending an inexpressible zest to our labours, and the thought that we should be returning in a few months to this same field, to harvest a crop which showed every sign of being abundant, filled our hearts with joy.

With our simple workclothes sticking to our skin, we gave no thought to the blinding rain that drenched us. Mother would break into a lively, catchy song and father and I would join in the chorus:

> *Kaï! Kaï batâ na n'dé!*
> *Ka nabé, touâ, magan nan!...*
> *Tcha! tcha! tcha!... tcha! tcha!... tcha! tcha!*
> *tcha!*

When all the seeds and slips had been planted, I was left in charge of the field to keep the birds from damaging the young shoots.

There were scarecrows placed all over the plantation, but the queleas and other greedy birds were so used to these that they perched on them brazenly and then swooped down on our future crops. It was absolutely necessary for me to keep constant watch over our field to prevent this flagrant pillaging. My job was to act as a living scarecrow, but my tender conscience was to be my undoing.

Perched high in my observation post which was built in the middle of the plantation, I scrutinised the land on every side with a keen and watchful gaze. To keep the birds away, I sometimes shouted noisily or sang loudly; sometimes I clapped my hands in time to a mocking song that I made up, jeering at the greedy creatures. But most often I played my reed-flute, that my friend Bossou called a *kpété*, and warbled a Fon song which I was very fond of, although I didn't really understand the words. Bossou had taught it to me. He was a boy from Abomey whose parents had come to settle in our region. It went something like this:

> They are from the city and they pick
>   quarrels with me,
> These town kids always pick quarrels with
>   me.
> I don't mind whether anyone greets me or
>   not;
> I don't mind whether anyone is interested
>   in me or not,
> I don't care a rap.
> Look at the net lying idle in the river,
> Is it angry that it has caught no fish?
> Is it pleased when it is full?
> It's just the same with the elephant:
> He is happy just to exist and is unconcerned
>   with the little creatures round him.
> He asks no more than to live with his father
>   to a certain age.
> What can others do with me or against me?
> Men who are by nature bad, what can they
>   do against me in this world I live in?
> Nothing! They too are mortal creatures like
>   me.
> We are all doomed to oblivion,
> And I am the net lying idle in the river,
> I am the elephant, without concern for the
>   little creatures nor for any other animal.

Bossou, who is still alive, is two years older than me. At that time he was a brawny youngster of medium height, quite well proportioned although his head was too round and hard. His features were finely chiselled and his hair was thick and frizzy, for all the world like a mass of tiny black marbles. In fact Bossou was a typical youngster from Middle Dahomey. At the time I am talking about, his father owned a large banana plantation on the western boundary of our field. This proximity favoured our friendship. We saw each other frequently and spent much time chatting. He could speak fluent Hausa, Bariba, Nago, Yoruba and many other dialects of the northern regions, whereas I was incapable of uttering a sentence in Fon without making the grossest mistakes. We always conversed in one of the northern dialects, for my sake. He taught me how to shoot with a bow. I have many happy memories of Bossou, but there was one occasion when he nearly came to grief.

One day he passed through our field on his way to his parents' banana plantation and he stopped under my lookout to tease me:

'Hail great king! Art seated so early on thy lofty throne?' he quipped.

To which I retorted in the same tone: 'If I was a Fon and a prince of Danhome it certainly wouldn't be long before I was elected king!'

Bossou laughed and then scolded me as usual for not making an effort to learn the Fon language. Then he left his kpété, his little harp, called a *tôba*, his bow and his quiver at the foot of my lookout and went off saying, 'I'm just going round the banana plantation; I'll be back in a minute and we can chat.'

A little while later, while I was playing my kpété, I suddenly heard a piercing scream, like someone in pain and distress. I interrupted my tune, grasped my flute in my hand and listened. Another anguished scream went up. I recognised my friend's voice and, not stopping to wonder what had happened, I scrambled down from my perch, seized my machete, grabbed Bossou's bow and arrows and rushed off into the plantation, over a hedge of brambles and cochineal cactus which scratched my legs.

About thirty yards in front of me I saw Bossou bound hand and foot by four monkeys, who had wrapped their long tails tightly around him like ropes. Another two monkeys were lashing him with their tails. Meanwhile the rest of the pack were pillaging the plantation. Some snatched bunches of fruit and made off at full speed; others hopped up and down and capered around, hugging their booty to their chests and uttering little cries of delight at getting the better of a human being and reducing him to helplessness.

Crouching behind a banana palm, I took an arrow out of the quiver, stretched the bow, took aim and shot. The arrow sped away and struck a monkey full in the eye. The creature leapt into the air, let out a howl and fell with thrashing limbs. I shot another five arrows, one after the other; six huge monkeys yelled, shrieked, barked or howled like dogs in their last death throes. Then the whole marauding band was seized with panic and made off in disorder.

But a strange and surprising thing occurred: they grabbed the bodies of their dead comrades and dragged them off. I was deeply moved by this human reaction in the midst of their distress; but there was no time for maudlin sentiment – the important thing was to rescue Bossou. I freed him from the monkeys, shooting down two of the ones that had tied him up. These I carried off home by their tails and we ate them. A week later I made Bossou a present of the two fine ash-grey pelts which father and I had stripped from the corpses of his assailants.

But first I had to help my friend hobble home. Then I went back to my parents and told them the story of Bossou's unfortunate experience and my part in his rescue. Bossou's mother and sister had done a good job of picking off most of the cactus prickles and bramble thorns that had stuck into me, teasing me as they did so on my resemblance to a hedgehog or a porcupine. Mother managed to remove the last of them. The rest of that day father had to keep watch over the field himself.

The next day I took up my watch again, but armed with firecrackers that Bossou had taught me how to make.

You must first have a large hollow key into which you stuff sulphur scraped from the heads of nine or ten matches. To this you add a tiny pinch of sand. Next you tie about twelve inches of strong string to the ring of the key and attach the other end of the string to a big nail, just long enough to fit easily into the hollow of the key. Then you stick the tip of the nail in the barrel of your makeshift

gun and let the string act as a sling by which you carry it.
If you want to drive away birds and monkeys, all you have
to do is to take up your position at the foot of a tree or
near a small rock against which you strike the head of the
nail very hard so that the point suddenly shoots into the
barrel, setting off an explosion in the mixture of sulphur
and sand, so spreading panic among the creatures.
Since Bossou's misadventure, I never went off to the
field without taking half a dozen of these firecrackers, well
loaded. My friend also had his share and we took a
mischievous delight in letting off our explosions which
echoed from one field to the other, provoking terror in
the hearts of the marauders.
As the birds took flight we would aim our arrows into
the air, sometimes bringing down partridge or wild
guinea fowl; but most often our bag consisted of
woodpigeons and queleas.
I mentioned that my father also owned cattle. When I
was not keeping watch in the field I used to take the herd
out to graze in our sweet grasslands at the foot of
Kinibaya, one of the highest mountains in the area. This
pastureland stretched for more than two hundred yards,
bounded on the right by the mountain, on the left by the
stream that runs from the source of the Kiniba. Seen from
a distance or from the mountain, it was a sea of rich,
green grass. I loved taking the cattle there. I loved to slip
on my woven cotton _boubou_, pick up my kpété and tôba,
fling my crook across my shoulders and set off with our
four dogs, whistling or playing a merry tune on one
instrument or the other. I loved to sit astride Faya, our
huge, bearded, black ram with the twisted horns and the
thick coat, who bore me off proudly to the pasture. It is
true that I did not take the animals out every day, as father
also liked to do so himself, but when I was out with them
my unbounded joy could be divined from afar from the
sound of my playing. But when I was perched up in my
lookout, what pleasure I felt as I gazed out over this vast
expanse of ripening grain, where the frail stalks of fonio,
maize, millet and sorghum danced to and fro, like fly-
whisks waving with the slightest breath of wind, glinting,

shining, sparkling in the burning northern sunlight ...! I watched our crops ripening, looking forward to that great day on which all our hopes had been pinned ever since we began the sowing: the day when we would start to bring in the harvest.

A little before daybreak, partridges and guineafowl would rend the air with their regular, explosive screeches. Cockerels would add their voice to the chorus; then there would be silence for a time, till the orchestra started up again with even greater gusto, as if the musicians were aware of the need to celebrate the birth of a new day. Thousands of birds woke to join in the chorus. Soon the whole countryside was one huge festival, in which men and women, as they in turn woke, could distinguish the voices of their favourite birds.

Mother would rise, stretch, yawn, her eyes still heavy with sleep. Father and I were up first, and would be off to the kitchen to cut up the quarters of a young goat that had been skinned, drawn and hung the night before.

As I recall the history of our family, one year was very like another, with only slight variations. But the year in which I turned ten or eleven is printed deeply on my mind. It was the eve of the harvest; we had killed two huge porcupines whose meat was to be added to that of the goats which we had already slaughtered. As was our custom, father and I, helped by our friends, had also built in the middle of the plantation a sort of shelter out of banana leaves and trusses of straw. It was here that all the workers were to partake of a generous feast on the day harvesting began, when half the crops had been gathered in.

When mother was dressed she went into the kitchen and three or four of her friends came to help her prepare the food which we were to eat out in the fields. Father and I helped put out all the necessary ingredients needed by these energetic, devoted assistants to practise their culinary skills; then we set off, accompanied by a band of workers comprising more women than men, for harvesting, in our part of the country, is more especially women's work.

Snares without End

We arrived with baskets and machetes. As the sun rose higher in the sky it glinted on the golden leaves of the standing corn and the silvery plumes of the maize cobs. Grassy fronds swayed in the soft breeze, rustling loudly as if rain was falling somewhere in the distance.

The women's nimble fingers grasped each stalk, stripped off the ears and dropped them into the baskets with movements so rapid that it was scarcely possible to distinguish their hands rising, slipping quickly along the stems one after another, and down to the baskets again. Only, where a moment ago the corn stood weighed down with heavy ears, now grain stalks swayed lithely in the breeze with a sadly short-lived suppleness, for they were soon to fall beneath our machetes and lie as useless straw in the furrows ...

So we advanced across the field, stripping and cutting down every cereal stalk. Behind us they strewed the earth, like the countless victims in the aftermath of a desperate battle, to use the words of my father who had retained terrible memories of his experiences in the war.

As each basket was filled, the women would take it and empty it behind the shelter, where huge heaps of grain gradually piled up. The air around us resounded with lively songs, taken up time and again in chorus and prolonged in echoes. The birds circled around, alighted, took flight again and hovered overhead, singing merrily.

At midday we ate with gusto, then set to work again. Towards evening, the greater part of the harvest for which we had invited our friends was gathered in. But we were often obliged to continue working late into the night, and it was not unusual for the moon to rise and find us still busy bringing the corn into the granaries.

We had six granaries which still exist: they consist of a sort of round turret with no opening, covered by a conical, removable thatched roof, on top of which a little earthenware pot was placed to keep out the rain. We would climb on ladders to fill the granaries, three of which were built of mud and three with a double wattle wall built on piles. We removed the roofs and replaced them as soon as the granaries were full. After this our helpers ate, and father gave each one a basket of sorghum, millet, fonio or maize and they went off, filling the starlit sky with their cheerful songs and their peals of satisfied laughter, lit on their way by the moon's silver beams. In the distance the rapid, lively beat of tomtoms told of the rejoicing of our neighbours who had also brought in their harvest.

The cereals that had not been cut were sold to other folk who harvested them. We also sold part of the grain crop stored in the granaries, as well as half our tubers. The tubers that were needed for our personal use were dug up a few at a time, as they were required; we did the same thing with the produce of our vegetable garden. We also sold our surplus dairy produce.

Life was pretty good. Yes, indeed, it must be admitted that life was good. Bakari was well off, Mariatou was well off, and as for me, young Ahouna, I considered myself well off too, reckoning that what belonged to my parents belonged to me, since Séitou no longer lived with us. We were happy.

Chapter 2

We did not always enjoy such peace and serenity, with no more ripples to disturb the peaceful tenor of our life than ruffled the calm waters of the Kiniba as they flowed between its verdant banks. How I envy those people whose existence is uneventful, even and transparent as the panes of glass in your window, set between two rows of metal bars; a life devoid of misery and misfortune such as they say the abode of Allah to be. I also admire those people who deny that evil exists at all, and think themselves clever enough to convince others that this is so. I too would dearly have loved to be able to be so firm a believer in universal good, but when I was barely thirteen all the forces of evil took possession of our home, seared my flesh, setting its brand not *upon* but *within* my heart and my very entrails. And this, I must admit, just when I believed us all to be so happy and my parents to enjoy such wealth.

One morning, early in the harvest season, when my father went to open the cowshed he found two cows lying dead, with black, protruding tongues, bared teeth and glazed eyes that still bore the expression of acute suffering. Overcome with surprise and distress he called me – I had never seen him in such a state – and asked me where I had taken the cattle to graze the previous day.

'Why, in our pasture, father!' I replied, surprised at the question, and added, 'What's the matter, father? You look very upset.'

'Look, son!' he said, opening the cowshed once more.

I burst into tears at the horrible sight which still seems to be before my eyes. Still weeping, I drove out the rest of the herd. As soon as they were outside thirteen of them set up a continuous, loud lowing; their eyes took on a rabid stare and they leapt into the air to fall heavily to the ground. My parents and I watched trembling, weeping and praying to Allah to save our beasts, for we knew from their jerking limbs that these thirteen cows too were dying. Their tongues protruded, already turning black, and saliva streamed from between their clenched teeth. Some of them were biting off their own tongues. They were lying on the ground, jerking convulsively like fetishists in a trance, when suddenly two of our three bulls made straight for us. We just managed to avoid them, but they were not attacking us. They continued their mad rush to be brought up short by our *naseberry* trees. These they nearly uprooted, then they circled round several times, leapt into the air and fell down, bellowing furiously, to lie stiff and foaming at the mouth.

At the sheepfold the same fearful sight met our eyes. Faya was dead, with two thirds of the flock. I don't know if I have mentioned our farmyard – well, it was almost completely wiped out. Except for three hens and two cocks wandering miserably around, there was not a creature left alive there. Oh! I can scarcely bear to think of that period of our existence.

Our whole household was plunged in grief. My father ran round in circles, like a man demented; then he pulled up short and, to our astonishment, he, who did not believe in witch-doctors, ran off to call Adanfô, a man from Agonli who lived in our area and had the reputation of being a great sorcerer.

Adanfô arrived, undid a raffia bundle from which he set out bones, minute calabashes, an 'agoumagan' – his instrument for looking into the future – and all the rest of his paraphernalia. Then he consulted the gods.

Adanfô, the soothsayer, was a man of slender build, and of graceful, unruffled demeanour; he would have been most handsome, had he not had a head like that of a wild boar. About a quarter of an hour after the beginning of his operations, he informed us – without having any previous knowledge of what had occurred – that the 'coal sickness' had come upon us.

'This has already brought many victims,' he said. 'I hear cries of distress, father, mother, son moaning with grief, lamenting and calling on Allah to help them, as they think all is lost; but the evil thing is still abroad and there will be still more victims if we do not make haste to drive away this terrible sickness.'

The words were scarcely out of the soothsayer's mouth when my mother ran up, shaken with sobs, tears streaming from her eyes.

'We are ruined, ruined!' she exclaimed. 'Another cow and two goats have just ... just ... died under my very eyes! It is all wrong! It is unjust for us to be so sorely tried in less than one day!'

Adanfô gazed at us, his eyes bright with triumph, and with his canines projecting over his lower lip he looked more than ever like a wild boar.

'Yes, everything that you have just told us is taking place here, on the other side of the house,' my father said. 'I have all the more reason to believe your words as you could not have known why I sent for you.' Father's apparent calm was belied by his red eyes that shone with the tears which he would have shed had it not been for the presence of the sorcerer.

Was it really the will of the gods? Were these the tricks of a man wishing to take advantage of a fellow-man struck down by misfortune? All I know is that he decreed that we must sacrifice a black she-goat and a black ram. 'No one must eat their flesh,' he ordered, 'for I shall have put the "coal sickness" upon them. Then we must give the entrails and the viscera to Tolègbâ, the fetish who protects the whole of the village. The she-goat's carcass must be thrown out at the crossroad where it will be eaten by dogs; that of the ram must be cast into the stream that runs into the river Kiniba, whose waters will carry it into other waters. After that the *soothsayer* must be given a white she-goat and a black cockerel. Finally, you must go and gather in the bush a large amount of a special herb that I shall show you after the ceremonies; this must be ground into a powder and mixed with the water in the troughs where your animals drink. Then, every morning, for three days, before dawn, you will add to this infusion a pinch of a black powder that I shall give you presently, and let your flocks drink this mixture. In this way you will never see this sickness nor any other attack any creature

in this house as long as you live!' So spoke the soothsayer.
My father acquiesced. As none of our surviving animals
was of the colour so strictly defined by the gods and their
representative, we had to purchase the ones required and
the sacrifices were made. I am thirty-three; it is eighteen
years since I lost my father, and more than twenty since
our herds were ravaged by the coal-disease – anthrax, it is
called – and from that day no signs of this epidemic were
seen in my father's compound, that my mother, Séitou,
Camara and myself eventually inherited ...

Did Adanfô's cabalistic words really play any effective
part in ridding us completely of the anthrax? I don't
know, but I don't really believe they did. But I certainly do
believe that the leaves ground up and mixed with the
water that our beasts drank were far more efficacious
than the soothsayer's hocus-pocus. What had the offering
of she-goats and the ram and cockerels to Tolègbâ, and
the dogs and the river Kiniba and the soothsayer, got to do
with the ravages caused by this epidemic? Really! These
Dahomean witch-doctors are damn tricksters, real liars!

My father took good care not to fall into their hands
again after the sacrifices. As he left, Adanfô said, 'Bakari,
you are likely to have other misfortunes; beware of
cassava meal; according to my calculations, you were
born under the sign of Gbégouda and this oracle forbids
those he protects to eat cassava meal.'

My father smiled and said nothing, but as soon as
Adanfô had gone he warned me, 'Beware of these Fon
people, especially when they are soothsayers. They are all
bright, hard-working, brave and full of good intentions,
but they are cunning tricksters and love to brag; when
they become soothsayers their double-dealing is only
equalled by their zest for the job. A real Fon is like a leech
as soon as he is inspired to become a witch-doctor: he
doesn't let go his victim till he has sucked his blood to the
last drop.'

I have always remembered this warning, but I have
known so few Fons that I could not judge them all solely
by my father's generalisations, which were possibly
motivated by the instinctive mistrust that the people of

the north feel for those from Middle Dahomey and even more so for those proud inhabitants of the south. Besides, my friend Bossou, in spite of being a Fon, is quite different from the ones that my father knew.

I have never had much faith in all those Dahomean gods, but I must now give them credit for possibly not liking the soothsayer's exploiting methods: after having driven the epidemic out of our home, Adanfô was unable to protect himself from the disease, to which he fell victim two weeks after his visit to us. But Gbégouda, the oracle under whose aegis my father was supposed to have been born, had his revenge.

A month after the outbreak, the harvest was due to begin. Everything was ready as usual; our people were waiting for us in the courtyard of the house; the sun had risen, but it suddenly disappeared and the sky grew quite dark; the air became curiously heavy and oppressive. We heard a distant rumble, quite unlike the sound of thunder. Besides, it was the dry season, and it would have been quite astonishing for a storm to break out suddenly like that.

In the cowshed, the sheepfold and the farmyard, which had been disinfected by the sanitary inspectors whom my father had sent for from Founkilla at great expense, our surviving animals that were still recovering did not seem excessively agitated.

But the sky had rapidly lowered, the rumble had grown till it resembled the sound of an enormous swarm of bees, a gigantic buzzing. As the meaning suddenly became apparent, panic-stricken cries of distress were heard:

'Locusts! locusts! locusts!'

Everyone immediately dropped their baskets and seized empty receptacles, iron hoes, anything they could lay their frantic hands on to make a noise with; they also grabbed pieces of wood and began to make a deafening din as they ran towards the field, beating the receptacles as hard as they could. Some seized wooden clubs and also rushed towards our plantations.

My mother ran around frantically, without any fixed idea as to what she should do or where she should go. My father waved his arms in his distress, running hither and thither, his boubou floating in the wind, shouting, cursing the locusts, calling on Allah!

I was quite determined to do what I could to help, to show myself able to rise to the occasion, capable of heroism. Well, had I not routed an army of monkeys when I was not yet twelve years old, and saved the life of my friend Bossou? And now I was a big fellow, I was strong with good, sturdy muscles; I was quite a man: I was thirteen!

I rushed into my parents' iron-roofed hut, seized an old turban that my father had given me, and wound it around my waist. One long end of material hung down in front of my genitals; I passed this between my legs and tucked the end into the sash made out of the turban. I left the other end of the material, from which I had improvised a G-string, dangling over my buttocks like a tail. Then I took my bow and three quivers full of arrows, some of which were tipped with poison prepared by my father.

Thus rigged out as a young warrior I made my way with determined gait towards our field.

The sky which hung low above our heads seemed suddenly to crash to the ground; the sun reappeared and the sultryness vanished. I reached the field; my father caught sight of me; he clasped me affectionately to him, saying in a voice touched with emotion, 'My poor boy! I admire your courage, but neither a bow nor poisoned arrows are any good against the locusts. Stamp your feet, make a noise with a stick; that's the only thing you can do. Look at our field, our fine field, that we have pinned our hopes on all these months. All ruined! all lost! I'd have liked to set fire to it all, but we ve still got the tubers in the ground ... Oh! Allah is against us, Gbégouda has got it in for me! Do what you can, my child, get to work!'

I was very upset that I had armed myself for nothing to try to rout the locusts as I had done the monkeys, but I did my best. There were locusts everywhere; the grain field was covered with them, crawling, hopping, jumping from ear to ear. They made a noise like the snapping of hundreds and hundreds of thousands of fingers; like the cracking of hundreds and hundreds of thousands of nuts; like the nervous clicking of scissors; like strenuously tearing new calico: it was a snapping and a rapping, a rustling and a roaring, a creaking and a squeaking, a rattling and a rumbling. The locusts went rampaging on, harvesting in their fashion ... The ears of grain vanished in their path, the stalks fell, cut into tiny pieces.

We shouted and yelled, crushing the filthy creatures which seemed to multiply in spite of our furious efforts. The huge, grey-green insects crawled over our legs. We crushed them with more violence and using more strength than we would have needed to kill a wild beast.

All in vain! In next to no time the harvesting was over, the field was completely devastated and what was left of the swarm took to the wing again as if obeying a rallying cry, some imperative call to arms, bearing disaster with them in their flight.

Now we plumbed the full depths of wretchedness. Our store of grain from the preceding year? Faugh! My parents with their usual neighbourliness had made loans to friends who were also completely ruined and so were unable to repay their debts. Our remaining animals? My father had had to slaughter several, first of all so that we could eat, and then to get a little money.

About this time I made my first trip to Abomey in one of Houraï'nda's big lorries, to buy maize, millet and yams. Houraï'nda was the chief of the Founkilla district; the driver's name was Samba. Two of Samba's wives used to accompany him with orders from the local people, coming back two days later. We normally did the same as the other folk from our village, asking Samba's wives to do our purchases for us. But I had been begging my father for a long time to take me to Abomey, where my friend Bossou was born, and to Bohicon, which he had often told me about himself, so he asked Houraï'nda if I could go with Samba, not because of the sacks of maize, millet and yams we needed, but so that I could see the country. The chief agreed and we set off.

I sat in front, in between the driver's two wives; we

were squashed tight, as in a vice. The rough, empty road stretched out in front of us, never ending. I won't tell you about the country we travelled through, nor of the stop we were forced to make when a pride of lions took their time crossing the road in front of us, or rather stood in the middle of the road to look at the lorry and roar at the throbbing of the engine. I won't tell you of the wild guinea fowl, the hares and the agoutis that the lorry ran over. Samba and his wives were sorry that they could not stop to pick up their victims. 'What a waste of good meat!' they murmured bitterly every time a guinea fowl was caught by the lorry or we ran over a hare or agouti.

We left Founkilla about eleven at night and reached Abomey about nine the next morning. The countryside seemed vast and flat and the earth redder than at Founkilla. The market at Abomey, which is called Houndjlomê, is the biggest that I have ever seen, with its many thatched or corrugated-iron roofed sheds. The market soon got busy. I went from stall to stall, satisfying my curiosity. Every second more people arrived, heavily laden with goods which they unpacked, spread out and advertised loudly. There were men and women selling grain, tubers, fruit, and varieties of vegetable oils; there was meat and fish, both smoked and salted, fried and grilled, even powdered. Everyone was chattering; no one seemed to be listening to what his neighbour was saying. Men selling fetishes and wooden statuettes, like these here around us, sat boasting of the virtues of their wares which were spread out before them: bones and antelope horns, skulls of hippopotamuses, crocodiles, alligators, birds and of many other creatures, including humans, together with a host of little bottles filled with black powders of supposedly infallible potency.

At the Houndjlomê market I first saw a woman wearing trousers. She was a white woman, the wife of the Abomey district governor, so they told me. She was wearing a lovely pair of khaki trousers; her fiery red hair fell over her shoulders, hiding the collar of her man's shirt. She was with her husband and led a big dog on a leash. Astonished at the sight of such a pretty woman in this get-up, people rushed to get a closer look at her, then hastened back to their wares. Others meanwhile took advantage of the disorder to steal a bunch of bananas, a basket of maize or oranges, or a grilled agouti. As soon as the victims of this pilfering realised what was going on, they started yelling and shouting curses to high heaven, then they ran to pour oil on this or that fetish, praying to them to bring down punishment on the thieves, or even to kill them. But before they could get back from the fetishes, many more goods had disappeared of course. It might have been more use if they had all stayed to look after their wares and left the gods alone.

As Samba and his wives had gone off to finish the orders for the people of Founkilla I had to stay and look after our purchases and protect them from the expert hands of the Houndjlomê thieves, so I could not go and admire the lovely hair of the Governor's wife. I would have liked to have seen it too, out of curiosity. But I asked a Fon boy what all the fuss was about.

'What are all the folk running off for?'

'Haven't you been to see?'

'No, Allah preserve me!' I said, holding tight to a sack of maize.

'You haven't missed anything. It's only a woman wearing trousers.'

'That must be a very rare sight, since everyone's rushing to see her.'

The youngster, with the quick wit of all Fons, retorted, 'A very rare sight? ... Pooh! A woman in trousers! D'you think she's got anything inside there that can move?'

I burst out laughing and the youngster went off. A little later the white couple passed quite close to me and I could admire the lady's fiery red hair.

We left Houndjlomê about one o'clock. Samba was taking the daughter of one of his friends back to Founkilla from Abomey so there wasn't room for me in front and I had to travel with the goods he had bought, under the tarpaulin that covered them. Actually I preferred this shelter where I should have had a good night's sleep amidst the smell of guavas, oranges and grain. But we had scarcely been five hours on the road, with nine or ten still to go before we would be home, when in the half-darkness under the tarpaulin I saw the head of a viper emerge from between the sacks of maize and millet. I nearly screamed aloud in panic. But in some inexplicable way I recovered my self-control and stared hard into the eyes of the snake. It slid a little further out, rearing its head, feverishly darting its forked tongue in and out. I made as if to throw an imaginary stone at it; it slid towards me; no sooner had it reached the spot where I had been than I leapt to one side and seized it by the neck and the tail. I squeezed; it spat at me, wriggling and twisting to get free. I squeezed and pulled as hard as I could, my long hard nails digging through its skin and into the flesh. What a job I had to dispatch that dangerous reptile! I knew that vipers were poisonous but I would never have believed that it could be so strong and so resistant. I sweated as I pulled till I heard its bones snap, and it ceased struggling.

The viper was dead, but I held tightly on to the two ends for the rest of the journey, with my nails dug deeply into the body from which sticky blood continued to ooze. It was as if I was afraid it would come back to life and attack me again if I threw it into a corner of the lorry that was travelling along at full speed. Naturally I did not close my eyes all the way back to Founkilla.

No sooner had the lorry pulled up in front of our house in Kiniba, and Samba had come to take off the tarpaulin, than I jumped down with my viper in my hands. My mother screamed with fright when she saw me; I threw the snake down, and the driver, his wives and the girl they had brought back from Abomey took to their heels. My father assured them that the snake was dead and they came back. They asked me what had happened and I told the story of my struggle. Some neighbours, for whom Samba had brought back supplies, having heard the noise and the lorry hooting came up with their lanterns; father told me to tell them about the viper, which I did, adding a bit to the story.

We unloaded the sacks of grain and yams with the help

of our neighbours, whom we helped in turn to carry in their supplies. The next day the whole of Founkilla knew that I had strangled a viper! Everyone spoke admiringly of me; youngsters and adults came to ask me to tell them of my exploit, and each time I added a few more details to the tale; but I never forgot to keep to the essentials of the truth, because that was what really interested me.

But now I was happy: I had the reputation for being a serious lad, honest, open, sincere and hard working and, what is more, I could say to myself, 'We have been unfortunate, but now we are going to have stocks of grain and tubers, oil and all the other things we need. We can renew our herds. Life is beginning again!'

Life was beginning again, it is true; but it was too soon to rejoice.

Chapter 3

You remember, when Séitou went to live with Tertullien, this introduced a European into my father's household. By some error of judgement, my parents and I thought this would protect us against the ill treatment and victimisation that was often the fate of our compatriots. We had a white man in the family! From now on the sun would shine only for us, we would be able to grasp the moon; the stars which shone through the darkest nights, vying with the moon for brightness, were our stars; the waters of the Kiniba, which ran through our pastureland, seemed extraordinarily pure, transparent and limpid; the sight of that majestic river flowing slowly between its grassy banks, babbling among the frail reeds and rushes bending in the slightest breeze, would remind us that all was well with us, because of Tertullien. We based our happiness on a foolish illusion which increased day by day till it exceeded all limits. So my father would walk proudly, his head high, his chest out, dressed in his rich robes, trimmed with arabesques and embroidered with gold and silver thread. Swollen with arrogance, he thought himself a sort of unofficial deputy district chief, the third in the hierarchy of gods in Founkilla, after the District Commandant and Houraï'nda, the chief. Indeed, everyone took it for granted that when the patriarch Houraï'nda died my father would be the best man to succeed him as district chief. Was Bakari not most neighbourly and generous? Had he not fought in the Great War, and won medals to show for it? He was upright, respecting Allah and all men of every age and social class; and to set the seal on his happiness, a white man was in love with his daughter, had taken her as his mistress and she had borne him children. He was the father-in-law of a European, a white man was his son-in-law; he was the grandfather of three little half-breeds. In truth there was no room for doubt: Bakari was a most fortunate man; he would be our next district chief. Peacefully flowed the Kiniba.

This was indeed what the people of our village thought, knowing nothing of what Séitou had suffered since Tertullien abandoned her. We did not disillusion them about the reality of the paradise in which they imagined us to be living. Among ourselves, we had long ago given up any illusions. And then, two years after the plague of locusts which I have already told you about, we were forced to change our ideas even more radically.

One morning, about five o'clock, two district guards knocked at our door. My father got up immediately, thinking that people had come to ask him for help. He opened the door and saw the guards, who enjoined him to follow them forthwith.

'Why?' he asked in astonishment.

'Your name appears on the list of this year's recruits for forced labour!' replied one of the guards, happy to exert his authority over a white man's father-in-law.

'You must be mistaken,' said my father, surprised to hear them speaking of forced labour to him, Bakari, a rich man, and one understood to be Houraï'nda's successor.

'Mistaken? That's a good one! That's how a white man's wealthy father-in-law speaks! Up! Follow us.'

'I'm not following you; go and tell Houraï'nda that Bakari refuses to obey you.'

'We're not sent by Houraï'nda, it's the Commandant himself,' one of the guards replied angrily.

'Well then, go and tell your Commandant that I refuse to obey his orders; tell him I am the master in my own house, I pay generously those who work for me, and I always settle my taxes regularly. You can also tell him I wish to make it clear I am not the kind of man who undertakes forced labour, unpaid labour, and that this is not the way to treat an old soldier!'

This insolence must have exasperated the guards, but they controlled themselves and left.

'What is all this about forced labour, Bakari?' my mother asked after they had gone. 'We are going through a real period of misfortunes.'

'I don't understand it!' he said. 'I've seen people working with these idiots of guards standing over them and threatening them, but I've never tried to find out whether they were prisoners or not. Oh! There is something wrong here! Something badly wrong, my poor Mariatou ... I'll go and see Houraï'nda!'

As soon as the sun rose he donned his finest boubou, wrapped his turban around his head, took his ebony cane with the silver knob and went off to see the chief.

'They were at your place early this morning?'

'Yes, very early. And you should have heard the way they looked and spoke to me! The insolence of wretches who have only done their military service, and never fought in the war, where you and I had the honour of killing the enemies of France!'

'Yes, it's a sad business! Now that the war is over the white men haven't got any consideration any more for those of us who did so much to help them to overthrow their enemies. Times are changing, Bakari; times are changing. And with a speed that terrifies me. A year ago, the Commandant often asked my opinion about certain of his plans; now he patronises me, decides everything himself, leaves me out of everything. Someone must have told him that Houraï'nda didn't insist on all the people in his district doing forced labour. This is partly true and partly false; Houraï'nda has a sense of respect for people and an understanding of their dignity. Forced labour always seemed to him an unreasonable thing for the white men to demand, but as it forms part of the orders that Houraï'nda must obey himself, and see that others obey, he submits to the decree which instituted the system, as well as to many other unreasonable things. The only people Houraï'nda exempts from forced labour are the rich; then Houraï'nda sends for the man in question and says to him: "This year your name is on the list of people who have to work without pay. It's a disgrace and completely unreasonable to be obliged to work in this way; but as you are rich, I think that you would prefer to pay some needy person who is capable of doing this thankless job for you, rather than exposing yourself to public shame." The rich people Houraï'nda made this suggestion to always accepted it, and poor folk did the necessary work in their place. That's why no one can ever say he has seen a rich man from Founkilla slaving away with those idiot guards standing over him – those men who go and get themselves circumcised in Abomey or in the south, so that they can pass as real men here, where no one worries about circumcision. Houraï'nda certainly doesn't think they are real men; they are either busy cuckolding other men or being cuckolded themselves; and if they don't fall into either of these categories, then they are eunuchs. Houraï'nda will get his own back one day. Someone's been telling lies to the Commandant and he's taken away my duties, without warning me. When Houraï'nda asked him what was going on, he answered in an overbearing way: "I don't want to hear any more about differences between rich and poor!"

' "But the poor get the benefit from what I do for them; someone who bears me a grudge has been giving you the wrong impression. Houraï'nda acts in the best interest of the poor and they are glad about this. The proof is that many of them come and ask if I haven't got a replacement for them to do!"

' "I don't give a damn! These are my orders, as they have always been: if it's somebody's turn to work, then he does the job and that's the end of it! Good-day, Houraï'nda!" '

'What must I do, Houraï'nda?' asked my father, when the latter finished this long speech, in which he frequently referred to himself in the third person, as the Mossi and Dahomean kings are said to have done in olden times.

'Forget your riches and your position and do as the Commandant says. You have known hard times, but you have built up your fortune again. Well, pluck up your courage and go off to do the forced labour with the idea that it is not you yourself doing the job but some impersonal *thing* inside you!'

Father returned home, very angry. The next morning, the Commandant's white horse and the horses of his two guards stopped outside our house. They dismounted and

---

the white man came straight to my father, who was giving orders to his workmen.

'It seems that you refused to obey my orders, Bakari?' he shouted in Hausa, which he spoke fluently.

'I have never seen a man of my condition lower himself to do the type of work that you invite me to do,' my father said coolly, which must have irritated the white man.

'Well, then! You'll be the first!'

'I have people I pay to work for me; they can replace me.'

At these words, the Commandant's whip struck my father six times across the face. He tried to defend himself, but the guards seized him. The Commandant shouted an order and they stripped my father naked in front of everyone and pushed him into his room, where they forced him to put on one of the old boubous which he used to wear to work in the fields. A few minutes after this humiliation, they brought him outside again. What! you frown, Monsieur Houénou? May Allah be my witness, together with the spirits of the people who watched this scene, as well as those who were present at what followed. I have only one aim, to tell you the absolute truth.

'And now, will you do the work, like all the niggers, or won't you, Bakari?'

My father remained silent. The whip whistled around his bare head.

'Will you work or won't you, you idiot, you proud old fool, you old peacock?'

Bakari did not reply. Ten times he was asked the same question, with no result, while the Commandant's whip cut into his face, which was always so gentle and calm, so nobly framed by his beard and moustache which I so admired. Blood spurted out from his ears, from his head; tears of blood poured down his face ... Oh! how I hate to talk of these things! I'd like to wipe them out of my memory for ever, but as I tell you about them I see it all again, I live through the whole scene, that is why I weep like a child, as if this happened only yesterday.

My mother, in her extreme anguish, did not even have the right to cry out; the guards forced her to keep silent

Snares without End

and she was reduced to weeping silently, without opening her mouth. As for me, I could not bear to gaze for long on the sight of this humiliation of the only human being, besides my mother, who I really respected; so I fled into the bush, where my howls of misery and pain echoed through the empty air. For long hours I wailed without restraint, in long-drawn-out cries, sharing my most intimate emotions with the plants, the mountains, the beasts and the trees that I knew so well. I cried my laments to the Kiniba, whose waters seemed to flow rapidly for the first time.

I returned home. I drove our new herd out to graze. Oh! such a meagre, insignificant herd now that it really isn't worth mentioning. My mother came out to me in the pasture. She was completely ravaged by grief; I threw myself into her arms and we wept long and loud. She tried to console me and I tried to console her, but we only wept the more.

As we parted she bade me look after the beasts well, but I really had no heart to remain out in the pasture. To try to cheer myself up, I put my pipe to my lips, but I could only manage to play the most melancholy tunes which tore at my heartstrings and brought on more floods of tears. I could no longer bear it, my heart was beating fit to burst with my distress. I put my pipe back in my pocket, left the beasts in the pasture and ran across the fields and the hills to the place where father was now employed in slave labour for the government. Mother had told me that she had finally prevailed on him to obey the Commandant's orders, out of love for me and for herself.

I found the place. Hidden behind a tree, I watched him toiling with about forty men equipped like convicts. They were clearing a space about eight yards wide, which stretched out indefinitely in front of them; they dug and turned the earth, digging up roots and stumps of trees and any obstacles that their picks and shovels encountered. Some of them were chanting:

> Earth, what harm have I ever done you?
> Would I be digging now, if I was not forced
>   to?

Snares without End

If the Commandant had not ordered it,
    would I be digging now?
The Commandant spoke the word:
The earth must be laid bare,
The earth must be dug,
The earth must be turned,
The earth must be levelled,
And then turned again,
And then excavated,
And then it must be sieved,
And then once more levelled,
And then we must sprinkle it,
And then beat it hard:
For we must keep working!
The Commandant said you must become a
    highway,
And I must obey,
And you will be a highway.
Earth, what harm have I ever done you?
Would I be digging now, if I was not forced
    to?
If the Commandant had not ordered it,
    would I be digging now?

But most of the men worked in silence. A leaden sun
shone down on their bent backs, that dripped with sweat.
The guards walked backwards and forwards, brandishing
their whips made from wild boar hide or a horse's
phallus; they yelled orders, mocking the rich men over
whom they exercised their command like eunuchs.

From time to time my father brushed away the flies
which stung his ears, still covered with dried, coagulated
blood. He half straightened up, resting his hand on the
handle of his pick, as he might have done on the silver
knob of his ebony walking-stick. Many people had come
to watch the members of their families who were forced
to work like slaves, but they were not allowed to talk to
them; the cursed guards threatened them with their
whips if they approached. I stared hard at my father, and
he looked up towards the tree behind which I was
crouching, as if I had actually called out to him. Our eyes

met, and I was suddenly blinded by a flow of tears. I buried my face in my hands and wept silently.

'Get on with your work, Bakari!' yelled one of the guards.

'I am tired; I think I have the right to straighten up for a moment, haven't I?' my father retorted.

'Get down and get on with your work, Bakari! That's an order!' the accursed fellow screamed again, a man who had not even fought in the war, but had been appointed as a guard by the Commandant simply because he thought he had sufficient courage, strength, cruelty and viciousness, just like all the guards recruited from my region.

My father did not answer. I could feel his anger rising at the way the guard spoke to him as if he were an equal, or even a servant. The man fell on him with his whip. It was bad enough for the Commandant to beat Bakari; he was a white man and they are entitled to do what they like with us blacks; but to see a man who was nothing but a district guard act like that, a eunuch who could have been our servant – that I couldn't stand. Unarmed as I was, I was tempted to hurl myself at the fool and attack him with my bare fists ... A child's anger, helpless when directed against parents, or against an authority like this eunuch; I had to control myself and keep quiet, trembling with fury. Suddenly I saw my father draw a knife from the pocket of his old boubou. I stifled a cry of terror but at the same time I was glad, glad that he was about to fling himself at the bastard and plunge his knife in his belly, till he was as full of holes as a refuse bucket stuffed with rotting garbage. But he did nothing of the sort. All the people working on the road shouted when they saw my father standing nervously grasping his knife. Some of the guards, who had more sense than the one who gave himself the airs of a chief, told my father not to take it to heart, not to think any more about his wealth, to forget who he was and to submit to the law like his fellows. Nothing in life lasts long, they said; everything comes to an end, like burning straw, and so it would be with this forced labour that he was rebelling against, and which would only last for three months, after all!

Three months! what a curious mixture of humour and sympathy! My father looked at them wildly, there was madness in his eyes and his lips foamed with rage.

Tiba, the vicious guard, had ridden off to inform the Commandant of his little altercation with my father. He returned with the white man; they reined up their horses and dismounted. One of the guards shouted an order and all the labourers except my father straightened up to greet the Commandant, who shouted angrily, possibly because my father had not greeted him, 'So, Bakari, you tried to kill Tiba?'

My father did not reply.

'Answer, can't you? Are you going to answer me? You wanted to kill him, you fool, you dirty nigger! You wanted to kill him, did you?' he yelled, as he rained blows on my father under my eyes that were blinded with tears.

And he went on raining blow after blow, flogging him as I have never seen a man flogged in my life. But my father stood his ground. And finally the Commandant, breathless and sweating from wielding his whip, stopped to wipe his face with his handkerchief and hitch up his trousers.

'Show me your knife!'

At these words I trembled more than ever, afraid that Bakari would refuse to obey, and to provoke another rain of lashes about his head which was already covered with bleeding gashes and weals, but he did as he was ordered, and I felt a moment of relief – relief which was short-lived.

'Now kill him; kill Tiba, do you hear! Go on, you damned rich fool, you coward, you!'

The lash whistled once more round my father's ears, from which the blood again began to flow. For the first time since the anthrax epidemic and the ravages caused by the locusts, I saw tears flow from my father's eyes. He looked down at his knife. I walked towards the worksite.

'Go away, Ahouna!' he sobbed. 'Your place is not here.'

Unable to restrain my tears any longer, I burst into loud

cries of distress. People turned to look at me. The Commandant shouted for this little whippersnapper to be taken away. He exaggerated; I was getting on for fifteen; it's true that I was not as big or as muscular as boys of my age sometimes are, but I·was far from being a 'little whippersnapper'. Two guards made for me; I backed away. Suddenly I saw my father raise his knife, I shouted out, pointing to him, but before anyone had time to see what was happening, it was too late!

My father had plunged the knife into his own heart! Blood was flowing furiously; people rushed towards him; I saw him fall, like one of the huge baboons which I used to shoot down with my bow and arrows from the top of our fruit trees. Father lay in a pool of blood. Everyone was suddenly silent except the Commandant, who expostulated, shouting insults, calling now on the guards, now on the labourers as his witnesses.

'The bastard! did I kill him, now? Isn't it true, Tiba, I never touched him! You there, you all saw that he stabbed himself! It wasn't me. I didn't kill the bastard!'

And I started running like a madman, waving my arms in the air, howling my misery and my grief, running through the fields like a robot, over the hills, from village to village, from hut to hut: 'My father is dead! Bakari has been killed! The Commandant killed him! Bakari has been stabbed! He plunged the knife in his heart, but the Commandant drove him to it! I saw it all. My father died under my very eyes. Come! Come, everyone, and see what the District Commandant of Founkilla did to an old soldier! to a man whose daughter was married to a white man!'

I let Houraï'nda know; I let Séniki know, and Boubakar. I shouted the news at all the doors. I announced the news to my mother, who fainted dead away. I was afraid that she would also die and I flung myself down beside her, shouting at the top of my voice. When she came to, she began to weep most strangely.

We ran to the worksite where my father was still lying in the pool of blood which had scarcely coagulated, with the knife still through his heart. Someone had put a large banana leaf over his face; flies were buzzing around the corpse. The whole of Kiniba was at our sides, weeping without restraint.

Houraï'nda was in a furious rage, but he wept too, in spite of his dignity as a chief. He then ordered eight strong fellows to carry away my father's body, to be buried that same day in the room which my mother still occupies.

Houraï'nda threatened the Commandant, telling him that he would write to the Governor in Porto-Novo, that he would go and see him himself, that he would complain to journalists he had known in Cotonou, and that the Commandant's career in the country wouldn't last long. He told the labourers, who had dropped their tools, to go home and never again submit to this white man's slavery.

The Commandant shouted; Houraï'nda shouted; they argued angrily, but in spite of the Commandant's protests the band of forced labourers dispersed and this job of making a road was left unfinished.

Two or three weeks later, the Commandant was sent back to France. He was replaced by another man, more intelligent and more humane than his predecessor. He thought it more reasonable to get the work of making the new road, that had been begun by my father and other rich men, finished by folk who were unable to pay their taxes, and by convicts who had always been subject to work of this kind. So forced labour took on a different form in our area.

Chapter 4

Bakari's death brought my sister back into the fold. It had
thundered throughout the night; flashes of lightning had
rent the darkness while the sky trembled and moaned.
From time to time, as it lit up, it had seemed to stream
with blood. The mountains too had resounded, as my
poor father would have said, 'With the angry sound of
guns'; but no rain had fallen ... The thunder continued
to rumble until dawn, the mountains to reverberate as if
with cannon shots which were caught by the echo and
carried down to the village, whose inhabitants trembled
with apprehension. Animals and birds were silent,
poultry-yard and herds alike overcome with alarm.
Suddenly, blinding sheets of lightning illuminated the sky,
which let out a mighty roar, yawned indecently and then
opened up its floodgates; the waters spilled out as if from
thousands and thousands of huge pitchers, suddenly
overturned.

As I could not go off to our fields to check on the work
done the previous day by our hired labour, I stayed at
home with my mother. My father's death had completely
disfigured her. Whereas she had been particularly
beautiful, tall, supple, with rippling muscles, scarcely
looking her age, now she had wasted away; her cheeks
were sunken; her formerly smooth brow was furrowed
with wrinkles; she no longer bore herself proudly
upright, gazing confidently before her, but bent her head
fearfully to the ground, avoiding meeting your gaze. In
her bereavement for her husband, Mariatou left her hair
dishevelled and unkempt, looking like a beggar or a poor
madwoman. She never left the house, scarcely ate. If she
did her best to look after the home, it was out of love for
me. If she had been alone, she would have let herself fade
away altogether in the mental and physical confusion that
my father's death, eight months previously, had brought
about in her life. She spent whole days crouching on a low

stool, leaning her elbows on her knees, with her arms across her chest, gripping her shoulders, shedding floods of tears and keening slow plaintive dirges.

I did not care for these songs of mourning which seared what I must call my soul, with their anguished, monotonous chant. But that day my mother was not murmuring any dirge; she was talking to me about life, which was, she said, 'A series of nameless absurdities'.

'Life, my dear little Ahouna, is a wasteland of rotting refuse, in which men devote their energies to futile, vain things, and build their hopes on these. And yet you must continue relentlessly pursuing these trifles, if you want to go on living and feel that you are in fact alive. Everything is linked to these terribly meaningless things.'

We watched the rain still falling in torrents, streaming through our yard, barring the air with a steel-grey lattice. After talking to me of life in general mother went on to speak in a tone which indicated how fundamental this was, of the importance of never quitting 'this wasteland of rotting refuse' without leaving any posterity behind. This assertion, which she did not explain to me, then led on to her telling me to begin to think about marriage.

We had just reached this point in our conversation when a lorry, coming from Parakou, drew up in front of our house. A man, a woman and five children alighted, entered the gate and were just crossing the yard when mother jumped up, shouting, 'Séitou! daughter! come in, children; come in, all of you! Make yourselves at home!'

We immediately understood that the handsome man who accompanied my sister was her new husband and that, in addition to Tertullien's children, she had had two more by him.

We welcomed them happily, lifted up each of the children in turn, embracing them affectionately. Our house, of a sudden, became once more merry, lively, noisy. Pure, limpid and fresh as the spring waters of the Kiniba as it leaps down the mountain, human happiness once again lit up my mother's sunken, gaunt countenance. I was so happy to see her like this that I burst into tears. Séitou wept too. She wept endlessly as she gazed at the settle on which our father used to rest in the evenings, smoking his pipe and telling his beads.

My mother sprang to life. It was astonishing how active she suddenly became! She bled two chickens, cooked them with Séitou's help, boiled some yams, peeled them, mashed them up in a mortar, and quickly prepared a sauce for the chickens, in which she put some sesame balls. We feasted on this repast, which was the best our house had seen since Bakari's death; and all the time the rain never ceased falling.

That evening, my sister and brother-in-law told us how they had heard of father's death.

I told you that Houraï'nda had threatened the Commandant. He had let Parakou, Abomey and Bohicon know of the tragedy that had cost my father his life. He had been to see journalists in Cotonou; he even requested an audience with the Governor of Dahomey, and when this was granted he went in person to Porto-Novo. Two journalists came from Cotonou to Kiniba to question my mother and other witnesses to the tragedy, including myself. Why, I did not know at the time. It was only after Séitou's and Camara's arrival that I learnt that the news had spread through Africa, and so reached my brother-in-law, who could read and found out about it from the newspapers.

You say that you remember reading about it too? All the better! Camara did not get on very well with his family, so he and his wife had decided to come to Kiniba.

'Mother, brother, I abandoned you,' Séitou sobbed, 'but I have come back, hoping you will forgive me; take pity on me and take us back into our father's house.'

'You are welcome, children. You are all my children,' mother replied, her eyes misty with the tears that she tried vainly to hold back. 'My only wish is for you and my grandchildren to live happily in this house that has been the victim of so much misfortune. Ahouna will marry too; he will have children and I shall die happy in your midst. Oh, how I wish that I may never again have to sing a song of mourning, but only songs of joy!'

'Life is a low-down trick played on us by Allah, but I

hope that your wishes will be granted, mother,' said
Camara.

Camara was a handsome, well built man who rarely
wore a boubou; he was accustomed to dress like most
men from the southern regions in shorts or long trousers,
shirt with rolled-up sleeves, khaki cloth cap or felt hat
imported from Accra, sandals locally made or bought in
the shops. He was typical of young men from the south,
such as we in the north imagined them to be. He chewed
his thumb, and a flood of bitter, painful memories were
mirrored in his black eyes.

'Yes, indeed, life is quite ridiculously absurd. I wonder
how and why Allah, who is supposed to be goodness itself,
can have created it so ... I never had any difficulties with
my fellows; I had many good friends; but it was my own
sister who brought me unhappiness. It was my mistake to
have been born ten years after her. Her excuse was that
she was long considered as an only child; but since I did
come into the world, why could she not forget herself a
bit, bury a part of her selfishness and recognise my place
in the family? Mariama had to have everything; I had to
give in to all her whims. I might have held my own
against her bullying, if it had not been that mother, who
was cruelly unfair, always took her part. "Poor Mariama
has no luck!" she would say. "She is forty and isn't
married! You know, Camara dear, that your sister is a
paragon of virtue; she loves you; you must forgive her
little faults. She is very nervy!"

'I forgave Mariama, but she did not become more
reasonable, probably because my mother was always on
her side. Father, who was very reticent, stupidly reticent,
never interfered. He was quite indifferent to our ceaseless
scenes and violent quarrels. Mariama took advantage of
this indifference to get all the more worked up against me
... Oh! she was a real devil, she couldn't help being
jealous of any girl she saw me with. Because she's an old
maid, she could not bear to see me with a girl. She enjoyed
herself with any man who happened to please her; that
was her own business, and I'm not criticising her for it.
But why did she have to tell dirty lies about me? That's

something that I've never been able to understand. Mother gave her everything; I had nothing. Up to the time I was twelve, or fifteen even – or older if I am not mistaken – most of my clothes were made out of my sister's reach-me-downs. I never had anything new, anything of my own that I was the first to wear. It was because of her that I left for Cameroon to work as a servant for a Syrian. It was in Cameroon that I made a bit of money after leaving my boss; and that's where I got to know Séitou. When I realised that I loved her, I asked her to marry me and she accepted. I was stupid enough to take her back to Conakry, because I wanted to get married near my own people, and I also wanted to have their opinion on my choice.

'So we arrived in my country. Séitou and her children lived in a house near the port, where she soon got a job in the sorting-office. One day, I told my parents of my intention to get married. My father, who never speaks when he has to give an opinion, to my great surprise frowned and shrugged his shoulders, and finally said that he had no objection, if I was sure that this was the woman I really loved. Mother tightened her lips, slapped her thighs, clapped her hands and declared abruptly that I could never marry a woman who had already got three children. Then my sister added, with her usual kindness and incorruptible virtue, "Three white men's kids, three little half-castes with different fathers. There's no doubt about it, this woman's no better than she should be, running after any white man!"

' "It's not true that Séitou runs after white men. Her three children were all from one husband, Monsieur Tertullien whom I knew in Cameroon!" I protested vigorously.

' "That's enough!" cried my mother, putting an end to our quarrel.

'Then Mariama began to conspire about my disgrace. Whenever she had a chance she spoke disparagingly of Séitou. People began to look at her askance, taunting her when they met, bursting out laughing and making sarcastic remarks when they saw us together with the children. Mariama was delighted at the results of her mean tricks, the silly bitch. But I took no notice of the gossip. My sole desire was to stabilise my relationship with Séitou, to stop evading the real issue and transform our courtship into what I hope will prove to be a lasting union. So I married Séitou, but that was my undoing.

'My sister stepped up her scheming. She managed somehow or other to get father on her side. He now never spoke to me except in most curt and, sometimes, ambiguous terms. He never expressed either approval or disapproval for anything I said to him ... I was very attached to my family; nevertheless I began to feel sick of living, not only in a corner of our home, where no one took any notice of us, but in a country where my sister's stupid observations and unbelievably offensive aspersions had made me a laughing-stock. Everywhere we went, Séitou and I met with nothing but contempt, malicious remarks and even open hostility.

'Have you ever watched a fly caught in a spider's toils? I have always felt for these insects which I do not hesitate to save when I find them still alive, struggling to escape from the snare. I mention this because, trapped as I was in the hostility of my family, I was like a fly caught and thrown by some sinister hand into a spider's web from which it cannot escape. I could see the threads being woven around me, paralysing me while the spider advanced ready to stifle me.

'One morning my father sent for me. I found him flanked by my mother and sister, who looked hard-faced and tense. In the eyes of all three of them could be read the decision that they must have just arrived at, calmly and with no heed for any tragic consequences. I looked at them, examining each in turn, and guessed from the expression in the two women's eyes that they must have put pressure on my father to take action.

' "Camara, you married this woman against our wishes," he began.

' "Why do you bring up that old story? We have been married for four years and we have two children. I know that no one cares for our children, but that does not worry

us. Why are you talking about Séitou now? – or rather
talking about her again?"

' "You might let *my father* finish his sentence!" Mariama
interrupted.

'Father lowered his eyes, then looked up at the two
women in embarrassment, as if to consult them.

' "I've given it a lot of thought before sending for you,
Camara. I find it most inconvenient for you to go on
living here with this woman; I can't accept the fact that
you, my son, married without my consent!"

' "You told me to marry Séitou if I was sure that ..."

' "I was joking!" he interrupted me harshly.

' "You were joking? ... That may be. But I did what I
wanted to do."

' "To prove what a strong character you were!" said
my mother.

' "To prove *to myself* that I had strength of character,
mother."

' "That's a good one! I'd always suspected something
like that," exclaimed my sister.

' "You shut up! Don't you interfere, you shrew! You
damned bag! You should be ashamed of your whoring!
Yes, everybody knows all about you! Get the hell out of
here if you can't stop sticking your nose in my affairs!" I
yelled, beside myself with rage.

'Mariama leapt at me, but my parents pulled her back;
she was weeping bitterly, shedding those tears which
came so easily to her.

' "You have now exceeded the bounds of my anger,
Camara!" my father exlaimed. "This is the last straw;
you must think about leaving us."

'I did not expect this outcome. I stared at him, and
stammered, "You're driving me out of my grandfather's
house?"

' "Yes, Camara. I say you must leave this house. What is
more, you will not have a penny from me. Goodbye!"

'I was disinherited ... and so I staggered out of the
house, as if intoxicated. Not that I had expected anything,
anything at all, from my parents; I had not relied on them
for my subsistence; still, the news of this unjust,

unreasonable disgrace struck at my very soul.'

When Camara reached this point in his tale, he fell silent, burying his face in his hands, but he did not weep. My sister, on the other hand, lowered her eyes and burst into tears. My mother rose, went over to Camara and put her hand affectionately on his shoulder, saying, 'I understand, son; this was all the harder to bear, as it was your own parents acting in this way; but try to forget all this distressing past.'

'But it is inhuman, absolutely unreasonable! Why turn me out of my own home because I married the woman I love?' he asked, wild-eyed.

'Everything in life is cruel, inhuman and unreasonable. I came to this conclusion the day my husband was forced to commit suicide; but since we must go on living the best thing is, at least as far as I can judge, to accept life as it presents itself to us, in all its absurdity.'

Camara looked overcome with sadness. I was distressed to see him so downcast. I went outside. Mother joined me in the yard. The rain had stopped; the sky was clear again, its dark blue spangled with stars; the moon was rising; the air was cool and pleasant to breathe.

Mother and I walked together towards our vegetable garden, where beds of huge ripe tomatoes, green, yellow and red peppers, onions and many varieties of spinach could be clearly seen in the starlight.

'What can we do to make life pleasant for your sister, her husband and their children, my little Ahouna?' my mother asked affectionately and thoughtfully.

Without a moment's hesitation, I answered, 'I like Camara very much; he seems strong and brave; his whole manner speaks of goodwill and stores of energy. Instead of using paid workmen for our farm, whom we also have to feed and give a share of the crops, wouldn't it be better to give Séitou and Camara some of our land, which my brother-in-law could cultivate for himself?'

My mother hugged me. We walked far that evening without exchanging further conversation, except, as far as I remember, just as we reached the foot of one of the naseberry trees which shade our yard, mother said, 'I see my husband's generosity in you. If your father had been alive he would not have thought twice before giving Camara some land. I heartily approve your suggestion, my boy. And as our herds are on the increase again, if you like we can also give Séitou and her children a couple of cows, four goats and a ram, so that her family can settle down and run their own life.'

'I certainly agree, mother. Our home has many spare huts; some of them need to be repaired straight away. We'll talk to Camara about it when he has seen the whole property and has got used to our way of life ... He must feel quite at home with us; I'd like him to find here all that he has been deprived of in his own home: affection, understanding, human sympathy and genuine love,' I said, happy and excited.

'I hope Séitou won't be sorry that she has come home; I also hope Camara will never be sorry he got to know us and I hope their children, my grandchildren, will be happy with us.'

'We'll do our best to make them happy, mother,' I said.

We went back to join Camara and Séitou; the children had long since fallen asleep. Mother told the young couple of our plan. My sister was so overcome with joy that she could not restrain her tears and had to go out into the yard where she wept unrestrainedly under the fruit-laden branches of the naseberry trees. As for her husband, he seemed in quite a daze. He just stared down at the ground and, to look at him, not knowing the happiness that overwhelmed him, you would have thought that some shock had deprived him of his wits.

Camara and I became great friends. He talked to me about life, about my sister and their children. He taught me how to wrestle, with all the different holds you use to throw off an opponent who is bigger and stronger than yourself, while I taught him to play the *balafon*, the kpété and the tôba. Referring to the last two instruments, he used to say, 'You'll turn the heads of all the girls in Kiniba and in the whole of Founkilla with those, if they are as sentimental and as full of feeling for music as the girls where I come from – those at any rate who haven't been made stupid with prejudice.'

'Do you think that prejudice is the cause of what you call the stupidity of the people of your country?'

'Prejudice comes from human stupidity, just as stupidity can result from prejudice. Some of my countryfolk are naturally stupid, but local prejudices have made them even more stupid and more malicious than they would otherwise have been,' he replied thoughtfully.

We used to go off together to the fields, and together we would drive the herds out to graze. He taught me to read and to get along in French. For eight years, he had been their children's first teacher, with the help of Séitou, who speaks French very well, at least in my opinion, and also makes herself understood in English and German, which she learnt in Cameroon. So together they were responsible for all their own children knew, as well as the children that I and Anatou were to have later. This teaching only ceased when all the youngsters went to the local village school.

Sometimes we went off to the pasture on horseback, taking Rémy, Jean-Claude, Mireille and Bouraïma. People who saw us, three astride each horse, smiled and joked with us and gave the children fruit. These inhabitants of Kiniba couldn't do enough for us since my father's death; they presented us with bunches of bananas, baskets of pineapples, avocado pears, naseberries, cashew nuts and pawpaws, which we found rather a nuisance, as we were not short of these things and did not really know what to do with them; however, we accepted them gracefully and gratefully. I remember that we either gave them away in turn to the youngsters whom we met on our way to the pasture, or else to needy folk whom we knew.

Some of our neighbours expressed their regret that my father was not alive to admire his handsome 'half-white' grandchildren; others stopped us for useless and endless gossip. We met crowds of people on our way; men going off in single file to work in the fields, with their hoes on their shoulders, their machetes in their hands; processions of women going off to the Kiniba Falls, with their

---

calabashes or their water jars balanced on their heads; youngsters armed with bows and arrows or catapults, the terror of the birds ... How far from them I felt myself to be, since I now considered myself to be grown up and mature, prematurely seared by so many blows of fate, cruelly branded with the seal of life! We exchanged greetings, which were at first noisy and then repeated endlessly in a singsong as is the Founkilla custom:

> *'Ma tan'g kali non ?'*
> *'Ma kam'g biô !'*
> *'Fô, orou,'*
> *'Fô, kpaï.'*
> *'Fô, orou,'*
> *'Fô, kpaï ...'*

We passed the Kiniba Falls. From its great height this vast spool of water unwinds into space, scattering its spray and enveloping the mountain in a fine, cold mist. I can still see in my mind's eye this immense sheet of water, emerging from the heart of the mountain and taking on, in the early morning light, the most magnificent colours I have ever seen: an extraordinary weave of ribbons in every shade of blue, yellow and red, with greens and blackish tints, mauve, purple, orange and jade ... I remember how Camara fell suddenly silent when he came upon this sight for the first time. He spent more than an hour gazing at the water, which was continually metamorphosed in the rising sun, and listening to the music of the falls – the monotonous, deafening cadences that lingered down in the valley in a soft, harmonious murmur, among the reeds and rushes and pebbles covered with threadlike water weed.

When my brother-in-law finally made up his mind to continue on to the pasture, he said something that made me very proud: 'So this was the scene of Séitou's home and childhood? I can understand her love for her native land. She never lost an opportunity of talking about it, and especially whenever she talked about you all.'

Up to the time when I left Kiniba, whenever we went off together to take the herds up to the pastureland Camara could never pass these falls without stopping to gaze at them for at least five minutes.

Our docile animals, who were quite familiar with the path, walked in front of us, accompanied by our four dogs who ran forwards and backwards, barking and keeping them together. When we got to the pasture, we left the dogs to guard them and set out to climb to the top of the Kinibaya mountain, which is about 1300 feet above sea level. From there we had a panoramic view of the whole village, lovely stretches of fresh, green vegetation, birds in flight, coursing deer, monkeys performing acrobatic tricks from branch to branch while the females moved around with their young clinging to their bellies.

Sometimes, as we watched these lively scenes in the distance, I took out my kpété and improvised songs, wild and sweet, primitive melodies, that enthralled the ear and which were the spontaneous expression of my adolescent heart. No, no! I protest, I do not deserve what Anatou did to me. It is possible that a monster is hidden deep inside each one of us, but no one has the right to awaken this monster, if we do not do so ourselves, or if it does not show itself of its own accord. How I could have wished – how I still wish, that no one had woken from its slumbers that monster in me, of which I was unaware! How I wish that it could have slept to eternity! But let us not anticipate the rest of my story.

Whether I played my kpété or my tôba – and I think of these melodies as having some divine quality, not to mention the tunes from the southern region that Bossou had taught me – the music I improvised moved Camara deeply. He used to gaze at me with a strangely gentle expression, smiling discreetly as if I were a girl, and would say, 'The more I hear you play, the happier I am to be in your midst.'

One day, when I was playing the tôba on the top of Mount Kinibaya, three or four years after my mother had mentioned the subject of marriage, he said that I ought to get to know a girl worthy of me, 'intelligent, understanding and kind, like Séitou. You are nineteen now and should be thinking of getting married.'

Snares without End

'How old were you when you got married?'

'Twenty-eight.'

'Then I'll get married too when I am that age.'

'It's not necessary to wait so long. I could well have married Séitou when I was nineteen, if I had met her and fallen in love and won her love.'

'Do you think that marriage is such a necessary thing that one should rush into it, Camara?'

'Yes, Ahouna. Family life, surrounded by children ... What a good thing! What pleasure! What joy! What happiness too! especially when your wife loves and understands you and you love and understand her also. Of course there are worries: the children fall ill; the produce of your fields, on which you depend for your income, does not bring in as much as you expect. But these are everyday occurrences. They are accidents like epidemics and plagues of locusts. You should get married, Ahouna.'

'Well, that's decided then! Since you are my brother-in-law – like a real elder brother who can give me only good advice – I'll get married when I meet a girl as intelligent, understanding, kind and beautiful as Séitou!'

'Good. Meanwhile, let's build a hut in the corner of this pasture, where we can shelter from the storms.'

'My father had built one, but the heavy rains and floods washed it away.'

'Was it on stilts?'

'No.'

'Well, that's how we are going to make it now.'

When we got back home I asked mother if she would like me to get married.

'In the name of Allah and your poor dead father!' she said, 'don't you remember that was what I talked to you about the day Séitou, Camara and their children arrived? I would be so happy to rock your children too on my knee, and to carry them on my back before I die! Then, in the next world, I shall be proud and happy to be able to tell my husband that I have fulfilled my duties as a mother and a grandmother!' And to her tears of grief as she thought of my father she added tears of happiness at the idea that I was thinking of getting married.

Two days after this conversation with the good Camara, we took into the Kinibaya valley long poles for making stilts, bundles of flexible sticks and bamboo, rolls of strong fencing, bundles of straw, everything necessary for building our shelter, and the next day the hut was finished. Camara made a little ladder with six rungs, up and down which we used to climb from our shelter. The children loved to play there and sit under the shade of the hut during the hottest period of the day.

A few days later, when the whole household came to admire our masterpiece, Séitou asked, joking, if that was where I would get married. To which I replied, in the same vein, 'I'd willingly spend all my life here, if the girl I loved was happy here. Love should require very little to satisfy it.'

Insh'Allah!

Chapter 5

We had good harvests; our cows calved, our goats bore kids, flocks and herds increased, our poultry-yard was once more well stocked. New blood circulated in the veins of man and beast. The Kiniba flowed majestically; the air was fragrant, fresh and invigorating. Money came in regularly and we were happy. Camara worked in the fields while Séitou took the eldest children to the Founkilla school, a good hour's horse-ride from our house.

Dressed in my indigo boubou, my kpété in one pocket, my tôba in the other, with my shepherd's crook across my shoulders, I would drive the animals out to graze. There, as was my wont, I dreamed or improvised melodies, songs that sprang from my young shepherd's heart. I also took my reading-book with me so that I could get on with the lessons that my sister and brother-in-law were teaching me.

One day, when I was trying to make out a nice story in *Mamadou and Bineta*, I began to perspire heavily. I felt as if I was suffocating, not from fright, for there was nothing to be frightened about in this little book, but from an uncanny, sultry heat. I lifted my eyes from my reader and saw that huge bronze clouds were chasing across the whole sky. The green, tree-covered panorama, which I loved to gaze on from the top of Mount Kinibaya, was terribly agitated. In the distance, beyond the rocky heights, herds of terrified deer raced across the plain, packs of dog-faced baboons and banana-eating monkeys leapt from branch to branch, yapping and yelping; the sky was full of birds, wheeling before the clouds. At the foot of the mountain the animals were becoming restive; they ran around, bleating and bellowing, as if they were all seized with the staggers. Then, suddenly, everything was silent; the sky was empty of birds; I climbed down to the valley, herded all the animals together and, with my musical instruments in my pocket, my crook in my hand, drove them all back to the sheds, bellowing and bleating, with the dogs barking ceaselessly to help me.

When I got back to the house, I realised that I had forgotten my reader. I would not have been separated from this little book for anything in the world; Camara had given it to me and I was learning so much from it. So I threw my crook into a corner of the cowshed and ran back to the pasture as fast as I could, with the wind in my back to help me, while thunder pealed around me.

I got back to the place where I had dropped my book; I picked it up, already somewhat torn by the wind. The sky was terribly black and lowering; it looked as if it would tumble down to earth any minute. I was about to retrace my steps when the air all around me trembled with deafening explosions that endlessly re-echoed louder and louder from peak to peak. As if by instinct, I threw myself on the ground and crawled forward. The din grew louder, the peals grew longer. The heavens were enraged; the air was in a fury. I crawled to our shelter, climbed in, trembling, and sat down. I was terrified of some unknown power, and prayed that Allah would not permit these awesome phenomena to destroy the fragile shelter. No sooner was my prayer ended than the most blinding and terrifying flash of lightning I had ever witnessed forked across the sky. I buried my face in my hands. At that moment a strange rumbling was heard; it seemed to come from the bosom of the earth. The shelter lurched on its stilts. Then a mass of rock rolled down the side of the mountain with a mighty roar, then another rumbling was heard, and everything seemed to be muttering and moaning around me.

Heavy, violent, torrential rain was suddenly unleashed; it seemed to be vomited from the heavens and thrown up from the mountains. The Kiniba, which could not be contained in its narrow bed, overflowed the valley. My chest seemed caught in a vice. But half an hour later all was calm. The air grew cooler and I could breath again. Then I took out my kpété and began to play the most wonderful tunes, that I felt could not possibly have come from me. I played till I was intoxicated with playing; I played myself into an ecstacy. Yes, that day I felt myself happy indeed, deliriously happy, for no cause, unless it was that I could fill the air with songs from my heart. Why did I not die that very moment?

The rain stopped. The sky once more turned a harsh, brilliant blue. The birds began to sing again. I climbed down from my shelter and returned home, fresh-faced, with shining eyes, my whole being exuding happiness.

'Where have you been, Ahouna son?' my mother asked sadly.

I immediately realised that she had been most anxious about my absence and that they had been looking everywhere for me.

'I went back to the pasture to fetch my reader that I had left behind, mother,' I reassured her, pressing her hand against my cheek.

'You really have got a passion for learning,' smiled Séitou, stroking my hair.

She seemed more beautiful and fascinating than ever and I thought to myself: 'I'll never marry unless I find a woman to love me who is as beautiful as Séitou.'

'You must have charmed the storm with the tunes on your tôba, in our little palace out there in the pasture,' joked Camara, holding little Ossaya on his lap and humming a tune which he had probably heard me improvise on the tôba.

'No, not the tôba, on the kpété,' I corrected him, stretching myself with contentment.

Then, taking up my instrument again, I played new melodies for them all. They were carried away with admiration. Séitou smiled, her eyes shining with joy; mother was entranced; Camara stared at me, fascinated, repeating, 'It's incredible, quite incredible, how you manage to express so many wonderful things just with a little piece of wood!'

The children gazed at me, wide-eyed, as if hypnotised. When I finished, or rather when I stopped playing – for I could have played on forever – the children rushed at me, covered me with embraces, asking me if I'd teach them to play the kpété. I promised I'd teach them the art, adding immediately, 'There are no secrets to this art. My friend Bossou, a young man who comes from Abomey, first taught me to play. What must have charmed you is just my vision of the world, heard in the form of a song from my heart. Everything is here,' I finished proudly, like a child, placing my hand on my heart.

I asked my mother if I could invite Bossou to share a couscous with us, to which she willingly agreed. My friend came to visit us a week after the storm, for the fifth time since my father's death. We hardly ever saw each other now as he was busy with his work as a young farmer, sculptor and apprentice *griot* and he had moved to a large property to the west of the Kiniba mountains, a good three hours' horse-ride away, when his parents sold their banana plantation next door to us.

I introduced my sister, Camara and their children to him. We chatted long over this and that and then we sat down to a good meal. We walked in the banana plantation where he had been attacked by monkeys, and which his father had sold to Assani, the most considerable itinerant merchant in Kiniba, who sold it in turn to Camara, being much keener on the life of a merchant than on farming. Camara still owns this land. Then we wandered into our orange grove, which was in full flower, fragrant with the sweet-scented blossom and alive with bees and wasps. We talked of flocks and herds, of wealth, of happiness, of women, to whom Bossou said he scarcely gave any thought, but that for the moment he took his pleasure where he found it, provided that the girl or the woman was pretty and willing. Naturally music formed an important part of our conversation, so as soon as we got back to the house I asked my friend to play for us.

He took my tôba and began to play. All eyes were upon him; we held our breath. His fingers danced rapidly from string to string with extraordinary skill, seeming now to caress the instrument, now to seize all the strings at once. Bossou conjured up visions of the south: the distant, continuous moaning of the sea could be heard in the midst of a voluptuous song of love or a song of war and death.

'Wonderful!' chorused Séitou and Camara.

'Are these melodies inspired by the south?' I asked my friend.

'Yes. The south once put its spell on me and I still feel a thrill when I think of all the amazing things I saw there. There is so much to discover and rediscover in Ouidah, Porto-Novo and especially Cotonou!'

'Now would you make up a new song, and improvise a tune on your kpété?'

'Certainly.'

Then he took his reed flute and we heard first a low sound prolonged for a long minute on the same unvaried pitch, with no inflexion in his breath; then he began to run his slender fingers in turn over the holes of the instrument. The vision of the south returned momentarily, to be replaced by evocations of the Kiniba Falls, the setting sun, the passage of time. Then he conjured up for us the image of a ravishingly beautiful girl, full of grace, draped in a magnificent *pagne*, of the kind they weave in Kana. She was looking for someone, a man she loved, and could not find. But did she even know the person she was seeking? Nothing in Bossou's melodies, played with such relentless mastery and artistry, gave any indication of the identity of this man, who must have been fairly young, Bossou's age, or mine, give or take a year or two ... The girl wandered endlessly, round and round, arousing our pity, while Bossou, conscious of the effect of his playing, continued to prolong her suffering. Suddenly she burst into sobs, in her distress at her hopeless search for the one she loved. The sobs were prolonged in painful moans.

My mother, Séitou and the children could no longer bear the sight that the melodies played on the kpété conjured up before their inward eyes, 'the eyes of their soul' as Séitou said. They were all in tears. Bossou noticed this and suddenly broke off his playing. But so as not to leave us with these sad impressions, he put the instrument to his lips, conjured up the south again, but this time a comic harum-scarum south, that made us all burst out laughing.

When he finished, Camara asked gently, 'The young invisible lover was yourself, I suppose?'

'Not at all. Ahouna knows me well enough to doubt my being able to make myself so mysterious.'

'But you must have known this girl, whose image I found so delightful – or at least have met her somewhere,' I said.

'Not at all! You asked me to improvise and I tried to satisfy your wish. But it's possible that in tracing this portrait of a girl, I thought subconsciously of nearly all the pretty girls I had known and even been in love with, when I lived in the south.'

'Really, you are badly bitten!'

'It's as irresistable as life itself, Ahouna. Once you've known the south, you can't help thinking of it; you can't understand what that experience has meant to me.'

Camara and I accompanied Bossou back to Kounta, glad to have spent a good Sunday with him. On the way back, we never stopped talking about him. When we got home, we were agreeably surprised to notice that the rest of the family were also still talking about him.

I would work in the fields with Camara; he would accompany me to the pasture when his responsibilities as head of the family left him free.

One day, when the weather was perfect and the sun seemed to linger indefinitely above the horizon, I was perched on top of the mountain, playing tunes on my kpété, that conjured up centaurs in conflict with amazons whom they could not overcome, when I noticed a female figure down in the valley. At first I thought it was an optical illusion, for with the exception of Assani and some three or so itinerant merchants who paddled past our property in their canoes, no one outside our family ever crossed the pasture. I went on playing, as I was making up a tune in Bossou's style that I was well pleased with; however, I went on gazing at the girl to convince myself that she was real.

She was in fact a real flesh and blood girl, who had looked like a child when seen from above. She had two oranges in her hands and juggled with them as she walked: two huge, ripe, greenish-yellow oranges. She stopped at the foot of the mountain; I was already making my way down, playing as I went. I saw that she was smiling at me, and with some regret I stopped playing and waved to her. She smiled still more and threw me an orange. An orange, as I've already mentioned, meant nothing to me; we had more than we needed at home. But to acknowledge the girl's friendly gesture, I quickly came down from my vantage point, where I felt high above the world. I came up to her, noticing that she had a slender, willowy figure, fine, bright black eyes and a pretty mouth; firm, nubile breasts rounded her cotton shift that was printed in subdued colours, depicting a scene with deer drinking beside a lake, covered with water-lilies in full bloom. Her lips were sensual; her slender fingers looked unused to work. I was struck by the long muscles of her half-naked limbs.

I picked up the orange and thanked her.

'Do you often come through our pasture?' I asked her curiously.

'No, Ahouna, but I always hear the sound of your instruments. You really play well,' she replied.

'But you know my name?' I exclaimed.

'Certainly. Aren't you Ahouna Bakari, the boy who strangled a viper several years ago?'

I was suffused with pride, but smiled discreetly. 'That is so, but I don't know you.'

'My name is Anatou.'

'Where do you live, Anatou?' I asked, gazing now at her magnificent eyes, now at her breasts that intimidated me.

'I live at the baobab village on the other side of the mountain!'

'The one that is hidden in a ring of baobabs that can be seen from the top of Kinibaya?

'Can you see my village from your perch?' she asked, trembling with pleasure which she did her best to hide.

'Yes, indeed.'

'So it's not surprising that we can hear your music so well, down there.'

'Will you come with me, up the mountain?'

'With pleasure.'

We clambered briskly up. At the top, I showed her the whole surrounding country. We could see the various villages that took their names from the surrounding trees: kapok trees, bombax, mahogany, baobabs. Anatou looked astonished. She gazed at her village, clapped her hands happily and cried out in her musical voice, 'There's our house! Can you see that house with the iron roof, with huts on each side of it, with little clay pitchers on top of each roof? That's where I live. That's Fanikata's compound; Fanikata is my father.'

'I see,' I said. Then, having discovered that her father's name was as musical as her own, I immediately composed a song which I accompanied with my kpété:

> Fanikata, Fanikata!
> Happy Fanikata to have a daughter,
> A daughter beautiful as the day,
> As graceful as my sister Séitou.
> Fanikata, Fanikata!
> Happy, happy, Fanikata,
> Your daughter is as lovely as my sister.
> Anatou has the look of a goddess,
> And the body of a goddess;
> For her alone will I sing henceforth,
> A song of ecstasy ... A song of ecstasy.
> Anatou, Anatou!
> Daughter of Fanikata,
> I feel my life has reached a turning point,
> Simply because I have set eyes on you,
> And I feel that I love you!

'Do you really?' she asked, with a strange surprise.

'Sincerely,' I replied.

'People must know each other before they can love each other.'

'It is possible to fall in love and then get to know each other afterwards.'

'That is absurd.'

Snares without End

'Are you afraid that you might be sorry that you met me and loved me?'

'Not at all. If I fall in love with you, I hope that I shall never regret it.'

'Now I know what I wanted to know. You can't ever love me,' I said.

In fact I felt that she did love me too, but was playing hard to get, while I was moving too fast.

'Don't be disagreeable and try to be reasonable. We only met under an hour ago and you are already talking about being in love with me. It is so difficult, so complicated to be really in love that it has to be thought about for a long time, because people never understand each other until they have known each other for a long time. Understanding is at the root of all real and enduring friendships, according to my sister.'

'You reason well perhaps, but too well for a girl as pretty as you.'

'I like you, Ahouna, so let's just be friends,' she said firmly.

I was deeply disappointed to think that she did love me but wanted to keep me at a distance.

'If that's what you want,' I said sadly; then I added quickly, 'I'd like to walk over to the baobab village.'

'Please don't.'

'I'm afraid I'll not see you again.'

'If you like I'll come and see you here fairly often. I like your music very much; I must confess in fact that I have been attracted by it for a long time.'

'Thank you. I'm glad you like my music, for all the melodies that I play come straight from my heart and my soul, and I play them exactly as I feel. With me what is instinctive, like my songs, is most sincere, and I act more often on impulse than on logic,' I said, sententiously.

She did not reply and I was rather ashamed of my grandiloquence. We climbed down the mountain together.

'May I accompany you a little way home?'

'It's not worth it, Ahouna. I'll go on alone. Besides, your animals need you here.'

She was right; I watched her as she went on her way. I remained in the pasture, rooted to the spot, my heart in a turmoil, overwhelmed with melancholy. I put my kpété to my lips and tried to play; for the first time I felt no joy as I caressed the instrument. I murmured,

> Fanikata, Fanikata.
> Anatou, daughter of Fanikata;
> Your lovely velvet eyes
> Have induced such feelings in my heart
> That I never knew could dwell in me.
> I love you, but I feel so sad,
> Anatou, Anatou,
> Daughter of Fanikata.

She turned round and smiled at me, waved a friendly farewell and disappeared. I slipped my kpété into my pocket, from which I had first taken the orange that Anatou had given me. I rolled the fruit time and time again between my hands, and as I handled it I felt as if I was caressing Anatou's whole body. Such a pleasant sensation, sweet and voluptuous at once, made me hesitate to eat the orange, although I felt like doing so. I took it home, took it to bed with me. The orange was metamorphosed: Anatou was lying beside me. I asked nothing of her, she gave me nothing; we were reasonable, good, but we talked long into the night and I was happy, divinely happy as I slept, for Anatou was there, sleeping beside me, and I could feel her body against mine.

I awoke, with my heart full of ease, my countenance suffused with bright, child-like smiles.

'You look as if you've been playing your kpété or your tôba in your sleep!' said Camara, greeting me with an early-morning handshake.

'Yes, I dreamed that I was singing a song of love, life and death all at once,' I replied with a smile.

'Of love? ah – ah! You'd better look out!' retorted Camara with a knowing look.

'Of life and death also!' I corrected him.

'That's quite logical: Love – Life – Death. That's a normal sequence. All other actions that people perform

Snares without End

only serve to link more closely these three fundamentals of human existence. We begin necessarily by life – whether happy or unhappy – and then we proceed to love, happily or unhappily also, and end in death, which needs no epithets. Everything leads inevitably to death.'

'I have never heard you speak like that. You talk like Anatou,' I let slip before I could stop myself, as I had no wish at that time to reveal the reason for my joy.

'Anatou? Who is Anatou?' he asked me curiously.

'That's Anatou!' I said, showing him my orange.

'I see!' he said, shaking my hand again, as if to congratulate me.

'There's nothing to see. I was just joking.'

'Perhaps. But in any case, you are in love. That's quite obvious.'

'Is love a mask that is worn by lovers?'

'No, not a mask. That would be most disturbing, but a mark, a seal.'

'A mark like you see on the European goods that Assani and the like cart around for sale? A seal like the ones on the statuettes that Fatchina carves?'

'Love is not a product for sale. Sometimes it turns into that, by accident or some strange chance, but it should not ever be so by rights. You will understand that later, Ahouna.'

'With all that it implies of happiness and unhappiness, for since I was ten or eleven, and especially since father's death, happiness and unhappiness, misery even, have been inseparable in my mind.'

'A little pessimism is fitting in a man who is conscious of himself, but you must not go too far, Ahouna.'

'I am clear-sighted, rather than pessimistic; I don't systematically see everything in the blackest light, but I insist on seeing everything absolutely clearly.'

'You are too much of a realist, Ahouna.'

I carefully peeled my orange, ate it with a feeling of awe, and curiously enough, from that moment, it was as if I was possessed. I felt the presence of Anatou within me; I kept up an interminable inner monologue with her. Anatou smiled within me, was living within me.

Chapter 6

Anatou came to see me fairly regularly in the pasture. I did not worry if she was late, nor if she stayed away. Sometimes she never came for days on end. But I was always pleased, delighted even beyond measure, to see her sitting beside me. We talked for long hours and I improvised tunes for her on one or other of my two instruments. Sometimes we just sat side by side, without exchanging a single word, strangely contented to be together.

One day, she asked me to sing her the song I had played the day we first met.

'But I can't remember it at all! All the music I fill the valley with is improvised.'

Anatou looked at me in astonishment and I guessed from the expression on her pretty face that it was most tactless of me to admit that I had forgotten that particular song, but this did not prevent her speaking more freely to me.

'Don't you really remember it, Ahouna?'

'Really, truly, Anatou. I'm dreadfully sorry.'

'Well, *I* remember it: that memory is engraved on my heart. I'm ... I could almost be jealous of it,' she said. Then she began to hum the tune.

At that moment, it came back to me, at first a vague memory, but I soon recognised what I had been trying to express and I played it again for her. She was sitting beside me, leaning her head towards mine. Then deliberately – for she did not draw back, as she would have done if it had been an unthinking gesture on her part – her body touched mine. I could feel her firm breasts. I was perplexed as it was the last thing I expected to see Anatou nestle close to me like this. I stopped playing and asked 'Anatou, is it true you just want us to be friends? Is it true you don't love me?'

'Don't be hard on me, Ahouna.'

Snares without End

She hesitated a moment and then added, 'At first, I just liked you as a friend, but now I think that I've really loved you ever since the day I came to see you here, the day we first met. I love you and this grieves me, Ahouna,' she murmured, with lowered eyes as if ashamed of this confession.

'Is it true?' I asked, suddenly brimming over with happiness.

For a moment I stared into space and then gazed at the Kiniba which seemed to flow imperceptibly. I placed my hand on Anatou's breast and felt her heart beating wildly. I repeated my question before she had had time to reply.

'Tell me it's true, Anatou.'

'Since I've said so, Ahouna, that means it is true.'

'But why does loving me upset you? Why are you unhappy, since you love me?'

'I don't know ... I don't know how to explain it to you, but I'm not so upset now that I've told you the truth; I think I was unhappy because I hadn't told you the truth earlier. It's a strange thing, I feel as if an unbearable burden had been lifted from my heart and my soul freed from suffering,' she said, holding me even closer.

I put my kpété to my lips and sang again the song that she liked:

> Fanikata, Fanikata!
> Fortunate Fanikata has a daughter,
> A girl as beautiful as the day ...

She smiled at me and I said, 'I am happy, Anatou.'

'I am happy too, Ahouna!' she replied, then added quickly, 'Don't let's say anything more.'

I put my kpété back in my pocket and laid my head on Anatou's lap, and we remained so for nearly an hour. Yes, I was happy. 'Life, Love and Death'. Life seemed to me to have been fused with love, swallowed up by love; would that I could have ceased living at that moment. Twenty years of life seemed quite enough to me, and it only remained to arrive at death. I even desired death, and wished that through some absurd accident Anatou and I could fall from the top of Kinibaya, where we sat, and die without ever regaining consciousness. I was still mulling over these thoughts when Anatou started slightly, saying, 'Someone's coming!'

I slowly raised my head, looked and said that it was Camara, my brother-in-law.

'Séitou's new husband?'

'Yes.'

'I often see their children; they are really lovely.'

'We shall have children also, shan't we, Anatou?'

She smiled her agreement, her eyes shining with happiness. We climbed down to meet Camara and I did the introductions. As usual, Camara joked, 'But you told me that Anatou was the name of your orange!' he declared with a broad smile.

Anatou burst out laughing merrily, showing a row of regular teeth of dazzling whiteness. I laughed also and added, 'It was out of discretion that I spoke symbolically. And then I wasn't sure that Anatou loved me. Now I am happy, Camara.'

'You must be careful of symbols; an orange can be very bitter or very sweet, without your knowing until you have peeled it. You can only tell by tasting,' Anatou said slyly.

'It can be a delightful mixture of the two flavours,' Camara observed subtly, to which I added, all my senses suffused with happiness, 'It takes a little of everything to make a world; and according to Allah, everything contributes to man's real happiness.'

We all three chatted together for a while, after which Camara drove the flocks and herds back and left us alone.

We walked towards the Kiniba and sat down in a patch of green grass on the bank, where a rock stood up from the river bed. I can still see the sheet of spray that spread out like rubies around this obstacle. We paddled our feet in the pleasant, cool water. Then I took out my tôba, gently stroked the delicate frets and the air was filled with anguished sounds.

'That hurts,' murmured Anatou.

'I'm sorry. I won't play it any more.'

'Oh yes, do, Ahouna; it is most sweet pain. Do play,' she

Snares without End

said softly, enveloping me with her fresh, thoughtful smile.

I thought of Bossou, conjured him up in my heart as if he were a presiding god, and began to stroke the frets again, the fine ones, the medium ones and the thick ones. I drew from them sounds which I would never have thought existed, which depicted the activities and the gestures from the south that Bossou had spoken of. I evoked the sea which I had never seen ... that I have still never seen, but whose distant thundering, reduced by distance to a whisper and a murmur, could be heard in my music. Every wave, as it broke on the shore, pronounced the name of my fiancée; the surf softly whispered, 'Anatou, Anatou ... Anatou, Anatou ... Anatou, Anatou!'

Anatou nestled close to me, her eyes filled with tears.

'How do you do this? How do you manage to say so many things, just with these rows of bamboo strips?'

I let the voice of the tôba answer for me;

> I do not know, I do not know,
> Anatou, daughter of Fanikata and Ibayâ;
> Your lovely velvet eyes
> Have awoken feelings in my heart
> That I never knew could dwell there.
> I love you and from such joy could cease to
>   live,
> Anatou, Anatou, daughter of Fanikata and
>   Ibayâ.

She squeezed my arm; I looked into her eyes and we exchanged a smile. Finally we lifted our feet out of the water and walked along the side of the stream.

Night was falling. The sun, like a huge, blood-red disc, was slowly disappearing behind the mountains, down there in the heart of the baobab village. A faint, blue, diaphanous haze rose up from the earth and enveloped the pasture, rising towards the top of Mount Kinibaya. The birds fell silent. The sounds of the night, faint in the distance, began to take over. We walked a long time through the pasture before retracing our footsteps. Then I suggested to Anatou that we should visit our shelter. She agreed and we climbed the steps into the hut perched on its stilts, and we sat down facing each other. The crickets set up their shrill, solemn chorus. The croaking of frogs and toads reached us from a stream not far from Kinibaya.

'Look, Ahouna!' Anatou suddenly cried, stretching out her hand towards the mist that grew denser as night fell.

The air was pitted with tiny fires, minute, pale blue sparks whose cool light was already visible. They all streamed up towards Kinibaya, settled and went on shining, became more and more numerous, clustered on the mountainside, covering it from its foot to its summit with amazing speed. Soon the whole of Mount Kinibaya was a-sparkle, for a whole army of fireflies seemed to have collected there, for the express purpose of offering us the sublime spectacle that we had before our eyes.

We climbed down from our lookout and made our way towards the illuminated mountain top. We climbed up with the utmost precaution, so as not to crush a single firefly. From the height we could see the lights of the different villages, the baobabs, the mahogany and kapok trees and all the others. Standing there, like a couple of divinities who had emerged from the womb of the earth, we stood gazing in admiration on this universe of glowworms, which seemed to express in their primitive fashion all that was deep and pure in the feelings Anatou and I felt for each other.

'I must go back home, Ahouna,' Anatou said in a voice choked with emotion.

And we climbed down the mountain again.

'I'll walk back with you, Anatou.'

'No, not back to my home.'

'To the door of your house, then.'

'All right.'

'Are you afraid of your parents knowing we are in love?'

'Not at all! Do you have to be ashamed of falling in love with someone you liked straight away and still like?'

'Of course not; on the contrary.'

Snares without End

'I've even told my mother about you.'

I controlled my astonishment, but could not hide my curiosity when I asked her what she could have said to her mother about me.

'That I loved you ... that I love you without knowing whether you love me also.'

'You are unfair, Anatou; you know that I have been in love with you ever since we first met.'

'That's true; only I wasn't sure then. Now I've no more doubt; I'm convinced that Ahouna, the poet, the son of Bakari and Mariatou, is in love with me. That's what I shall tell my mother, and she will let my father and all our family know,' she said in her soft, firm voice.

'I will tell the glad news too, to my mother and sister, who have no doubt that I am in love.'

I put my arm round her narrow, supple waist and we walked together in the direction of the baobab village, accompanied by the chorus of crickets and frogs.

That evening, of course, I got home late. A purplish moon was climbing up the star-spangled sky. The haze had disappeared, the earth was visible once more, the grass was cool and fresh. The soft murmurs of the Kiniba could be heard amidst the reeds and rushes. My heart was over-flowing with happiness.

The whole household seemed to be asleep, except that the light of a storm-lantern warned me that my mother was waiting up for me. I went into her room.

'Not in bed, mother?'

'No, my boy. Camara told me that you were chatting with some friends, so ...'

'I'm sorry, mother; I'll tell you the whole story, but first, I hope that you ate without me?'

'No, son. You know that I don't like to eat without you.'

'Oh, then please forgive me for keeping you waiting.'

'You don't have to be sorry, son. My whole life is a long waiting and a long patience which will only end with my death; that is the fate of all women worthy of the name of mother.'

I sat down on the ground beside her, put my head on her lap, and remained a long moment lost in thought, and then we began to talk and I confessed to her the secret of my heart.

'You will bring Anatou to meet us, won't you?'

'Of course, mother,' I replied, and we separated for the night.

A week later, I went to Anatou's home for the first time. The Fanikatas own no cattle, but they have very valuable farming property, acres of orange groves and karite trees, and great quantities of poultry. They are rich, but their chief source of pride is that they had lived for eight years in the south, and they could not help mentioning this in the course of their conversations.

Fanikata is an elegant, handsome man. He owes his light complexion to his mother who came from the Niger. Certain scandalmongers in the baobab village said that Fanikata's mother must have been put in the family way by some white man or other; but as he never took any notice of this crude slander the gossips soon had to stop their gibes. As for Ibayâ, she is a worthy partner to Fanikata: tall and slender, with Anatou's willowy figure. When I saw her for the first time, it was impossible to believe that she was the mother of five children, of whom Anatou was the youngest. The sisters and brothers were all married, and as they lived neither in the same village nor in the Younikili area, I could not make their acquaintance the day of my visit.

I soon felt very much at home in Fanikata's family. We talked of my father, whom my future parents-in-law had known.

'Oh, I remember that tragic day when your worthy father was driven by the shame of the taunts and outrages to which he was subjected, to put an abrupt end to his slavery by taking his own life. I was so enraged that I took my gun and my scimitar and swore to kill the white man and his accursed guards; I would have done so if my son Sylla and my son-in-law Idissou hadn't prevented me, by seizing my weapons. They even had to lock me up, like a madman.'

'So that was you?' I exclaimed in surprise and admiration.

'Yes, that was me, young man. I cannot think of the horror of that day without feeling suddenly beside myself.'

'I have heard of you, but I can't remember having heard your name, for I would have recalled it when Anatou told me that she was Fanikata's daughter ... I had heard that someone who had known my father Bakari and held him in great regard had been so filled with indignation that he had sworn by Allah to avenge his death.'

'That is so,' said Ibayâ, her black eyes flashing with animation. 'Although Sylla and Idissou had locked up my husband, he shouted that he must be allowed to go and kill the white man and his guards, even if no one was tempted to follow him. He insisted on avenging the death of the man who had been his comrade-in-arms in France, and declared that the violence of his anger would drive him mad if he were not allowed to destroy all the criminals; they must let him out and they'd see what he was capable of doing for a friend who was worthy of the name. He swore that he was beside himself, he was convulsed with fury, that he would die of shame and fury if they didn't let him go, in the full impetus of his anger, and kill off all those murderers. Oh, my poor Ahouna, we had a hard time controlling my husband as he let loose these torrents of bitter indignation.'

We continued to exchange ideas for a short time and then I took Anatou home with me. I introduced her to my mother and sister. Camara greeted her jokingly, 'Welcome to our home, Orange!'

Anatou who had been feeling somewhat strained, smiled.

'You know each other already?' asked Séitou, with her gentle smile that was so familiar to me.

'You know Ahouna has no secrets from me.'

'Now I know why you are always teasing him about oranges.'

I then told the whole family how Fanikata had reacted the day my father died. My mother, like me, must have heard of the fury of one of my father's friends from his army days, and when she heard this painful incident she was moved to tears.

Snares without End

Still under the influence of this emotion to which was added that of seeing me about to get married, she took our hands. in her own and said, with tears of happiness, 'In a week's time I shall go and call on Fanikata and Ibayâ, fortunate couple that they are. For my part, I can now only think of you two together. I unite you before Allah and before the shade of Bakari, who is not dead for me, for he is still present and living in my heart. Live long; live happily, my children.'

She rose and withdrew, hiding her face in her hands. Anatou's eyes were also brimming over with tears, which she was hard put not to shed.

My mother went to call on the Fanikata family. Everything went well. Henceforth it was known in the two villages that Anatou and I were to wed. In Kiniba, they teased me, saying, 'Your future father-in-law's a strong man, equal to any situation. If anyone was offensive to you he'd certainly come along with his double-barrelled rifle and his scimitar and avenge you.'

To which I retorted, 'That would be a real advantage. So then Fanikata could kill the tiresome fellow several times over, and be quite sure he was good and dead!'

In the baobab village they said when they saw me, 'Is he the one who's going to marry Anatou?'

'That's him! He's Bakari's youngster.'

'The lad who strangled a viper when he was barely thirteen?'

'Yes, indeed.'

'Poor little Anatou! It's to be hoped that he won't strangle her as well one day!'

Anatou and I saw each other every day. She came to our house for dinner on Sundays, when I was not invited to her house. The pleasure of our evening walks together was enhanced by some love song that I composed on my kpété or my tôba. We accompanied each other backward and forward from one house to the other; finally, in the order of things, I left Anatou at her parent's house and returned late home myself. Five or six times, as we walked to and fro, we were surprised by the sunrise and still had no desire to part. Fortunately my mother no longer waited up for me to eat in the evening or to go off to sleep. But I never parted from Anatou without playing for her the music I had improvised the first day that she came to see me in the pasture, the one about centaurs and Amazons. She liked that melody so much that I had to learn it off by heart, to please her, for this tune and the one about her and her father reminded her of two precious moments in our lives.

Six or seven months after my mother's visit to the Fanikata family, the end of the harvest time came round. The grain had been brought in; sales had been good; every farmer had paid his workers. Everywhere sums of money had been put aside for taxes and special occasions; those who believed in the gods gave thanks to them. With nothing to worry about for the moment, the fields were left until the first rains and the entertainments which take place at nightfall were organised in all the villages.

The rumour went about that Bossou was going to perform at the baobab village. He had become a well-known griot, having sung and played in Ouidah, Cotonou, Porto-Novo and Abomey and surpassed Tokpon-Kinigbé, who was considered the finest griot of the day. The memory of that evening spent in Anatou's village will remain engraved on my heart for ever.

Men, women, girls and youths who had come to hear my friend Bossou sat around the biggest baobab tree in the village meeting-place. There was an enormous crowd. The moon was high in the sky, shedding its metallic light over the whole of Younikili. For the last half hour, the village echoed with sounds, now joyful, now solemn, now enthralling and voluptuous, now lugubrious, that musicians beat out on their tomtoms with skilful hands. While waiting for the arrival of the Master, the assembled crowd sang songs that they all knew. Two girls, smartly dressed in the fashions of the south, entered the circle, holding in their hands dried gourds decorated with allegorical designs that were burnt into them and covered with a network of tiny cowrie shells. They waved these in time to the music. A thrill went through the crowd when two more girls appeared, followed by a youth with a white silk scarf tied around his head and another one with a red scarf. The two lads each carried twin gongs which they beat while the girls waved their gourds. The crowd lost control of themselves, their frenzy intensified. One man, coming from the same side as the preceding couple, turned cartwheels over several yards, jumped over the circle of onlookers and took up his place in the middle, intoning incantations to which the whole group responded by a song which none of the spectators knew, but which was very pleasant to listen to.

Just as the chorus was finishing, Bossou arrived with two apprentice griots. I caught his eye and we exchanged a smile. I was so moved that I could hardly breathe.

Bossou's head was bound tightly in twisted scarves of red, yellow and black silk. In one hand he held a black horsetail; in the other a white one. The stumps of the tails were bound with black and white leather thongs and decorated with cowries. Bossou climbed on to an ebony stool placed in the centre of the circle. The crowd fell silent. Every eye was fixed on the young singer; every breath was held; every soul hung on my friend's lips. His voice rang out, sweet and solemn, then enthralling and voluptuous; it told of things that could not otherwise be expressed. All felt their spirits rising up from the earth, possessed by the demon of the music and carried away on a long and magnificent journey. It seemed to me that I had never seen or heard Bossou sing before, so wonderfully rich was his voice that evening – it was a golden voice.

Towards the end of this inaugural song, Bossou raised the horse-tails, waved them skilfully about in the air and then suddenly lowered his arm. At this, the whole company sang in unison the same song that Bossou had sung in such a dazzlingly pathetic manner. Then the sound of the tomtoms and gongs blended with the tinkle of the cowrie-covered gourds, while a man seated beside a huge jar drew from it a most captivating murmur, by a stroking its brim with a fan of dried oxhide: all this gave rise to the most intoxicating harmony that I had ever heard in my life.

. Then there were droll songs, then songs of praise of Fanikata and Moumouni and well-deserved eulogies to the memory of my father.

Then came the dancing. Bossou sang, brandishing his horsetails, running hither and thither round the ring of spectators, who clapped their hands and stamped their feet in time to the beat. The moon hung in the sky above our heads. Bossou's voice rang out above the tops of the highest trees. I felt that he was singing for me. Excited by the music, enthralled by the sensual, thrilling sounds of the instruments, stimulated by my friend's irresistible voice, I leapt into the circle. Anatou followed me.

First we danced some distance from each other; we sketched the first steps, listening to what the instruments were saying to us, but we were especially guided by the booming voice of the biggest tomtom. Our steps became more definite, faster, more expert as we danced closer and closer to each other; then came the supreme moment: our feet, arms, hands, hips, our whole bodies moved in time to the music, expressing what I can only call our whole heart and soul. I had never been so supple. Anatou and I were now dancing face to face, my breath mingled with hers; the beat of the big tomtom came faster and faster, and we felt ourselves lifted from the ground to fall into each other's arms, to the frantic applause of the crowd that was delirious with joy.

We left the meeting-place and two months later I married Anatou.

Chapter 7

Was life pleasant? Why deny it? Everything we undertook was a complete success. Anatou settled down well in our home and she and I were happy together. My mother was very fond of her. She and Séitou were quite inseparable, like a couple of sisters; neither of them ever bought anything without thinking of the other. They dressed alike, with only minor differences. In Kiniba and at the baobab village everyone said that Fanikata's daughter was indeed fortunate – and I hope they still say the same thing.

Camara and I got on wonderfully; we consulted each other whenever we wanted to give our mother or our wives a treat. I had taught him to play the kpété and the tôba and he showed considerable talent. We never had the slightest argument.

Not being exactly impotent, I soon gave proof of my manhood. I shall remember to my dying day the kindness that Camara showed me and all the good turns he did me ...

Until the birth of our first child, who is now eleven, Anatou liked to come and sit with me in the pasture when she had finished her work in the house and nothing kept her there with Séitou. We were still very much in love and I would play her favourite melodies for her. Even when she was pregnant, and up to three days before the baby was born, she still came all that long way, which made me quite anxious for her.

Finally came the night when she gave birth after quite an easy labour. We called the child Bakari in memory of my father.

With the birth of my first son I not only experienced the joy of fatherhood, but I also felt as if a great weight had been lifted from me, as if I had carried the baby in my own belly for nine months; and it is no exaggeration to say that I had the same impression with each of my other children, two boys and a girl. My heart was filled to

overflowing with songs of joy which I would have liked to
send echoing through the whole village as my fingers
tripped lightly over the holes in my kpété or the bamboo
frets of the tôba. But for the first time in my life I felt that
if I tried to express in music the deep happiness which
caused me such inner turmoil, it would somehow lose its
purity.

As soon as everything had been cleared up after the
birth, I left the house at first light, while the ground was
still wet with dew, and mounted one of our horses. I
galloped off to the baobab village, borne by a new
momentum, with a soft, melodious music singing in my
ears: the last distant sounds of the dying night, the first
murmurs of the new day, voices which swelled, grew
more distinct and then died away in mysterious
whisperings, while this sweet harmony was broken only
by the sudden cry of a bird as it fell perhaps from its nest
or was attacked by ants.

I reached the Baobabs. The moon, which must have
risen very late, still hung high in the sky in which a few
stars lingered. I knocked at my parents-in-law's house.
Fanikata rose, opened up, saw me and before I could even
break the glad news to him he read it in my eyes that
sparkled with joy.

'Anatou's child is born! you are a father!' he cried.

'Yes, indeed! I am so happy, so happy, Fanikata!' I
declared in a voice still stifled with emotion.

He seized my hand and shook it, then we embraced
affectionately. Meanwhile Ibayâ had got up; she too
embraced me and then, clasping her hands together, she
gave thanks to Allah.

Taking no notice of his wife, Fanikata hurried off to
purchase from Tchiffi, a sheep-breeder, a pure white ram
whose magnificent fleece hung down to the ground. The
beast had whitish horns which seemed translucent in the
sunlight, streaked with tiny, light-red veins. Camara had
noticed this ram and had suggested to me that we acquire
it for breeding purposes, to improve the strain of our
goats. I had agreed and we were simply waiting to buy it
until the tax season came round; that is the time when

stock-farmers in the northern areas are prepared to accept reasonable offers for their animals that they have first habitually overpriced.

Fanikata returned from Tchiffi's farm, dragging the ram on a short rope. He gave it a drink and then held out a branch of tender green leaves that he had torn off one of the naseberry trees overhanging the entrance to his compound. The ram stretched out its neck, seized the branch and was just beginning to munch the leaves when Fanikata gripped it and slit its throat as a thank-offering, expressing his joy at having a grandson at last, as his other children had only produced daughters.

This grisly sight greatly distressed me, but my abnormally intense delight at being a father overrode all other feelings and my pity for the sad fate of the handsome white ram was short-lived; so I shook my father-in-law heartily by the hand by way of approval for his action.

'We'll eat this beast today at noon; its skin shall make a prayer-mat for Bakari when he is big,' declared Fanikata. By now Ibayâ was dressed and expressed her intention to return with me.

'I must go and see my little Bakari and his mother,' she said.

'You'll be back early to see to the cooking. We shall be dining off this animal in Kiniba.'

'Stop worrying about that and come with us!' Ibayâ said impatiently. 'We'll come back and see about Tchiffi's goat when we have embraced our grandson.'

I returned to Kiniba with them. The Fanikatas went back to the Baobabs. Then about one o'clock they came back to Kiniba with the meal prepared. Our house rang with peals of laughter and cries of merriment. Camara and I played the kpété and the tôba; everyone joked; the children ran around, jumping and capering, turning cartwheels and somersaults, shouting, applauding. Mother was everywhere at once, laughing, crying, sending up prayers to Allah, admiring the newborn babe, evoking my father's memory, telling the guests little anecdotes about her youth and her happy married life, that I had never heard her speak of before. The event which we were celebrating seemed to have revived in her widow's heart a world which she had thought dead for ever, and she chatted on endlessly, with astonishing animation and humour.

Each new birth in our house was naturally followed by joyous scenes of merry feasting. Fatou followed Bakari and then came Sikidi who is the spit image of her mother. Since I no longer believe in Allah, or in anything, I beg you, M. Houénou, to pray to your God, with whom I have no dealings, that my daughter should not be like my wife morally, and that none of our children should take after either of us.

After Sidiki's birth, Camara asked me if we should not carry out the suggestion I had made of enlarging our compound so that the children could have a room to play and keep their own little possessions in, 'without always being disturbed by the grown-ups', as Rémy and Jean-Claude used to say. I agreed; my mother, who had frequently had this idea in mind, was delighted. She even added, in front of Camara and me, that we should put an iron roof on this new building.

'If I remember aright,' she said, 'there must be about thirty sheets of iron roofing up in the loft. I recall that they were already treated with creosote, then my husband put them away, intending to use them for the roof of a big new hut.'

There were already three circular huts in our compound; the one which belonged to my parents, and where I slept until I was too big, was rectangular with a corrugated iron roof; this was the 'big hut'. We decided to add two similar constructions to the whole family compound.

'Then we shall need more sheets of corrugated iron than we have here,' Camara pointed out.

'Well, since we can afford it, let's buy them,' I replied. 'But one of us will have to go to Parakou or even as far as Abomey.'

'Finiki, the pedlar in the baobab village, goes to Parakou and Abomey fairly regularly now that he has a big lorry. Couldn't you ask him to buy the sheets of iron you'll need?' suggested Anatou.

'That's an excellent idea, Anatou,' Camara replied; adding slyly, 'that'll stop any business with vipers,' at which we all burst out laughing.

'So we give Finiki the money ...' I began when Séitou interrupted, but speaking directly to her sister-in-law, 'Would it be wise to entrust Finiki with money, Anatou?'

'I know Finiki well; he's an honest man. But at the Baobabs, no one pays him until he has brought back the goods. He even insists on giving invoices when he buys at a white man's shop.'

'Well then, Finiki must have enough cash in hand to bring us a hundred sheets of iron,' Camara said.

'A hundred?' exclaimed Séitou in surprise.

'Yes, since we intend to build two large huts like that of our parents, even a bit bigger perhaps, like the ones I've seen in Abomey!' I said proudly.

For the next six months, our place was filled with people: friends and neighbours engaged to help us build the ten-foot-high walls, and carpenters who in our northern region are also roofers, joiners and locksmiths. You say it's the same in the south? So this is nothing new to you ... The bricklayers, who are also very good house-painters, came last of all.

When the work was finished, Séitou and Camara moved into one of the new apartments and Anatou and I into the other. One of the huts that we had previously occupied was handed over to the girls, the other became the boys' room.

Before my marriage I used to take all my meals with my mother; in the evenings Séitou, Camara and their children used to join us for dinner. After I married Anatou I saw somewhat less of my mother, but she was too happy, so she said, to see me become 'a real man, now that I was married', to give much thought to her own isolation. In fact she hardly ever ate alone; her big three-roomed hut was always overrun with her grandchildren and we still had our evening meal together, as in the past.

Snares without End

Just one year after we moved into the new buildings, Moumouni was born. He is now two and a half. So, when my youngest child was nine months old, the drama began which has turned me into the man I am now.

One day when the sun had been shining brightly since five in the morning, I got dressed and took my kpété, my tôba and my crook. As little Bakari, who helped me from time to time, had already left for school with his cousins, I let the flocks out and went off to the pasture with a light and happy heart, taking the same path that I had traversed for more than twenty years without ever sensing any monotony. I did not even realise how far it was; I did not notice the distance and covered it as if it did not exist, with the impression that I dropped straight out of our house into the middle of the pastureland.

I climbed to the top of Mount Kinibaya. The sun was already quite high in the heavens. I stood there, gazing at the light that quivered beneath me, like a strangely transparent lake of glass. Through an optical illusion I imagined I could see, far off in the plain, a man dressed in an ample white boubou. Then my mind went back to the time, some twenty years before, when on such a day my father had talked to me of Allah, and had recited by heart a fine passage from the Koran in which the prophet Mohammed gives thanks to the Lord God for having created him a man and put him in the world to contemplate such splendours. As in a waking dream, I could once more hear the inflexions of my father's voice – now gentle, now solemn, bordering on pathos. I was moved to the brink of tears, and to prevent their flowing I took up my kpété.

No, that day I did not make up new tunes. But I recalled the song that I had composed when I first met Anatou, to which I added some new lines referring to my own parents:

> Fanikata, Fanikata!
> Fortunate Fanikata to have a daughter
> A daughter beautiful as the day,
> Graceful as my sister Séitou.
> Fanikata, Fanikata!

Snares without End

Happy husband of Ibayâ,
You have given your daughter to the son of
    Bakari and Mariatou;
Mariatou, Mariatou, sublime mother,
My joy is that you gave me birth
To see you dandle my children on your
    knees.
I feel life surge in my veins, I am filled with
    joy
When I see you smile, and I say to myself:
I am a man,
I am the husband of Anatou who wants for
    nothing,
Anatou, the wondrous daughter of Fanikata
    and Ibayâ.

I had reached this point in my composition, with inspiration coming as easily to me as ever, when I saw my wife coming towards me. She had already reached the foot of the mountain before I caught sight of her. I immediately thought that something must have happened to one of the children. I quickly put my kpété in my pocket and was about to rush down to meet her, when she signalled to me not to worry, and at the same time shouted to me that she wanted to come up to talk to me. When she reached me, somewhat out of breath, anger and hatred showed in her eyes. I was all the more surprised in that there had never been the slightest misunderstanding between us in the thirteen years that we had been together and I had left the house barely four hours before.

'What's wrong at home, Anatou?' I inquired, intrigued.

'Everything's all right, everything's quite all right!' she said aggressively, she who was always quiet and smiling.

I had never seen her angry. I did not dare ... no, it did not even occur to me to ask her if my mother or sister had made some slighting remark about her, as no incident of that kind had ever occurred in our house. Camara? but have I not insisted at length on my relationship to him? As for Séitou, she is always ready to help us; it was she who undertook to teach our children French, English and German, with her own, while they were still quite young. Séitou is kindness itself. My mother? I have told you enough about her. However much I try, I can find no words worthy to describe her, as I see her. So whatever could have happened at home?

'Why have you left the children to come here, Anatou?'

'They're playing with their cousins; they are all with their grandmother.'

'So, I suppose you felt like coming to keep me company here, like the old times? ... That's very sweet of you. I often think of those times, too. I was just calling them to mind just now, with the tune I was playing on my kpété, when I saw you coming.'

'Liar!' she exclaimed suddenly, pulling away her trembling hand that I had been holding in mine, while I wondered what was going on in her head.

I was so astonished that I could only cry, 'Anatou, my dear, whatever is the matter?'

'Liar! liar! liar!' she shouted furiously.

'I never lie, Anatou,' I replied quietly, trying to answer violence with gentleness.

'Oh yes you do. You weren't thinking of me when you were playing just now.'

'Please believe me, Anatou. I was playing for you, for your parents, and mine too ... not forgetting myself,' I replied firmly.

'That's not true. To me, you always seem to be trying to entice some woman. That's what you're doing, in fact; I'm convinced that you were singing for a girl you must have met since I stopped coming here with you.'

'Anatou, you are jealous?'

'Haven't I got the right to be jealous?'

'Yes, indeed. It's proof that you are still in love with me. It would be better to have to do with a stone than a woman incapable of feeling some twinges of jealousy and the same would be true of a man. But I think you are jealous of nothing, of a figment of your imagination. I love no one but you, and no girl or woman has been this way since you stopped coming to the pasture. Besides, this is not a public thoroughfare. You are the first and last person to come through here, in the time before we knew each other.'

'You're lying again, Ahouna! Your eyes give you away, your lips are trembling and crying out that you are lying. If you could see your eyes while you deny the truth, you would see the reflection of a girl who begs you not to hide anything from me any more. Why are you lying, Ahouna?'

A girl's reflection in my eyes? Bossou had already mentioned this strange phenomenon to me, but I had not believed him. His words came back to me suddenly and I repeated them to myself. 'Every man has at the back of his eyes, the perfect photographic image of the woman who has done him the most good or the most harm, or the one who has made him the happiest or unhappiest. This image only emerges at a certain moment of his existence and then becomes visible to everyone.' Well, I had done no one any harm and Anatou was the woman I thought I was making the happiest. I replied, 'I am not lying. If there is any image of a girl in my eyes, and you claim to see one, then she can only be you.'

'Hold your tongue, will you! You're still lying. You can't stop lying.'

'No Koranic law forbids me having two wives. But my father only had one. Your father also. Camara is Séitou's husband and not the husband of any other woman. Like them I have only one wife, you, Anatou, and I have no intention of burdening myself ... that is, of taking on another one.'

'I've always known that I was a burden to you. I know that one day you'll want to get rid of me.'

'Anatou! ... forgive me. That unfortunate word just slipped out. It was your goading that made me come out with that stupid remark; I didn't mean you were a burden to me; I've never felt that or thought that for one instant,' I protested.

'I feel as if ... I'm waiting patiently for the moment when you'll kill me to get rid of me ...'

'Anatou!' I cried, terrified at this terrible idea.

'Only I can't stand your telling me you love me, when you don't lose any opportunity of deceiving me with that girl you entice with your music.'

'Anatou!' I exclaimed again, unable to understand or even to guess at the reasons hidden behind this accusation.

'Hold your tongue! By Allah, hold your tongue! You're going to tell more lies. Ha! Ha! ... You never lie, you've never lied, you're not lying, this field is not a public thoroughfare, there's no road through here. All the same! Just look there, if you have the courage! Praise be to Allah!' she exclaimed and her mockery froze the blood in my veins.

I looked down the slope and saw a girl passing. Allah himself must have been against me. Never – and please forgive me for stating this again so categorically, but the facts require it – never had I seen anyone crossing our pasture since Anatou came there. Never had I seen this girl in Kiniba, nor at the Baobabs. I looked at her but had no idea who she was; I was dumbstruck to see her passing at the very moment when my wife was accusing me of a contemptible action which I had not committed.

According to Anatou, the girl smiled at us; I saw her wave as if to indicate that she would not disturb us, she was just passing by. I was overwhelmed. I could guess how Anatou would interpret this unfortunate coincidence.

'That *smile*, and the way she waved goodbye, that was all meant for you. This all implies that you are in league with her and have a secret code that only the two of you understand. Are you going to go on lying, Ahouna?' she said, trying in vain to wipe away the tears that now flowed freely.

'I have never lied, Anatou. I shall never lie as long as I live,' I declared; but my voice suddenly faltered.

'Oh! I can't bear it! it's terrible to hear you go on lying in the face of the truth. I have seen you in my dreams for a long time with that girl. At first, I didn't want to believe it; but it's always the same person I see mocking me, so I decided to come and surprise you. So I came! And I saw you. I'm certain my dreams were not just illusions; they reflected the reality. I can only give thanks to Allah who gave me the idea of coming here where I've finally seen everything.'

'Either what you are saying is a sacrilege, in which case I'm sorry for you; or you are quite sincere, in which case Allah himself is against me, innocent as I am ...'

'Allah is against you, because you're an untrustworthy sham!' she interrupted me excitedly.

An untrustworthy sham! These words shook me profoundly and I exclaimed, 'There is no man more sincere than I. I am innocent. I swear by our mutual love and on the heads of our children and by my father that I am innocent!'

'Poor Ahouna, the man I loved with all my heart, with all my soul and whose only love I thought myself to be!'

'Anatou, your dreams have deceived you. You are wrong to believe in them. I can invent illusions also, in which I imagine you making love to another man.'

'Only you wouldn't be able to face me with the real thing, as I have just done!' she declared haughtily.

'Because you would be able to hide your little game. I can't hide anything, for the simple reason that my heart is too open. You can even read in it what isn't there!' I said firmly, conscious of the effect that this thought would produce.

Anatou stared at me insolently. She fiddled with the scarf that she wore round her head, like the women from the south-east region, and nervously untied and retied the little pagne that she wore over her slip. She sighed and asked miserably, 'What do you mean? Hide my little game?'

'Why not, since you accuse me of such unspeakable things?'

'I accuse you of what's true.'

'A truth that does not exist. You've invented a whole story that seems credible but which is quite absurd in fact. Then, by dint of repeating it to yourself, you've convinced yourself it's true. You are terribly unjust, Anatou!'

'Monster!' she shouted.

'I don't deserve that, Anatou!'

Snares without End

'Monster! monster! monster ...' she repeated, hurrying down the mountainside, so fast that I was afraid that she might slip and fall to her death down one of the sheer faces of the rock.

I remained long bewildered by this quarrel. I tried in vain to see if there could be any foundation, other than Anatou's dreams, for the accusation she had made.

I would have liked to play my kpété or my tôba, but my heart was beating so violently that I felt more like weeping, as if I were still a child. I controlled myself. I sat down, my legs bent under me, my arms around my body, my chin on my knees. I must have looked like a bundle of rags dropped there on top of Mount Kinibaya. I stared into space seeing nothing, neither the little shelter on its stilts beside the stream, nor the cattle or sheep, nor the dogs that I used to love to watch gambolling in the grass. I collected my wits. The Kiniba river seemed to be swirling round in its bed. The light quivered before my eyes like vapour rising from a lake poised in midair.

As if it were a premonition, I saw in this atmospheric phenomenon the very meaning of my life: a slight, imperceptible quiver in time and space, as soon as the weather is hot, and which will disappear into oblivion without anyone caring. I suddenly had the revelation of the futility of my existence, the vanity and vacuity of all the actions I had ever performed and was still performing. I realised the absurdity of my personality being developed with the aim of making it endure as long as possible, so prolonging its very emptiness. I was basing my life on a fiction and did not know it. Emptiness, the only thing that really exists, for the very reason that it is all round us, had become palpable. I could touch it with my finger. Trapped as I was in the heart of the absurd, there was nothing left for me but to hurl myself into the void, to crash against the sheer face of Mount Kinibaya, like a pebble ricocheting across the surface of the lake, to fall dead, down below, among the animals in the middle of the pasture, from where from my earliest childhood I had lifted up my shepherd's heart in endless song, and where I had met Anatou.

But I recovered my self-control. I thought of my children who had not asked to be born. To kill myself would be to abandon them and make them wretched. And I adored them; I wanted to make their lives as happy as possible. I thought of my poor mother, about whom I worried every morning if she woke a little later than usual. My poor good Mariatou is so old – if indeed she is still alive – that I was always afraid she would die suddenly one night, without having the chance to look into my eyes for the last time and say a word to me. I thought of Séitou who is both a sister and a friend, of Camara whom I was so happy to see happy in our midst, of my nephews and nieces whom I love and who loved me too.

I should be lying if I claimed not to have thought of Anatou also. If I had taken my own life, I would have given her the impression that she had been right, that she had discovered a secret which did not exist, but it would also have made her regret her unjust accusation; she would have been consumed with remorse, inconsolable, miserable. All these reasons seemed more important than my own distress; I shook my head as an indication that I rejected this easy way out, stretched my stiff limbs, stood up on the top of Kinibaya, took out my kpété and recalling one of the Fon songs that Bossou had taught me, I intoned,

> *Yé do tome bo do ha ba mi wê,*
> *Yokpo le do tome bo do ha ba mi wê.*
> *A do gbé mi on, ahoo,*
> *Medé ma do gbé mi houn, ahoo*
> *Me ni gbo:*
> *Adjâ éba houékpo*
> *Adjâ lo non i houé,*
> *Adjïnakou ma non gon daa ton houé.*
> *Etêwê énasso mi do wâ?*
> *Nou tê kpossin gbêtô nasso gnin do wâ do wêkêmê?*
> *Adjâ éba houékpo*
> *Adjâ lô non i houé,*
> *Adjïnakou ma non gon dâ ton houé.*

I returned home, intending to speak to Camara, but I

thought better of it; he had had a hard time in his own country and with his own family because of his marriage to my sister; he had come to us and we had made him welcome; he had found with us all that he needed for his happiness and he was indeed happy. Why should I now inform him that for the last few hours I had become unhappy, and so inspire him once more with a pessimistic outlook on life? Why should I engender anxious thoughts in him which he could not help imparting to my sister and mother, which would have forced them to summon Anatou and me and ask questions which I could not answer, for the very reason that I was and am innocent of everything that my wife accused me of?

On my return from the pasture my children welcomed me effusively as usual, which always gave me the impression that I was returning from a long journey. My children's laughter and smiles and those of my nephews were that evening the sole satisfaction that I felt at being back home. An acrid humour seemed to be mixed with my blood and circulating in my veins. When I returned from the sheepfold I felt a sudden surge of revulsion against life. I tried to control these emotions, to which I could not give a name; I held each child in turn in a close embrace. I took little Moumouni in my arms and hummed a lullaby with words coming straight from the heart.

> The sun has set already
> And night enfolds the earth in her arms.
> Bakari still lingers at his play and then will
> go to sleep.
> Fatou will start to cry that he is not yet
> sleepy;
> Sidiki will fall asleep, nursing her wooden
> doll,
> And Moumouni will rest for long on his
> mother's lap
> And then will fall asleep too, with his
> thumb in his mouth.
> Deep night falls on the earth.

She embraces the earth with a mysterious
   kiss.
Like pure-hearted parents affectionately
   · kissing their children goodnight.
The children sleep while their parents watch
   and wake:
Hearts unhappy in their innocence cannot
   sleep ...

When she heard these last words, Anatou, who had
tried to look as if she was not listening, came and took the
child from me; she looked at me with revulsion
murmuring, 'I hope you're not going to give yourself
martyr's airs in front of everyone.'

'I am a martyr, because I am innocent. But don't
worry. I love my mother and sister and my brother
Camara too much to upset them with your foolishness.
I'm not the kind of man who resents seeing other people
happy around me,' I murmured drily.

Anatou gave me a contemptuous look and went to join
the children.

Now that not only Camara, but also Rémy, Jean-Claude
and Bakari, could play the kpété, we used to gather in the
evening, before or after dinner, to play together under the
biggest of the naseberry trees that shaded our courtyard.
That evening Camara started up a war-song of the
Almamy Samory Touré's army; the children played the
accompaniment, while I harmonised the tragic,
anguished implications of the song on the tôba. The effect
was overwhelming. Mother had to beg us not to conjure
up such melancholy memories.

The atmosphere at dinner was as merry as usual, but I
felt that my accustomed good humour was artificially
maintained.

When we were in bed, I lay close to Anatou, but she
pulled away roughly, betraying her aversion to me, which
I noted with bitterness. Contrary to her habit, she lay with
her back to me; I tried to place my hand on her shoulder,
but she drew further away. I did not insist, but I wanted to
ask her certain questions, so I called her name.

She did not reply, but I went on, just the same, 'Anatou,

are your dreams the only cause for your unjust accusations?'

She did not take up the words 'only cause' and 'unjust' that I had deliberately used.

'First of all I had certain premonitions,' she said in a surly tone..

'That doesn't mean anything. You've lived in the south a lot and you've made a point of imitating customs and ways of speaking which are quite different from ours. From what I've been told, people in Cotonou and the big towns in the south, who've been corrupted by white men's hair-splitting, talk of premonitions when they want to hide the real reason and motives for their actions. My sister was the wife of a white man. From her life with Tertullien she learnt to know a bit about the worth of such people. She has lived in the south as well; she knows their customs and has told me about them. Open your heart, Anatou; tell me what is going through your mind. Behave like a girl from the north and not a little snob, copying the south!' I said boldly.

'I'm not copying anyone. You're wrong to blame the southerners. I told you that I had a premonition, then I had dreams that always showed me what was actually happening; finally I decided to go to see the truth for myself; well, I saw it, I realised what the truth was. You can't deny what I saw. By Allah! Ahouna, that girl ...'

'I don't know her! I've never met her!' I declared firmly.

'Ahouna ... Why are you beginning your lies again? Why do you persist in lying? Take another wife, if you feel like it. By Allah, I would not despise her. But I can't bear you deceiving me and then denying it.'

Everything that I would have liked to say seemed suddenly repressed, stifled in my heart. I felt as if I was suffocating, worse than if my throat was caught in a vice. If I had had to undertake to go on talking – not to defend myself, for that was now completely useless as my wife was convinced I was deceiving her, but to try to make her understand once more that she was accusing an innocent man who loved no one but her – my tears would have prevented me from speaking. But was she – is she – capable of pity? And then, I was not at fault, I had done nothing, nothing, nothing! *That* was what I so much wanted her to know.

'Listen to me, Anatou.'

'Have you really thought about it? Are you going to tell me the truth, and nothing but the truth, or rather are you going to confirm what I know to be the truth?'

'I've nothing more to tell you, except that I am terribly upset, deeply hurt that you accuse me of something that has never even entered my mind. If you want to leave me for some reason that you alone know, then leave me. I shall not remarry, but shall remain alone with our children that I love and shall love till my dying day!'

'You're mad. You're talking out of your hat, as my sister would say.'

'All right then! Since I'm mad I shall go to see your parents. I shall tell them of your foolish behaviour, how you have become jealous without any valid reason that I know of.'

'So you need some support, people to back you up; you couldn't defend yourself alone against a weak little woman? Please don't go and upset my parents' peace of mind.'

'They must know what is happening.'

'It's funny. I thought you were more of a man than you seem to be now.'

This insistence on my weakness disarmed me and stifled all my affection.

Chapter 8

We lived for four months in this atmosphere of tragi-comedy: there was laughter in front of the rest of the household, jollity at meals in the presence of my mother, sister, Camara and the children; then, at night, we would lie back to back, one on each edge of the bed we still shared, without daring to exchange a word.

One day I had to remain at home to look after some of our cows which had calved and were not well, so Camara took the animals out to graze. I forgot to tell you that for some time – I can't judge how long but it seemed quite a long period to me – I did not see the girl crossing our land who Anatou alleged was my mistress. But that evening, when Camara came home, he told me he had seen a girl walking across the pasture. He had pointed out to her that the meadow was not a public thoroughfare and said he didn't want to see her there again. At which, according to Camara, the girl insisted that she often passed that way and said I had never made any such difficulties.

Although Anatou heard what my brother-in-law said, she pretended to take no notice. I expected her to return to the attack after three months' silence. But she did not do so.

The next day I rode out to the meadow on horseback, as I very much wanted to leave the dogs to guard the flocks and then to ride over to the baobab village to let my parents-in-law know what was happening, as I had really had enough of living with my wife under these conditions.

When I reached the meadow, the grass was still damp with dew and the rising sun had left a harsh red gash across the horizon, such a savage red as I do not remember ever having seen. I climbed to the top of Mount Kinibaya, from where I gazed long on the melancholy beauty of nature in all her splendour – melancholy no doubt in reflection of my own mood. I took up by tôba but I could express only distressing, mournful, despairing feelings. I put my instrument back in my pocket, drew my legs under me and curled up like a porcupine ready to defend itself. This posture seemed to me to indicate my complete collapse, which greatly displeased me: I think I have told you that I disapproved of revolt for revolt's sake. But instead of getting up, shaking myself physically and, what was more important, shaking off a sort of indescribable mental metamorphosis that I seemed to be undergoing, I remained in this curious posture.

The sun began to warm the air around me, but I could not feel its heat that must have penetrated me: I was shivering and perspiring as if smitten with a fever. My legs unbent from beneath me, as if of their own accord; my arms fell useless to my sides; I was in a state of utter dejection, incapable of any action; I could see myself lying like a heavy corpse that an eagle had dropped from its talons on to Mount Kinibaya. I even wished for one short moment that this bird of prey or some vulture should pass overhead, seize me and fly away with me. But at that instant the picture of my assembled children flashed before my eyes. I could see them orphaned, wretched, abandoned, in tears, their heads buried in their arms. This picture caused me even deeper distress than had Anatou's contemptible accusations. I tried to pull myself together, as I had done my best to do since the beginning of these events. I even tried to smile.

This smile awoke in me the memory of a past which quite sincerely speaking nauseated me: the memory of my early love for Anatou quickened and unfolded in my mind. I stood up, wiped away the burning sweat that streamed down my face, mixed, no doubt, with tears that I had shed involuntarily. I stretched my limbs, took out my kpété and did my best to improvise a merry song. Dragonflies with their curiously transparent, mauve wings skimmed through the air in their mating dance. I felt they were dancing to my music and this sight delighted me: I was happy to think I was of some use to these innocent, harmless creatures, disporting before my eyes.

Snares without End

I was letting myself be lulled into the belief that these simple, everyday sights could still procure me pure delight, when I was disturbed by one of the dogs barking, and turned round, curious to find the reason. I saw a female figure crossing the meadow; I recognised by her bearing and her silhouette that this was the girl who had first appeared three months previously. I climbed down angrily to the foot of the mountain and barred her way. She was extremely pretty and smiled at me pleasantly but that only made me all the angrier.

'My brother told you yesterday you are not allowed to cross this land,' I told her coldly. 'There's a path on the other side of the mountain.'

She gazed at me in disappointment, and I noticed that her eyes were a curiously light brown.

'I thought you were good natured. Doesn't your music express the deep emotions of your heart?' she said gently.

I was disconcerted by this remark, but I recovered my control and shouted at her challengingly, 'You're never to come here again, ever! Do you hear? Never! Now be off with you, immediately!'

'Why! You're really bad-tempered! ... I'd never have thought you capable of behaving like this ... What a pity; it's most disappointing. I do so like your songs and I only cross your land from time to time so that I can hear them better,' she said with tears in her eyes.

Both her face and her words expressed her innocence; I was upset at having to speak roughly to her, but I had no other way of definitely preventing her coming into our meadow. Besides I had no choice.

'I tell you you've got to go; do you understand or don't you?'

'Perhaps someone has been telling you I had designs on your flocks, but I assure you by Allah that I haven't any ulterior motives in ...'

'Shut up and leave me alone!' I burst out. 'Get out of here, you fool! I don't know what you're talking about with your ulterior motives!' I screamed.

Terrified, she now sobbed aloud. I was furious with myself for having spoken so roughly.

'I'm sorry, I'm sorry; goodbye. Thank you all the same for letting me listen to your music,' she said through her sobs and held out her hand which I shook mechanically. 'I don't blame you,' she went on. 'I swear by Allah, I really don't blame you. It's all my fault.' Then she turned and ran away quickly, light-footed and swift as a deer.

I turned too and was about to make my way up Kinibaya again when I caught sight of Anatou. I stopped short. She came up to me and said with a sarcastic smile, 'Forgive me for bursting in on you unexpectedly like this; you ought to have asked her to stay a bit longer so that I could get a good look at her. But, in any case, I think I'll recognise her again when I meet her.'

I could have slapped her, I was so irritated by her mock courtesy and cynical expression – things which I was sure she had learnt in the south – but I controlled myself and retorted in the same vein, 'I hope you heard enough to satisfy yourself, all the time you spent spying on us.'

'Me? Spying on you? You really must be out of your mind! That's madness itself, my poor Ahouna. You saw me coming and couldn't get rid of your mistress fast enough. And after behaving in this shameful way, you have the effrontery to say that I was spying on you! Really! I know you're capable of anything, but not of such childishness.'

'This childishness, as you call it, is on the level with the contemptible suspicions your deranged mind has been feeding on for the past three months, and that you've been making my life a misery with.'

'Coward! Idiot! Swine!'

I suddenly lost my temper and yelled at the top of my voice, 'Get the hell out of here, you too! Get the hell out of here, Anatou!'

Then, as I screamed with fury, I was suddenly possessed by an ominous thought that I tried to put out of my mind. 'Out of my way, out of my way, out of my way! Get out of my way, Anatou! You've gone too far ... you're driving me to ... out of my way!'

Panic-stricken, she ran wildly away, stumbling in her frenzy of fear. I must admit that the sight gladdened me. I rejoiced to see Anatou run away like that, rejoiced to the point of laughing aloud, a shrill, sarcastic, diabolical laugh which echoed all around. The dogs began to bark and then to howl dismally. As I approached them so they drew away. I called them by their names: 'Kina, Fatcha, Niki, Siguidi! Good dogs, you know me; it's Ahouna, your master. Don't you recognise me?'

They continued to back away, still howling dismally.

'Kina, Fatcha, Niki, Siguidi! You're upset because I've quarrelled with Anatou! But it's her fault, it's her fault if I've changed like this. Don't you be against me, too. If you didn't love me any more either, there'd be nothing left of me. I'd kill myself. Kina, Fatcha, Niki, Siguidi! good boys! Come, come!' I called, crouching down and moving towards them with outstretched hands as if begging for alms.

They ceased their howling. I crawled gradually towards them and they did not back further away. I patted them, stroked each one in turn. They let me touch them, but the flicker in their eyes and the feel of their coats betrayed their fear. It wrung my heart to see this, but I tried to convince myself that it was no doubt my own feelings that I read in the eyes and the coats of my canine friends. I called them softly again, 'Niki, Fatcha, Siguidi, Kina, don't reject me, I need your affection. Stay there and guard the flocks. I'll be back soon.'

I mounted my horse and galloped off across the mountains, valleys and plains to the baobab village. As soon as they saw me my parents-in-law inquired anxiously, 'What's happened? Are the children all right? And Anatou? And your mother?'

'Don't worry; there's nothing wrong,' I said calmly.

Ibayâ sighed with relief, Fanikata clasped his hands and said, 'Praise be to Allah!' I then told them of the moral climate in which Anatou and I were living, and the quarrel that I had just had with their daughter.

Ibayâ burst into tears; I did my best to console her and added, 'If you could help me to find out exactly what's going on in my wife's heart, then by Allah, by my father Bakari, and by my children, I'd do anything to make

Anatou and me happy again so that we can go on living together.'

My father-in-law murmured a name which I couldn't quite hear, then he said firmly, 'Everything'll be all right. Don't be afraid, Ahouna. Come and spend Sunday with us and the whole matter will be set right.'

'As I've told you, Anatou doesn't want you to know what's happening between us.'

'Next Friday I shall be in Kiniba; I'll take the opportunity to invite you over for Sunday.'

'Most important, don't say a word to my mother; she's very old now and I'd like her to die in peace, knowing nothing of my troubles. I don't want her to quit this world eating her heart out with sorrow at having to leave an unhappy son.'

'I'll see to it, Ahouna. Trust me.'

I returned to the meadow. The hours I spent there every day till Saturday evening seemed terribly long ... Naturally, our life at home continued in the same dreary, miserable atmosphere as soon as my wife and I were alone. We no longer slept together since the brief quarrel in the meadow; she took the only bed in our bedroom, while I slept on a mat on the ground.

On Friday afternoon, while I was busy picking oranges with Camara, my father-in-law arrived. All the children, Camara's as well as mine, rushed to meet him. He loved them ... he loves them all, and they all love him as well as my mother-in-law who spoils them outrageously. My mother, Séitou, Anatou and Camara chatted with him of this and that. He said he was on his way back from Founibé where he had been to visit a friend. Very diplomatically he behaved as if he knew nothing of my differences with Anatou and as he was leaving, with the full knowledge that Camara never went out without his wife, who was seven months pregnant and could neither ride nor walk the distance between Kiniba and the Baobabs, he invited us all to spend Sunday with him.

Camara replied, jolly as ever, 'Fanikata, happy man, forgets that my wife is my shadow and I never go out without her, and she can't move out at the moment.'

This evoked a happy laugh, after which Fanikata said, 'Well, Ahouna's shadow is perhaps less heavy and he can certainly move around with her. So I'll expect you Sunday with the children.'

'Fine,' I replied quickly.

'If there's nothing to prevent me on Sunday,' said Anatou.

'Your mother will be pleased to see you; it's quite a long time since you and your husband came to the Baobabs,' Fanikata said, embracing the children, and left.

Camara and I went back to the orange grove which is just behind the house. I intended to tell him what was on my mind. But what would he have seen except sadness, distress, affliction and despair? What good would it do? As my thoughts ran this way, once again I decided not to say anything to him, and like that curious plant, which Bossou used to describe as 'puritan', because its leaves curl up as soon as they are touched, I retreated within my own misery. And then, if Camara had known about this tragi-comedy, he would immediately have spoken to Séitou; then my mother would have heard about it. On the other hand, if my mother, sister and brother-in-law had the slightest inkling of the distress Anatou was causing me, they would no longer bear her all their affection and surround her with all their love as they still do now, while I am talking to you. And I wanted our whole household, with the exception of myself, to love Anatou; I wanted the affection that she had deserved till then not to be diminished. So I silenced my reason and my heart. I was possibly wrong.

Fanikata came to fetch us on Sunday about ten o'clock. He took Bakari and Fatou on his horse; Sidiki and Moumouni rode with me and Anatou rode alone. So we set off for the Baobabs talking of this and that.

During the meal we chatted gaily and then the children went to play in the yard. Moumouni fell asleep and his grandmother laid him down in the bedroom.

As if my parents-in-law knew nothing of the sombre matter that was tormenting me, I declared, 'This is

probably a rare opportunity and I'd like to take advantage
of it to describe to you the atmosphere in which Anatou
and I have been living for the past four months.'

This was a blunt, not to say somewhat peremptory way
of tackling the subject, but I felt that I couldn't proceed in
any other way if I was to leave Anatou under the illusion
that her parents were ignorant of the facts I was about to
repeat to them ... They appeared surprised and then were
all ears. These reactions, of which I could not fail to
perceive the comic side, nearly made me smile, but
Anatou got up quickly and tried to leave the room. Her
father stopped her, telling her harshly to listen to what I
had to say. My story took a long time, and I finished by
saying, 'I am pleased you allowed me to marry Anatou; I
am proud and happy that Bakari, Fatou, Sidiki and little
Moumouni are her children and mine, but I would be
even happier and think myself even more fortunate if you
could get her to open her heart in front of us all and tell us
exactly what she reproaches me with, and why she
delights in making my life a misery.'

Anatou defended herself like a panther, swore by Allah,
talked of premonitions, dreams, the girl who had fallen in
love with my music ...

'That's all just jealousy!' her mother declared.

'I'd have a perfect right to be jealous, but I'm not. It's
simply that I detest all this secrecy.'

'I've done nothing; I'm not hiding anything; I have no
secrets. The only mystery in my mind over the last four
months has been you!' I replied without flinching.

'You hide nothing except what you don't want me to
know,' she retorted sharply.

'Ahouna would have a perfect right to take a second
wife if he wished, even a third as well, like your brother
Sylla and your brother-in-law Idissou. If he hasn't yet
done so, it's surely because he prefers to follow his worthy
father Bakari's example, and that of Camara, who's a real
brother to him, and my example, too,' Fanikata said
roughly.

'I've already pointed that out to her, but she refused to
understand what I was saying,' I remarked.

Snares without End

She looked at me with hatred in her eyes and, turning towards her father, said, 'I'm sorry, father! You attribute ideas to Ahouna which he certainly doesn't have; that's not his conception ...'

'What do you know about it, my girl? Why do you systematically doubt everything your husband tells you? Ahouna has already told you what your father has just pointed out to you! So what now?' cried Ibayâ.

'I've told you what I know, and I've got all the necessary proof. If Ahouna doesn't take a second wife it's so that he'll have less responsibilities: isn't it easier to sleep with lots of girls, or even with someone else's wife, than to have all the trouble of a second wife?' she asked.

'Anatou!' I cried, shocked by the depth she could descend to, to lend substance to her accusations.

'Even if that were true, would Ahouna not have the right and the liberty to do as he likes? You are really beginning to annoy me seriously, Anatou!' said Fanikata; then turning to me, declared, 'Ahouna, my son – for I think of you as such – you are a man, that is to say, you are free to do absolutely anything you dream of, as long as you don't harm anyone. You're not the slave of a woman who seems to have lost her senses, or who is trying to find an excuse to leave you.'

Ibayâ burst into tears and said through her sobs, 'We made a mistake in leaving her so long in the south! She's picked up all the stupid hair-splitting, all the desire to have the last word that is thought clever there!'

'The south is not responsible for your daughter's outrageous behaviour, the shocking things she has stooped to! I have lived in the south also, in Ouidah, Cotonou, Porto-Novo, even in Dakar. What is more, I lived in France where Bakari and I fought in the war. I went to Paris and stayed there for months on end. I had white mistresses, as I told you. Did this experience of the world make me arrogant and insolent towards other people? ... Did it make me take leave of my senses? ... I know your secret, my girl. You may be sly as a fox, but you are dealing with someone even wilier than you, because he's older and has more experience. Instead of playing hide and seek, you'd do better to tell us the truth, namely that Pylla is back in the district. Well, as they say, first loves are not easily forgotten. Tell your husband the truth and stop side-tracking with false accusations.'

'I knew absolutely nothing about Pylla's being back in Younikili!' cried Anatou, in a panic.

What! Could Bossou be right? I suddenly saw in the bright pupils of Anatou's eyes the reflection of a young man, like two miniature portraits: a smart young Poullo, dressed like a white man. My curiosity was aroused and I asked, 'Who is Pylla?'

'He's a Poullo, Anatou's first love!' Fanikata replied angrily.

Pylla was indeed the name my father-in-law had muttered a few days ago and I had not quite heard.

'You were both very fond of him; I can still remember your disappointment when I refused to marry him!' Anatou retorted with her habitual sharpness.

'Are you sure that you don't think he would make a good husband since he came back to Younikili or rather to Founkilla where he's living now?' asked Ibayâ.

'I tell you: I had no idea whether he was back or not, until you just told me so yourselves. I couldn't stand him with his self-satisfied airs, and I shan't change my mind about him.'

'That may be! So, you're enjoying torturing Ahouna out of sheer shameless effrontery, then, are you, you unnatural daughter?' cried Fanikata.

'I'm not shameless, father,' she retorted.

Fanikata rose suddenly and slapped her repeatedly across the face. She ran and crouched in a corner of the room, howling with pain, and with the wild appearance of an animal at bay. Ibayâ's tears flowed ever more freely, and little Moumouni, wakened by our raised voices, also began to cry. I got to my feet in protest. 'I'm sorry, Fanikata! I didn't bring my wife here for you to ill-treat her. I only wanted you to try to bring about a reconciliation between us ...' Fanikata interrupted me, 'Either this girl is a dangerous lunatic and should be shut up in an asylum; or else – what seems more likely to me, in spite of her denials – Pylla's return has awakened her old love and this is the sole reason for her devilish tricks!'

'Compose yourself, Anatou. I'm really sorry about all this ...'

'Leave me alone! ...'

'Let's go home! ...'

'Leave me alone, you monster! ...'

'I accept everything that you say ... I'll do anything you like ... We'll go and live in the south. In a few weeks I'll tell them at home you're ill and we should go down to the south so that you can get the necessary attention ...'

'Leave me alone! In Allah's name, shut up and leave me alone ...'

'No one at home knows anything about the miserable state of things between you and me ...'

'For God's sake, shut your mouth! shut up! shut up! or I'll burst out laughing.'

I did not insist.

'This monstrous creature wants to destroy you before she leaves you. You'd better look out, my poor Ahouna!' said Fanikata, suddenly terribly weary.

'Allah is with me, if it's true that he sees clearly into men's hearts,' I replied sadly.

Absorbed in their games, the children, Allah be praised! had not for one moment wanted to come back inside while we were in the midst of these arguments. I went to fetch them. Each of us tried to put on a smile and we rode back to Kiniba with my father-in-law, who immediately returned home without making the slightest allusion to what had occurred.

At bedtime I lay down as usual on my mat on the ground, to which I had now grown accustomed. I even preferred the hard surface of our bedroom floor to the warmth of Anatou's proximity. If we had become reconciled, as I had so sincerely wished, it would have taken me more than a month to get used once more to the softness of the bed and Anatou's body smell.

Days went by; to me they seemed monotonous, interminable. All the activities which since my earliest childhood I had performed with such enthusiasm and joy now seemed dull, meaningless, to the point of irritation.

'You are working too hard, you look tired; you ought to rest a bit, Ahouna,' Camara said one day.

'I don't feel at all tired,' I replied, putting on a bit of liveliness; but as my voice sounded in my own ears, it betrayed a certain fatigue in spite of myself.

More than ever, at that moment, I wondered anxiously if I should not reveal the distress that was eating away my heart, instead of obstinately refusing to say anything to anyone at home. I chose to continue my silence.

'That's the way things always happen. One gets worn out without noticing; when one loves one's work passionately, one keeps on at it; then comes a day when one collapses with fatigue. That's how Diara died, the best and only friend I had in Conakry. As from tomorrow, you'll stay at home, until I think that you're fit to start work again. I'll manage everything,' said Camara, in the brotherly tone that brooked no argument.

'All right, but really, I don't feel at all tired.'

'Can't be helped! Come and eat; the women are waiting for us.'

'As from tomorrow, until I think that you're fit to start work again!' he said. Camara, my brother, will you ever see that day? That day will never come. What are you thinking, now that I am no longer with you?

That night, after supper, I lay down on my mat, but I could not sleep. I sat up with my hands on my knees, like a clay god. In the middle of the night Anatou got up, possibly woken by her ridiculous dreams or by some urgent natural need. She saw me and recoiled instinctively with fear and revulsion; then, as if her mind were wandering, she said in a voice which betrayed her anguish, 'Please, Ahouna, please don't kill me!'

'But what's got into you, Anatou? I've no intention of making any attempt on your life; I don't wish you any harm!' I said dejectedly.

'Oh, yes, you do! you do want to kill me! Look in your eyes! You're no longer the man I loved and who loved me, the man who married me! I can see crime quivering in your eyes. In the name of Allah! in the name of our children, I implore you not to kill me!' and, trembling with fear, she backed away.

I stood up suddenly, intending to appeal to her to be quiet, for fear her mad cries should wake the whole household, though fortunately everyone seemed more dead than simply sleeping; but as soon as she saw me stand, she screamed, 'Murder! murder!'

I started, no, I was terrified. Did I then regain control of myself as I had done on so many occasions? I no longer know. I rapidly slipped on my boubou and picked up my crook which I always dropped in a corner of the room when I did not leave it in the cattle shed. Suddenly a dagger hanging on a nail on the wall caught my eye; it had belonged to my father and was never taken out of its sheath. I went and took it down without knowing what I was going to do with it. I grasped it, feeling the blood pulsating in my fingers as they tightened around it; my heart was beating violently. Anatou panted as she beseeched me not to kill her.

If I had dared to stay a second longer, now that I could feel crime circulating in my veins, I would have killed my wife. I could already see her lying in a pool of blood ...

'No. I will never kill you, Anatou. You are my wife, the mother of my children. Goodbye!' I said.

Then I made for the door, opened it and went out, shutting it quietly behind me. Then I left our compound and disappeared into the starlit night without any idea as to where I was going. One of our dogs set up a dismal howl. It was Niki; I recognised him by his interminable howls, interrupted from time to time by doleful, lugubrious moans, with which he expressed his misery.

Chapter 9

I walked all night without stopping to rest. I had not a penny in my pocket nor had I taken my kpété or my tôba. Daybreak found me in Itcha, a little town about thirty miles from Kiniba. Famished and parched with thirst as I was, the sun seemed to beat down more relentlessly than ever, but I continued walking. Round midday I met a group of youngsters coming out of school, skipping merrily about like young goats; each one of them reminded me of one of my own children and set me thinking of those young mouths for whose birth I had been responsible, now abandoned in Kiniba, where they must be pestering their mother with questions, to which she would not reply. They must certainly be asking everyone in the house, especially my poor, revered mother, Mariatou, where their father was; and Séitou, why I had left without giving them a hug as I always did; and Camara, if he was going to meet me in the pastureland, or somewhere else; whether I would be back soon; whether we would ever be sitting round the big naseberry tree in the evening again, playing the kpété and the tôba.

I reproached myself with having abandoned them thus. It was unreasonable not to have thought of them before I left the house; I might perhaps have changed my mind; I might perhaps have wandered around all night and then, as soon as everyone was awake, I would have gathered them together and told them honestly what had happened; there would have been sighs of distress, expressions of exasperation, tears and cries. There might have been a question of breaking with Anatou for good, but all that would not have lasted long; Anatou might have left me, but sooner or later calm would have been restored to my heart, to my mind, to my children's minds and to the whole household. I reflected on all that, I felt that it would not be long before I turned back, while all the time, in spite of myself, I continued on my way.

I strode hurriedly along, pursued by living tableaux that were enacted all around me. Séitou followed me, her body weighed down by her pregnancy, accompanied by her other children. She implored me to tell her what was wrong, asking me if her presence in our father's house upset me; if so, she would agree to leave so that I could be happy with my wife and children. My nephews and nieces wept, my own children too, and all begged me not to leave them. Camara pointed out that I had given him back a taste for life, the joy of feeling himself a man, that *I* should not now despair just when *he* had got used to our home, where he had learnt to appreciate real happiness. My mother, poor old Mariatou, tugged at my boubou, trying to hold me back; her mouth trembled as she grasped her withered, pendulous breasts in both hands, saying, 'This is how I fed you, this is how I fed you, my little Ahouna. Tell me what is wrong, what is in your heart. I am a woman, I am only a woman, I am your old mother, nearing the end of her days. I want to die in your arms, so that I can take a good report to my Bakari.' She groaned, tragically, her eyes flooded with tears, while I hastened further and further away, fast, fast, fast ...

I had eaten nothing, but I walked on with an empty stomach. I stopped wherever I was overtaken by darkness, then resumed my way when the cock crowed for the last time.

Three or four days after I had left Kiniba, I arrived in Abomey. It was not the Hounjlomê market day. I roamed for a short time through the streets and then walked on as far as Bohicon. The town seemed very busy to me; I wandered there from street to street till I reached the station. I had never seen a railway station before, much less a train. There were a lot of people who seemed to be expecting something, but nothing in their expressions gave me any inkling as to whether it was a happy or unhappy event they were waiting for. I mingled with the crowd, wondering what would happen. Suddenly the ground began to tremble; I heard a shrill, prolonged scream; curls of smoke spread through the air, from afar. The train arrived, huge, dusty, seeming to go on for ever. Instead of astonishment, I felt complete indifference. People alighted, or got in; others, almost in rags, rushed up to the new arrivals, spoke to them, took charge of their luggage and stumbled off in front of them.

A traveller came up to me, said something to me in the Fon language, which I scarcely understood; I still can't really speak Fon fluently, that is to say correctly, as you no doubt notice. So he made signs to me, like you use to a deaf man. I understood he was asking me to carry his luggage home for him. Ashamed, humiliated, deeply distressed, I nevertheless accepted: I was hungry and I hadn't a penny.

'*Epkin!* It's heavy!' he said in Fon.

I nodded. I knew the meaning of that word that I had often heard Bossou use in respect of anything heavy or which he thought impossible to do. I lifted the load on to my head. It was indeed terribly heavy. I walked in front of the traveller for about an hour, with him indicating the way. When we reached his home two youths helped me down with the load. I felt a great sense of relief, or rather a feeling almost of weightlessness, that I cannot describe in words. I had difficulty in getting my breath after being relieved of that heavy weight, as if a vice in which I had been tightly clamped had been suddenly released; but I could still feel the weight on my conscience, although the physical burden had been lifted and I had freedom of action again.

I heaved a sigh of relief, asked for something to drink and was given a bowl of cold water that I greatly appreciated; this was in fact the first drink I had had since I left Kiniba four days before, with the exception of my own urine that I had been obliged to quench my thirst with the first two days. Then I was paid for my services as porter and went on my way.

Seventy-five centimes seemed precious little for having nearly collapsed under that diabolical load, but as I was penniless I had to be satisfied with such meagre earnings. I bought three akassa balls and some fried fish which I ate voraciously. I had fifty centimes over, which I pocketed and went on towards the south.

My windfall lasted for three days. Then, penniless again, I went and stole cassava from the fields and ate it raw. Look at my hand: you see this terrible, deep scar? That came from catching my hand in a snare.

One day, when I was absolutely starving and at the end of my tether, I saw a field of cassava and selected a plant with thick foliage; I bent down to pull up a tuber. Well, it happened that a snare had been set at the foot of the plant to protect it against agoutis and porcupines. No sooner had I dug my fingers in the loose earth than the trap was sprung and caught my hand from which the blood gushed. I nearly screamed with pain, but I gritted my teeth, prised open the blood-stained snare and threw the calamitous object down under the cassava plant. Then I went on my way again.

I walked the whole of that day with neither food nor drink. The people I met looked at me askance, with fear in their eyes, as if I were a dangerous madman or a wild beast; then they hurried on, some even taking to their heels. I was deeply hurt to be treated in this way. Twice the thought of suicide crossed my mind. But to take my own life did not seem the proper ending to this sorry enterprise that I was launched upon, as my footsteps were urged onwards by some inner force to an outcome which was as yet hidden from me.

Night fell, and once more gave way to daylight, in the regular, monotonous metamorphosis of time that ever runs on and is never still, except for those who live in the absurd illusion of filling time by forcing themselves to do something, to perform certain actions, which is as futile as it is incomprehensible. I had just reached this harsh but true conclusion when I saw four farm-workers in a field, gnawing greedily at an agouti which they had roasted on a fire, of which the embers were still glowing. I cast covetous eyes in their direction. Tortured with cruel pangs of hunger, I slowed down and tried to linger near them. They caught sight of me, stared for a moment, burst out laughing and then broke into that eternal Fon language that I had been hearing ever since I left Abomey. They finished their meal, lit their clay pipes and sat smoking; then they returned to work. I thought of going up to them and indicating by gestures that I would like to help them with their work so that I could get a bit of food; but I decided not even to try this, as it seemed to be hopeless. For these Fon people were already near enough to the southern areas to have sneered at me and treated me as if I were mad. And then, to tell the truth, I was now much physically weaker and my morale was much lower than during my first four days' walking, and I would not have been capable of doing much, even if they had understood what I was trying to say and had taken me on. I would also have liked to break into one of Boussou's songs,

Yé do tomê bo do hâ bâ mi wê
Yôkpô lê do tomê bo do hâ bâ mi wê.

But would I have managed to say anything else in Fon, if these well-fed farm-workers had decided to strike up a conversation with me? No. There was certainly nothing doing there ... I went on ...

I crossed an area where I saw a veritable army of tiger-beetles crawling all over the corpse of a man and eating away the flesh. Was it the body of some criminal who had been executed and thrown there? Was it a madman, whom these creatures had overrun while sunk in innocent slumber? Was it a man consumed with worries, undermined with despair, weary of living and who had voluntarily surrendered to this terribly army? I could not say. But I stopped to watch these greenish creatures relentlessly pursuing their grisly task, to convince myself once and for all of the vanity of man's existence, of the futility of all the reasons we give for our existence, of the meaninglessness of everything in human life. This, I was now positive, was one huge snare laid for man by Allah.

Under my curious gaze the beetles stripped every scrap of flesh from their victim's bones. Only when they had finished did I go on my way, thinking now of the field-

---

workers eating their agouti and smoking their pipes, now of the efficacy of the tiger-beetles.

Night overtook me in a district called Zounmin. I walked along endless trails hidden in thick tall grass; I walked beside fields of maize and cassava. Still tortured by pangs of hunger, I went into one of the fields, though afraid of catching my hand once again in a trap that might be hidden just beneath the surface of the ground. I approached a cassava plant, but this time I did not even have time to bend down and dig around the root. Arrows seemed to rain down on me, shooting into my forehead, my side and thigh and causing me to jump aside, out of range.

I'm not lying – why should I lie? I have never lied in my life, no matter what Anatou might think. Look at my forehead, my side and my thigh: you see the little scars as if nails had been driven into my body? There are the marks of porcupine quills. The stupid creature was right there, with its snout buried in a cassava plant that it was munching away when I arrived. When he caught sight of me he curled up into a ball ready to defend himself. Famished as I was, and thinking only of food, it never crossed my mind that a porcupine might be lying in ambush for me. I bent over the plant, but instead of taking flight the animal shot its quills into my body. I was driven to fury and would have fought back, but it grew bolder and shot off several more quills, all of which reached their mark.

I was vanquished not only by my wife, but also by the meanest of rodents. I was in great pain and distress, caused more by this defeat than by hunger, but I had no option but to leave, cursing Allah who seemed bent on my downfall.

I was exhausted, terribly wasted, drained of all resources and humiliated at being defeated by a porcupine. I managed to pull out the quills and sank down at the foot of a huge mangrove beside a river. If tiger-beetles had come and swarmed over me, if crocodiles had come to devour me, I swear that I would not have stirred; I had no more will to live, no desire to

Snares without End

struggle against anything ... I no longer want to live, you understand? I am a useless, absurd, nonsensical creature.

But neither beetles nor crocodiles came. Did I fall asleep? I have no idea. About three o'clock the moon, which had risen without my noticing, was high in the sky, shedding the splendour of its beams on the water, whose almost motionless surface was covered with wide-leaved waterlilies with half-opened white, red and black blossoms. A slight breeze bent the rushes and rustled through the other foliage. I caught the sound of footsteps approaching along a path a few yards from where I lay. I emerged from my hiding-place intending to set out on my way again. But where?

When I reached the path I saw a woman carrying on her head a large gourd which I realised some minutes later was filled with palm-oil. She caught sight of me and dropped her load in a panic so that the oil was spilt in the grass, and took flight, shouting, 'Stop thief! A ghost, a ghost! Murder! Help!'

I could hear Anatou's voice in these accusations and mad screams, and, suddenly overcome with a nameless fury, out of my mind with rage, I unsheated my dagger and ran after the woman as she fled screaming.

Why should she think me a thief? Had I stolen anything from her? Why should she think me a ghost? Had she ever seen a buried corpse emerge from the ground and go on living? Why did she call me a murderer? Did she know me? From where? and when? And who did she mean that I had already killed?

I caught her, threw her roughly to the ground and sat astride her belly. She tried to placate me, speaking softly, shamelessly begging me to take her with my penis and let her go. This suggestion exasperated me even further; I seized her by the throat and plunged my dagger in up to the hilt; then I drew out the weapon.

Blood flowed freely from her throat, mouth and nostrils. A few moments later, as I took to flight, I learnt my victim's name: it was Kinhou.

Kinhou, if Fon names mean anything, must stand for

Snares without End

Because-of-Hatred. I stood up with a feeling of satisfaction: I had now, as Camara would have said with his usual intuition, burnt my boats.

'Anatou, Anatou, what have you done to me? What have you done to my soul? What have you succeeded in doing to me? Why did you keep on telling me, not so very long ago, that there was another expression and another heart behind my gentle expression, my soft heart and the spell-binding harmonies of my music? This was the monster that lies hidden in each one of us. You woke the monster in me; but what of yours? Has the real monster that lies hidden in you shown itself yet? Is it this monster that urged you to bring about my downfall? What do our children say? And what do you answer them?'

'Ah, marriage,' Camara said to me once, 'seems to me far too important a thing for one to think too long about it before entering into it.'

I know better now: a whole life would not be long enough to prepare for it, even if one thought seriously about it for twenty-four hours every day ...

I was talking thus to myself, as if suddenly eaten away with remorse for having finally committed the act of which I had been accused for the last five months, while at the same time my heart was beating for joy: I felt light as swansdown, happy as a god, if any exist. Yet, I felt rid of an enormous burden with which I had been weighed down since that night when, driven to exasperation by Anatou's ravings, I had taken down my father's dagger and grasped it in my hand. I had freed myself of the burden which was stifling me a few minutes before; I had finally assumed my destiny and I felt free, extraordinarily free. To feel oneself *this* or *that* is to show oneself as such, instead of denying oneself; that is the essential thing, I said to myself again.

My soliloquy was interrupted by the shouts of men rushing towards me, alarmed by my victim's screams. When I saw them I took to my heels, without really knowing why, as it was now quite useless to try to escape; but perhaps I did not feel any desire to be arrested, ill-treated or perhaps put to death by people who were interfering in a matter that concerned only my victim and myself. So I had to get away from men's cruelty and their stupid justice.

I threw myself into the river and began to swim. My wasted body, thin and supple as a snake, ploughed through the water, while my ragged boubou dragged in my wake and billowed out on each side of my threshing limbs like countless wings. The moon sparkled cheerlessly on the surface of the water that lapped around my body as I swam on. As I concentrated on my movements, I was suddenly seized by an impossible desire to watch myself swimming through the water, to see my own body advancing through the deep blue of the stream. But I suddenly heard loud noises; the bastards were swimming after me; they had jumped into the river and were thrashing about like drowning men, upsetting the calm waters. This seemed a most regrettable lack of discretion on their part. Just then I felt a tug at my clothes. I managed to put on a burst of speed and just reached the bank in front of me; as I clambered up, I left behind a piece of my tattered boubou in the jaws of a crocodile that was about to grab hold of one of my feet. This was the weight that I had felt tugging at me, but it must have been quite a small one or I would not have got away quite so easily.

In this way I managed to make my escape across the marshes, which stretched along this bank of the river, losing as I fled still more scraps of my pitiful garment, with my accursed pursuers still at my heels.

I can still hear their angry shouts ringing in my ears: '*Tâ dou non!* After the madman!' '*Houi!* Kill him!' '*Mêhoutô!* Murderer!' '*Yovo!* White man's property!' I was well aware of the meaning of these words as I had heard them many times since I left Abomey. So I knew full well what fate awaited me if I was caught. I girded up the last vestiges of my strength in an effort to save my life and disappeared into the bush where I have been wandering for the last three days.

So, that's my whole story. You know who I was, where I have come from, how I became a murderer and the reasons for my action. You took a man into your home who looked like a beggar and you fed him; he is infinitely grateful to you. But what good will it do me to have gorged myself as I have done? I thought I was already dead, and now I feel that I'm simply dying by degrees. The real tragedy is beginning here, in your house. Time will prove me right. You said it would be possible to try to save me, that you would find a lawyer to defend me. A lawyer? What good would that do? Everything was settled twenty years ago, and all I had to do was to wait for the disaster to occur!

And so he ended his story, sobbing like a child.

Chapter 10

Although I was outwardly calm and unmoved, I was nevertheless profoundly shaken by Ahouna's story of how he became a murderer. I clasped my hands, closed my eyes and tried to achieve a state of complete composure, as if sunk in prayer. In a remote voice, from the depth of my meditation, I told my guest to trust me, to agree to stay a week or two, or even a month, in Zado and then I would go with him back to Kiniba. I added, 'No one will know anything about your adventure ...'

I was stopped short by Ahouna's sardonic smile; I realised I had made a blunder, and once again it was clear to me that this extraordinary man was endowed with a deep psychological insight. I would have liked to offer some other solution but I was weary and feared that any suggestions I could make would be mere words. I stood up and went to fetch a mattress, a mat and a pagne from the bedroom. I gave the pagne to Ahouna who took it with indifference but thanked me. I unrolled the mattress on the ground and laid the mat on it, then, as is our custom, I begged my guest to lie down to rest and bade him spend a peaceful night.

Ahouna forced a wry smile. Custom and peaceful nights were far from his thoughts. Although he could be fairly certain he was out of danger, he was nevertheless very puzzled to see me living alone in this large farm surrounded by vast cultivated lands. The room in which we had spent long hours in conversation and where he was to spend the rest of the night scarcely put him at his ease. Why was this room filled from floor to ceiling with books, packages, bundles of papers, statuettes, human bones and skeletons of wild animals, as if I were one of the peddlers of cheap goods that he had met at the Hounjlomê market?

I left him without giving him any explanation.

The distant crowing of a cock disturbed the quiet of the

night. Outside the moon shed a silvery light. I went to bed and put out the lamp. I must have fallen asleep immediately and had a long dream: I was taking Ahouna back to Kiniba; his house resounded with cries of joy because he had returned to the fold; Anatou wept and begged his forgiveness. My friend begged me to spend a few days in his area. I accepted, and without wasting any time I indulged my passion: archaeological research and the collection of Dahomean statuettes and objets d'art from the third to the seventeenth century.

Used as I was to distinguishing ancient routes from ordinary paths, I discovered in Kiniba a site which I began to excavate with the help of Rémy Tertullien. We uncovered a jar full of cowries. It was a 'treasure chest', cowries being the money used by the first inhabitants of this region now known as Dahomey. Encouraged by this discovery I continued my excavations, finding other objects of no great importance, till suddenly I came upon the remains of a whole compound with graves and funeral offerings. More than thirty feet below the surface a rather unusual object came to light. It was a copper plate on which was engraved a buffalo-toad, a pool, a well and a footpath; then a man crushing the toad at the side of the path; and finally the creature lying flattened. This series of pictures has a meaning; it was the chronological reconstruction of a Dahomean fable that dates back, I think, to the nineteenth or the beginning of this century. A buffalo-toad was fished out of a pool where he was croaking and thrown into a well; he beat delightedly on his belly, jeering, 'But I'm just as happy here as I was in the pool!'

The man then fished it out of the well and threw it onto a path, edged with green grass.

'I've still got the best of it!' the creature croaked, exulting.

Exasperated beyond endurance, the man then stamped hard on the toad on the edge of the path. At which the reptile declared cynically, unconcerned, with its last breath, 'Heavens above! now I'm invulnerable, but you're not!' Then it died.

This black humour dated from about the eleventh century, as was proved by the copper plate. The craftsman was a goldsmith from Abomey of whom I had several masterpieces in my collection. But how did this valuable object come to Kiniba? Had there been Fon people in this area? Had some inhabitant of Kiniba gone in the past to where Abomey now lies, and bought the plate there? A hundred hypotheses passed through my mind, but I discarded them and came up from the deep excavation. Delighted at having discovered in Kiniba one more reason for repeating sincerely to Ahouna that life was worth living, that he should take no notice of gossip and make the most of all the moments of happiness that every man is continually offered, I hugged my lucky find to my breast, and hand in hand with Rémy I went cheerfully back to find Ahouna.

At this point in my dream I woke up, to find my right arm across my chest and the other held slightly away from my side. I got up and very quietly opened the window of my bedroom, so as not to wake my guest, whom I supposed to be sound asleep.

The sun burst into the room like a hunted beast in search of refuge, filling it with a gentle, caressing warmth. A sensation of well-being suffused my veins, making all my senses alert. I felt happy to be alive, but even more so at the thought that Ahouna owed his life to me.

I went into the living-room to tell my guest about the dream I had had and to persuade him to let me go back with him to Kiniba. Ahouna was not there. What is more, he had not unfolded the pagne nor touched the bed I had taken the trouble to prepare for him and for which I had spent some considerable time moving my collection, which was arranged according to centuries.

I devoted the whole morning to looking for him or waiting for him to return, but in vain. The afternoon brought no better luck. Not knowing what to do, I took out my kpété. Ahouna had told me of his love for this instrument, which I too could play quite well. I put it to my lips and sang in each of the ten or eleven African dialects which I speak fluently:

Snares without End

A mêdjlovi gné m'gnié ...
Ma non miangbô
Nè mialébé na m'sé,
Mi fio m'afô tépé, afô non nan! ...

I was telling Ahouna to come back. We are all strangers on earth, seeking everywhere for true happiness. Where is it? How can one recognise it and grasp it? No one knows! But come back Ahouna, my brother, come back. You must make a fresh start, and it is here, in Zado, that the path to happiness opens up for you, maybe.

Did he hear my appeal? I think not, for he would surely have come back ... Exhausted, I gave in, dropped my flute, got out my chair, put it out on the verandah and lay down. The sun was setting beyond the bush and dipping slowly into the midst of the tall trees. The screech of wild guinea fowl and partridges announced the end of the day. I gazed at the sky, bloodstained by the evening sun. I love this scene, these bird calls, this sight that is so typical of the approaching night; not for their exotic element – which means nothing to me – but because they express my very being, my innermost soul and my perfect intimacy with this perpetually sun-drenched earth that is always filled with laughter.

But that day I felt somewhat indifferent to the magnificent sight of the setting sun. Suddenly I shivered and was seized with a feeling of impending disaster. Why? I had no idea. I do not believe in premonitions, but the more I tried to discount the feeling that overwhelmed me, the more irresistible it became. This irritated me. I took down a book I had been given by Bernard, one of my best friends in France. It was *The Imitation* ...

I lit a cigarette and opened the fine edition with its sober, deeply significant gouache illustrations. The more I read on, the more strength I found to continue my search for Ahouna, the more reasons for not losing heart and, when I found him, trying to make him happy. But I suddenly lighted on a terrible sentence that I had to re-read several times, because it confirmed what Ahouna thought of himself: 'Know and believe firmly that your life must be a continual death ...' Yes, but Ahouna did

not believe in God. What support could he find? At this
thought, the sublime book dropped out of my hands and I
protested with all the strength of my soul: 'No! No! Not a
continual death but a continual life, for it is not given to
everyone to believe in God.'

At this point in my thoughts, I heard the noise of
motorcycles. There was a knock at the outside gate and I
went to open it. It was Inspector Vauquier with three
native policemen and two other blacks, dressed like
wrestlers and armed with machetes.

Vauquier knew me. He was a good-looking redhead
from Valence. He greeted me, as always, most
courteously. He talked about excavations, congratulated
me on my latest article in L 'Art Nègre, then, showing me a
scrap of cloth, asked, 'Do you recognise this bit of rag,
Monsieur Houénou?'

I took the scrap of cloth.

'Where did you find it?'

'So you do know it?'

'I recognise it ... It's a scrap of the clothes worn by
Ahouna, a poor fellow that I met yesterday on my way
back to Zado; I brought him back here and gave him
food, and he told me his life story. I offered him
hospitality, but he left before daybreak while I was still
asleep. He never touched the pagne or the mat ... come
and see!'

'You are very unwise, Monsieur Houénou, with your
incorrigible trust in people. Those you see and come in
contact with, even those you talk to can never be the ideal
people you look for in art ... Do you know that you
sheltered someone who could have killed you before he
fled? Do you know that the person who claimed to be a
victim of misfortune was a murderer?'

'Yes, I do know; he hid nothing from me, at least, I
gather so ... but where did you find this piece torn off his
boubou?' I asked coldly.

'It was torn off his back as he fled through the bush. He
can't have told you that little detail.'

'Yes, in fact, Ahouna did tell me that he fled through
the bush and the swamps where his skin was lacerated and

his garments were torn off,' I replied calmly; then I asked the important question that emotion had put out of my mind, namely who had told Vauquier that I had taken Ahouna back with me to Zado.

'You were seen together,' he answered, adding, 'You see, art speaks and reveals its secrets to the "happy few"; but men betray you and give you into the hands of your enemies and slander you as well, when the mood takes them. You should learn to know men as well as art.'

Then I listened to what my two compatriots had to say, the ones who were dressed for wrestling. The names of the muscular youths were Tovignon and Houéfa. They were the second and third sons of Madame Kinhou, Ahouna's victim.

Vauquier told me not to spend the night at Zado alone, as was my custom, as Ahouna might come back and kill me. He asked me to help them look for the criminal. I agreed and we left.

We searched all night without finding Ahouna. Meanwhile I had the opportunity of proving to Vauquier my acute knowledge of the people and the customs of my country. How can you tell a man who is engaged in both archaeological and sociological research that he is an ignoramus and doesn't understand the mentality of the people he writes about in his articles? I had learnt the logic of the West, to which I had added that of my own race, after I returned to Africa. Thus equipped I had gone in search of my country's depth, sensitivity, originality which, as I had learned from the French poet Baudelaire, must be 'drawn from the sacred hearth of primal sources of light'.

Vauquier had to admit my case, after I had suddenly brought him up short before certain men we met who would have pillaged and plundered several houses if we had not anticipated their intentions and stopped them ... As the next day dawned I left the group, intending to go to Kiniba. But when I got back to Zado to change my clothes I felt so exhausted that I locked myself in and fell asleep without undressing.

I slept late, in fact until I was woken up by the sound of Vauquier's voice.

'You really are an obstinate fellow, Houénou,' he said in an anxious tone as he struggled to get his breath. 'I've been terribly worried about you.'

'Art hates hot-heads, people who cannot sleep. I needed rest; I'm not in the habit of spending the night tracking down thieves and spotting sorcerers on their way to their haunts,' I replied with a slight smile of satisfaction.

Vauquier unbent.

'True enough. I recognise your power now, but you are something of a riddle ... Anyhow, I came to let you know that we've found your Ahouna.'

I started.

'Where is he?'

'He's been fixed to a cross, according to the local custom, and four policemen are taking him to Ganmê,' he replied, as if describing a humanitarian action.

The earth seemed to tremble under my feet and I felt giddy. Vauquier left and a few minutes later I jumped on my bicycle and rode in the direction of Ganmê.

From the distance I could hear the beat of tomtoms, announcing a death!

> *Klim!...klim, klim, kingo!*
> *Klim!... klim, klim, kingo!*
> *Gangan!... glam, gangan, kingo!*
> *Kingo!... kingo, kingo! kingo!*

Heartrending, deeply despairing sounds, making you aware of the presence of death which touches you as it passes. Oh, how terrible is the language of the tomtoms, when one understands it!

I thought first that it was a band of fetishists going to bury one of their number, and I made way for them. But I heard the mournful beat of the tomtoms all the way to Ganmê and there I came face to face with the truth of the matter. People from Zounmin were escorting Ahouna to the police station from where they delivered him to Toupilly who was to put him on show for the town.

Chapter 11

'Ajotó! Mehutó nu e hùi
Ajotó! Mehutó nu e hùi!'

A dense, sweaty crowd swarmed round Ahouna, filling the air with their sneers and angry shouts. He had been hoisted on to a cross made from two pieces of rough wood and, with his head exposed to the harsh African sun, was being carried through the streets by six muscular fellows, stripped to the waist.

'Kill him! Kill him! Kill him!' yelled the crowd.

As the procession passed the only church in Ganmê, it was seen to be accompanied by two police inspectors – one white, the other black – and five native constables.

A slight breeze blew from time to time through the scorching air, as it usually does during the season of extreme heat, sweeping up a mixture of shrivelled leaves and rust-coloured dust. Faint, continual moaning sounds, common during the hot weather, could be heard, like the distant beat of tomtoms.

At that moment, a black priest belonging to the African Mission emerged from the church, saw the procession and approached with his white cassock flapping around him. He asked anxiously, 'What has he done?' as if he could not understand what the crowd was shouting about.

The priest was a sturdy man of medium height, with black woolly hair, a thin sad oval face suddenly clouded by a look of terror as he found himself so close to reality ... The Scriptures had told him of the life of Christ, but he had always thought it absurd that a man should be crucified because he taught the truth and did not share the opinions of the sages. So the Reverend Father Dandou could never look on the big black marble crucifix in the Ganmê church without an intense shudder. He could not imagine a life-sized man being crucified, except inside this church. So this scene, so like the one in which the hero was the Man he worshipped, upset him so much that he could only keep on repeating, 'What has he done? What has he done? Whatever has he done?'

Then he elbowed his way through the dense crowd and approached a young man to whom he put the same question. The latter merely shouted in his ear, in chorus with the rest of the multitude,

'Thief! Murderer! Kill him!

'Thief! Murderer! Kill him!

'Kill him! Kill him! Kill him!'

Father Dandou was not satisfied! No, the former Ouidah seminarist could not understand what was going on, although he spoke the same language as all these blacks who were yelling and sweating under the leaden sun. He couldn't understand because the sight seemed inhuman, and so was beyond his comprehension. Prompted by his curiosity, he addressed one of the six bearers of the sinister burden, repeating his question, 'What has he done?'

The prisoner, staggering under the weight of the cross, stared at him in bewilderment, then shouted angrily, 'You shut your mouth! ... Who are you anyway? ... A priest? ... You call yourself a servant of God? You liar!'

Father Dandou felt a great shudder through his body: it was as if someone had just shouted at him a truth that he was trying to ignore and he felt his heart bleed. But he was beginning to understand the meaning of the crowd's hostile yells. It was suddenly made clear to him, as if in a revelation, that a murderer was being exhibited to the whole town before being brought to trial. He was about to mutter his apologies to Affognon, when he was interrupted by the latter shouting at him again, whereby another truth was revealed to him, 'Have you ever been forced to carry a heavy cross like this? Have you ever carried *your own* cross, you damned lying priest? ... I'll bet you haven't. Well then, take it! Here's *your true cross!*' And with these bitter words he slipped from under the cross and thrust it upon the priest, who seized it hurriedly. The load was suddenly jerked out of balance, causing a mutter from the other bearers and a drawn-out moan of pain

123

from Ahouna. Father Dandou placed the pad on his head and now he was bearing the terrible load, as if he too had been one of the thieves forced to parade Ahouna through the streets of the town.

The crowd had paid no attention to the altercation between Affognon and the priest but, seeing a white cassock under the load, stopped short in bewilderment, and for a long minute there were no more shouts. Almost complete silence reigned over Hounhoué Square, a sort of vast intersection surrounded by huge, shady baobab trees, through which runs a fairly straight main road. As soon as Affognon was free he took to his heels, knocking over one or two onlookers in his path. The black police inspector and several policemen rushed after him, and the crowd, suddenly shaken out of their stupefaction, set up shouts again of 'Stop thief!' 'Arrest the blasphemer!'

A large number of curious bystanders joined in the pursuit, to assist the burly, broad-beamed policemen who panted after Affognon without catching up with him. The prisoner ran like a deer, slipping between the houses with their walls of clay and roofs of thatch or corrugated iron. Several doors had already been barred; no sooner had the rumour from the crowd spread than every house feared to shelter a blasphemer even more than harbouring a thief. There was no need to know if Affognon had profaned against God or any of the local gods: the important thing was that he had desecrated something sacred. So Affognon could not gain access to any house, because both Christians and fetishists in Ganmê kept their respective faiths solidly anchored in their hearts.

However, chance would have it that one door was ajar; the thief caught sight of it and burst into the house. He was met by a huge, sharp-nosed dog which leapt at him, as if he had been lying in wait for him, and sunk his teeth into his chest. Affognon finally managed to beat him off with his fists. The dog's howls brought the owners running but Affognon, his chest streaming with blood, like a wounded boar, had already scaled the outer wall, which crumbled behind him. In his distress he had forgotten that he had got into the house by an open door.

He ran down a narrow lane winding between the houses. A little band of naked urchins with swollen bellies saw him and began to shout, 'Here he is! Here's the thief! Catch him!'

Affognon lashed out at the brats, felling several of them, scrambled over another wall and dropped down into a Voodoo convent. He found himself inside a wash-house where naked postulants were bathing. The women rushed to grab their pagnes which they wrapped round themselves, setting up loud cries of fright and shouting curses that rose above the thatched roofs of the surrounding houses, overhung with gigantic roucou trees, which spread a thick, swaying carpet of shade all around.

The sight of these handsome female bodies, nearly all quite young, gave the rogue a strange thrill; he would have liked to linger over this exciting spectacle, but he thought better of it: he had not a moment to lose. He shook himself to get rid of the embarrassing sensation and all the feeling of a moment before vanished. He left the washplace and was making for another part of the convent; but the Voodoo men, alerted by the postulants' cries, had already opened a little interlinking gate, adorned with multicoloured cloths, palm-branches, goat's skulls, and the blood of fowls that had most probably been slaughtered in the course of that day.

They bent nearly double to creep under the low gateway and leapt into the postulants' courtyard, which was swarming with bare-breasted women. All the men wore strings of white cowrie shells across their chests, brandished clubs and tomahawks, chanted incantations and called down horrendous curses. They searched for Affognon in every corner of the convent, but he had already scaled another wall and dropped down at the foot of an enormous iroko, a fetish tree, against which he leaned.

He examined his chest where the dog had bitten him so severely and his grazed limbs from which the blood poured and which were beginning to be painful.

'Poor Affognon! Why were you born? What joy have

you had out of life? You've simply dragged body and soul through thirty-five years, of which ten only were easy and pleasant; since your childhood you've had nothing but trouble and failure; life has been one long abomination. Think of your name, what irony! *"a step in the right direction, a good start in life, success, a happy life"*! When you're nothing but a miserable wretch ...'

He looked up to the heavens which he could not see clearly through the foliage which formed a dense parasol above his head. Exhausted, he slowly lowered his eyes again and crumpled up at the foot of the tree. He was trying to find a position in which he could stretch his limbs a little when he suddenly heard, scarcely ten yards away, 'Here he is! Get him!'

His extreme fatigue suddenly vanished and he resumed his futile flight, escorted by shouts, angry yells and hostile cries. He zigzagged through two or three lanes and dashed back like lightning across the main square, where the crowd had grown extremely dense and where there were many curious onlookers keen enough to set off after him. Affognon collected his last ounce of strength and rushed straight into the church: here suddenly was the answer to his search for asylum, an end to his desperate flight. Had he not been taught as an adolescent, 'We are all children of God and he recognises us as such'?

But since his life had become one long series of abominations he did not think of himself as anyone's child, not the child of God or of any of the local gods. He believed in nothing. He was only concerned in finding a refuge somewhere. He had previously caught sight of a tiny thatched temple in which was enthroned a clay god with an enormous phallus, which made him both extremely important and worthy of the greatest veneration; Affognon would have taken refuge there if the door had not been too low and the building too small to house one more body.

Now he gazed at the huge black marble crucifix; an optical illusion gave him the impression that the Christ was still bleeding, that the great shining eyes suddenly stared at him and riveted him to the ground. Affognon even had the feeling that he had been run to earth, stopped dead in his tracks by the Christ, and was so terrified that he said aloud, as much out of astonishment as confusion, 'You too?'

But as he spoke these words his sensations and vision became more acute: he saw the body of Christ become detached from the cross, stoop down towards the ground, raise his head with neck outstretched, blood dripping from his open mouth, and stare straight into Affognon's eyes. He screamed and fell heavily to the cement floor of the church where the crowd had already gathered.

The black inspector, who had panted after him all the way, never losing sight of him as he fled, now caught up with him and pulled him to his feet, saying, 'Very funny, eh! Who d'you think you are? Everyone in Ganmè knows you're not a Christian. What d'you think you're doing here after giving your job to that poor priest who can't wait to get rid of it? You've made trouble wherever you've been and then to crown it all you come and give the good Lord a piece of your mind in his own house! Well, your little game's up now, good and proper. So off with you!'

He handcuffed Affognon and they left the church, followed by the idlers who hurled insults at him for a blasphemer.

They returned to Hounhoué Square where the missionary was still staggering under the heavy burden. No one, not even one of the Catholics who happened to be there, had offered to replace him, as the parade of the cross seemed to be under an evil spell. The onlookers also had the idea that it was a good thing for the sixth bearer to be a priest, a man who was supposed to be near to God!

Mauthonier, the European inspector, was not at all pleased to see Father Dandou so laden. The sight was beginning to embarrass him, but he was forced to look on: he was helpless. So as soon as Affognon was brought back he lost no time in ordering him to take his place, and be quick about it, but the prisoner refused categorically.

'I tell you to go back to your place, and double quick!' shouted Mauthonier.

Snares without End

'Never!' retorted Affognon, firmly.

Mauthonier gave him a clout about the ears, with the remark that if he wanted to act the gentleman and give himself the pleasure of rebelling, then he shouldn't have stolen a couple of goats and a sixty-six-pound sack of maize.

'If I was forced to steal, it was because of one of you white men!' retorted Affognon.

Mauthonier's reply to this insolence was to fetch him another couple of clouts and to ask him to explain himself.

'Explain myself? You're not going to humbug anyone here with the impression that you don't know the truth?' he said arrogantly; then he managed to cry out with the firmness of a man who knows he's in the right, 'Who's the cause of all my troubles, if it isn't that damned slanderer, that mad Bouquineur with his bunch of black and white prostitutes?'

Mauthonier, with the now silent crowd, listened contemptuously to the charge, the burden of which was not unfamiliar to him. Annoyed that Affognon spoke out so boldly in front of everyone, while the Reverend Father Dandou was still sweating under the heavy cross, Mauthonier concentrated all his strength in his hand and gave him another hearty clout, accompanied by a kick where it hurt most and a request to shut his mouth.

'Oh, knock me about if you like! I despise you! You're not even a man. You've never been circumcised! What would an uncircumcised dog like you mean to me?'

At these words, two policemen, prompted by an excess of zeal, hurled themselves at the refractory prisoner, and began to lay into him. At first, Affognon shouted that they could kill him rather, he wasn't going to carry that cross again; but as the blows rained thick and fast he gave in, crying like a child, or rather as if he were going out of his mind, 'No! No! Don't beat Affognon like that! Affognon can't stand any more! He can't take any more! No more! Never again! You understand?' His voice weakened and he whispered now, as if in a dream, 'D'you understand what that means? Not to suffer again, any more? Affognon didn't ask to be born ... He's a man like you, only he hasn't had a chance. D'you understand? D'you understand ... ?'

His words made some impression on Mauthonier, who ordered the policemen to stop. It was clear the inspector was struggling to suppress his feelings of pity. The black inspector, for his part, had nothing to say now. He too knew Affognon's story and was sorry that he had finally caught him, after nearly half an hour's chase, but he was only doing his job. He too was making an effort to control his feelings and resented the constables' excess of zeal. He looked at the prisoner as if to implore him, 'Affognon, brother, take up the cross; let the poor priest be rid of it!'

Mauthonier, realising his colleague's feelings, came up to him and shook his hand without meeting his eyes.

'No ... Affognon won't carry anything more! He can't bear any more!' replied the prisoner, groaning as if he were dying.

Father Dandou, still sweating under the load, was also at the end of his tether, and suffered still more at the sight for which he felt himself alone responsible. In vain he had shouted and begged them to leave Affognon alone, to have pity on him. Now he added, 'It isn't his fault. He wouldn't have run away if I hadn't stopped to question him. I am the guilty one. In Christ's name leave him alone, or else beat me instead of him. He doesn't want to carry this burden any more, he is quite right. I have the terrible load on my head and I shall carry it wherever you wish. Let's move! Move on!' he declared firmly.

The procession set out again, silently, sadly, almost lifelessly, with Affognon beside them, his wrists handcuffed.

The crowd had thinned out. Few people followed the procession. Curiously enough the bearers scarcely perspired; even the two in front seemed as fresh as when the procession first set out, or as if Ahouna's weight had suddenly got less, and so they did not seem to be labouring beneath such an unwieldy burden.

Passers-by hid their faces in their hands or looked the other way, or turned their backs to the street so that they

Snares without End

would not have to gaze on this Via Dolorosa.

As the procession advanced, thatched roofs gave way to huts with corrugated-iron roofs; the baobabs shading streets and houses gave way to kapok trees, bombax or irokos. Inquisitive folk came out of their houses or glanced rapidly through half-opened doors and then slipped furtively inside again.

At one point several men were seated in a circle at the foot of a roucou tree, playing *sigi*. As the procession passed they stood up, registered sudden shock at the sight that met their eyes and sat down again quickly; dropping their eyes to the stool on which they were playing, they declared that they had seen nothing – may the gods preserve them from seeing anything! Further on, under the dense shade of some mango trees, little groups of women and girls were merrily pounding millet or maize; at the sight of the procession they dropped their pestles, clapped their hands to spread the alarm, uttered cries of panic and scattered at full speed. Elsewhere people stood stiffly to attention as the procession approached, some of them motionless in respectful attitudes, others crossing themselves sadly – touching tributes to the man they presumed dead already, on the part of these living statues, deeply marked by their European education and Christian upbringing. But as soon as these 'emancipated' people realised that this was not a funeral procession they were ashamed of their reaction.

A man of medium height, with regular features, dressed in a khaki suit with a light-grey felt hat, broke away from the passers-by and rushed towards the procession. He took off his hat to reveal thick, black, woolly hair with a straight parting above a high forehead. He was clean shaven and wore gold-rimmed spectacles, a magnificent necktie and highly polished shoes. Everything about him indicated a man of property or an important African bureaucrat.

The sight of the Reverend Father Dandou, labouring beneath his burden, had awakened memories of the hours spent at catechism and shaken his conscience. He was taken back to his adolescence and words he had not heard for twenty-five years: 'The priest is the representative of Christ on earth; he who makes any attempt on his life makes an attempt on the life of our Lord; he who does not come to his assistance in time of distress disobeys the injunctions of the Son of God.' Gontran was shaken.

'What has happened, Father?' he asked the missionary.

The man in the white cassock, whose gaunt profile had caught Gontran Kouvidé's gaze, mumbled that it was nothing.

'This is a disgrace! A disgrace for Christianity, an affront to our town. Whether you like it or not, I won't let you proceed on this Calvary. Give up your place under that shameful burden!' he said peremptorily.

Mauthonier ordered the procession to stop.

'No, Gontran,' replied the priest. 'I admire your generosity and I'm grateful to you for your offer. I don't know where this procession is going, but I couldn't forgive myself if I let a man in the position of Monsieur Gontran Kouvidé take my place here.'

'Christ did not refuse Simon's help – though I don't imagine I'm Simon.'

'Who would dare to call himself our Lord's equal? No one, certainly, and me possibly least of anyone ... Come, don't let's use fine words; the load is heavy and we may still have far to go. On we go, my friends!' said Father Dandou, firmly.

But Gontran prevented him from moving by seizing the little pad where the cross rested on the cleric's head, and was so insistent that finally the latter gave in and removed his head from under the load.

Beads of sweat stood out on the face and hollow cheeks of the liberated priest; a thick vein protruded from his high, intelligent brow and branched out round his head and neck like the delta of a meagre watercourse ... The priest felt the blood throbbing through his arteries; he clasped his bony hands and stammered in a sad, strangely gentle voice, 'There are very few men like you, Gontran.'

At this moment the bell began to toll for a funeral at the Cathedral of the Immaculate Conception, the melting pot of Ganmê catholicism. Father Dandou suddenly remembered that he had to conduct a burial service. For a short moment the bells became fainter, and then rang out again their doleful dirge. 'The imperious call of the dead who are now at peace and know naught of the present which continues for all eternity; do they remember their past?' reflected Father Dandou ...

The bells still pealed, awakening answering qualms of conscience in the priest's heart which bled at the strain of his conflicting duties. As he no longer bore the burden of the cross a choice was open to him; he could return to the sacristy, where the choirboys waited impatiently for him to start the funeral amid the lamentations that arose amid the tolling of the bell; or else he could accompany Ahouna who was bound on the cross, his face exposed to the merciless sun, and with large green flies fighting for invisible specks on his beslavered beard.

Father Dandou gritted his teeth, nervously tugged at the sleeves of his cassock and said to Gontran, 'I'm staying with the procession.'

Gontran Kouvidé, chief accountant for a large English firm, was a prosperous man; he owned fertile lands and the three largest buildings in Ganmê; but he was also modest, generous to a fault and earned reproaches for being too devout, too observant a Christian. His reply was that no one could be too observant a Christian and added ironically that he had always been sorry that he hadn't been born a practising Voodoo, which would have allowed him to spend idle sybaritic months in a monastery where he would have the right to gaze on many a feminine beauty!

This was the man who was now carrying this sinister burden; but he had no time to reflect on this; scarcely had he walked fifty yards than a man elbowed his way to his side through the still silent crowd. This man was in his forties, wearing black shorts and a red, sleeveless vest under which swelled a colossal torso, with muscular arms which seemed to be trying to burst out of the armholes. His heavy neck seemed carved out of rock; his thighs, calves, toes and fingers were like wrought iron ... It it were not for his head, with its crop of flattened woolly hair and his eyes whose gentleness contrasted with the rest of his body, Dagbénon would have looked more like a monster than a human being.

'No, boss, this is really going too far! You're never going to carry a load like this in my presence.'

'You're on duty till lunchtime, Dagbénon,' said Gontran.

'You're also on duty till lunchtime, sir.'

'You are paid by the hour, Dagbénon.'

'Don't let's chop logic, boss. I know I'm a mere workman, but I'm not a slave to my bosses, nor a slave to money,' declared Dagbénon firmly.

Gontran looked at him admiringly; the priest ran his eyes over him in astonishment; this man's words were a sudden revelation to him of the meaning of charity and humanity that he had been preaching to his flock.

Gontran looked at him again and shook his hand. Then he turned to the priest, bid him go back home, put on his felt hat and turned on his heels.

But Father Dandou did not go: he could not leave Ahouna. The procession set off again.

An hour later, Ahouna was brought back to the front of the police station from which the procession had started out three hours previously. It was a large, stone single-storey building with a tiled roof. Ten steps led up to a vast waiting-room where two ex-servicemen were sitting on rickety chairs, in opposite corners, looking permanently bored. All the offices opened off this room, and the deafening sound of typewriters could be heard.

Toupilly, the police commissioner, a rotund man of forty-five, bald as a vulture, was informed of Affognon's attitude.

'What!' he roared. 'A thief, a prisoner, a layabout who revolts? Who's he revolting against, heavens above!'

He rushed at Affognon in a sudden fury, fetched him a couple of resounding clouts, and gave him several hearty kicks in the backside.

Affognon sank to the ground. Whether it were true or just a ruse, he cried that he had been kicked in the privates, that his genitals had been crushed.

Snares without End

'All the better! You dirty nigger! Lock him up with this little shrimp of a murderer!' yelled Toupilly again.

The policemen carried out the commissioner's orders enthusiastically, while Toupilly launched a few more kicks at the malefactors as they were borne away. But there was a strange expression in the eyes of the policemen: a short time ago they had been keen enough to lay into Affognon, but now they were shaken by the commissioner's brutality, shocked and extremely irritated by the expression 'dirty nigger', but their anger was powerless: they were born to obey, made to carry out orders. Even Mauthonier was displeased; he said nothing, but his displeasure was visible from the way he looked at his compatriot and colleague.

Chapter 12

'Wherever have you been, my dear fellow?' Gommier, the parish priest, asked Father Dandou when he got back to the presbytery. 'They've been looking for you everywhere, and when you didn't turn up Father Noutché had to conduct the funeral.'

'I am extremely sorry,' said Father Dandou sadly.

'What happened to you? You look most upset!'

'It's nothing,' he answered faintly, lowering his eyes.

His whole expression betrayed an indescribable lassitude; he was gradually overcome by a giddiness, against which he had been struggling ever since he left the police station; his muscles gave way, while he tried in vain to control his nerves; the whole room began to reel around him, faster and still faster. Suddenly, he collapsed on the floor.

Gommier leapt out of his leather armchair. A native of Saint-Etienne, tall, slender and remarkably elegant, he had a swarthy, freckled face, surrounded by a thick beard. He knelt down beside Dandou's prostrate form, which he tried in vain to lift; then, supporting his brother-priest's head on his right arm, he asked, appalled, 'What's the matter? Whatever's the matter? Should I call a doctor? Tell me what happened.'

Father Dandou was sweating abundantly; he did not seem to hear Father Gommier's questions, but he tried to murmur some words which the other did not quite understand. He made an effort to raise himself, and Father Gommier helped him on to a couch, facing his own armchair. The black priest felt a hot flush of shame suffuse him at the thought that he had collapsed like that in front of his brother-priest; he hid his face in his hands, remaining so for a long minute; then he pulled himself together and told Father Gommier what had happened.

'I heard the shouts and realised immediately they were parading a murderer through the town before executing him,' Gommier observed when Father Dandou had finished his story. 'But it's very unlikely he'll be executed, as the French law is now in operation here and has the full approval of the African assessors themselves. So we hope the old law of a life for a life won't be enforced; the murderer will most likely be condemned to hard labour for life ... And I'm sure you're not sorry you took up that cross, are you?'

'No, I'd have no regrets for what I did; I wouldn't be ashamed of it, if it weren't for what happened to Affognon afterwards. But now I feel responsible for poor Affognon's added misfortunes, so I do deeply regret having taken on that abominable cross.'

The funeral knell began to toll again. Father Dandou got up; in his exhausted state he staggered like a man the worse for drink, but managed to stay on his feet.

'Sit down, my dear fellow; you are too tired ... Father Noutché will finish the service.'

'No, thank you, Father, I feel better,' said Father Dandou, passing his hand over his clammy face and he went out.

At first the service went badly. '*Libera me ...*' The relatives of the dead man were in floods of tears; the organ wheezed, setting one's teeth on edge. Father Dandou stumbled over the prayers; he recalled the sight of Affognon being beaten up, of Ahouna slavering on the cross; he felt once more the weight of the cross on his head, heavier than before.

'*Domine, Jesu Christe ...*' The organist threw himself into the music; the organ wheezed still more, sadness and sorrow stirred the hearts and the deliberate tolling of the funeral knell made the sight even more moving. A woman moaned; a girl sobbed. Father Dandou himself seemed plunged in sadness, but this was because he was thinking more about Affognon and Ahouna than of the death of the rich man half the people present were weeping for.

Father Dandou read from the Gospels, then insisted on the necessity to pray for our own dead, as well as for those who have no one to mourn them: 'but how much more

---

Snares without End

important it is to love the living, to understand them and to help them! The task of a Christian worthy of the name does not consist only of loving; still less of loving such or such a one because he is our neighbour, or because he is rich: it consists of doing good disinterestedly.

'Yes, indeed, we never know if we are doing right, even when we think we are, so that while we think we are obeying God we sometimes transgress official laws as well as the decrees of the terrestrial city. It is not easy to reconcile these; in the same way, the Christian is often driven to wonder anxiously if he should not obey only the dictates of Christ ...

'To be sure, dear brethren, we must obey Him, but always with the certitude that the true law is spiritual and few indeed understand it. We must obey Him and never forget that, like Him, we are of this world, made of flesh and blood, sold into the service of sin.

'Let us consider all the generous, unprecedented acts He performed so that mankind should be happy and quick to understand! Let us consider all the evil that men do in His name. But let us consider also all the children who were slaughtered because of Him! Ah! whether we would have it so or not, the essential thing is to love God; but it is even more essential to love Him only insomuch as you love men, even as he himself commands ...

'All you do and all the tears you now shed for the man who is lying dead before us, belong of necessity to the domain of useless things, if but lately, that is to say, yesterday, you did not love this man when he was still living in our midst, or if you loved him simply because he was rich and was useful to you ...'

Twilight was falling on Ganmê; the market women and girls were already setting out their wares for the evening market on reed or bamboo slats balanced on three-legged stands. Night set in; thousands of stars twinkled in a clear and cloudless sky; the flames from lamps, tiny clay pots in which burnt cotton wicks soaked in palm-oil, flickered at the slightest breath of wind, went out, were relit immediately, and seemed thus to obey some code.

Snares without End

The market women crowded the *mâro*, the evening market, shouting their wares, advertising their products at the top of their voices; purchasers wandered about among the stalls, paused beneath the lamps in front of the goods, asked the price of different articles, protested that they were too dear, argued, laughed, bargained, obtained little reductions and made their purchase; or else they sulked, grumbled, grew angry and departed into the starlit darkness at the foot of the mosque.

There were cakes for sale, fritters and akassa balls, fried or smoked fish, slices of boiled or fried yam and cassava. Some of the women sold a stiff maize porridge and different kinds of sauces; others offered cooked meats and delicatessen. Some displayed grocery and haberdashery; in fact everything that could be found in the daytime market was on sale here in the mâro.

It was not long ago that Affognon had been in the habit of wandering among the lanterns to purchase his evening meal ... The place would become very busy and crowded about half past six, when the train had come in; the porters, happy to be relieved of their loads, would come to spend part of their earnings on the purchase of their supper. This was the time when the police increased their vigilance as they circulated between the stalls.

On the other side of the mosque the thick shadows cast by the bougainvilleas hid many a loving couple who whispered their confidences to the discreet walls. It was not long ago that Affognon had also made love in the shadow of the wall, held his mistress for one night in his arms, hidden by the flowery darkness of the bougainvilleas.

The muezzin, clad in his flowing white boubou, emerged at the top of the minaret, his head tightly bound in a white cotton turban. He bowed down to the four points of the compass, raised himself to face the immense expanse of twinkling lights of the town ... He lifted his arms to heaven, spread them and embraced the air with a gesture of compassion. The holy man's voice rose slowly from the top of the minaret, musical, warm, harmonious; then becoming shrill, moving, full of pathos, to fall again into persuasive, loving and sensual cadences as he called the faithful to the last prayer of the day.

It was not long ago, at this hour of the evening, when the market was closed, that Affognon would be crossing the mâro square, accompanied by a young black girl whom he was taking to share the bed of Bouquineur, who was ashamed to go courting a nigger-girl himself.

Ganmê prison was a large building, painted black. Its outer walls, the tops of which were protected with broken glass, were overhung with huge, shady trees – avocados, mangoes and naseberries. Ahouna's arrival and Affognon's revolt had aroused much agitation, but this had quickly been suppressed and calm now reigned.

A light was still burning in the 'special cell' occupied by Boullin, a thirty-five-year-old European, condemned to fifty years' hard labour. In the Africa of that period, the colour of his skin gained him certain privileges, and there were days when he did not work at all, and shut himself up in his cell, reading or writing. His greatest pleasure was to get to know what he called 'big-scale thieves', 'out-of-the-ordinary criminals' and to record their case-histories in notebooks which piled up under his bed. He never imagined he would die in prison, and thought that after he was freed he would publish his memoirs in several volumes, under the title of 'Fifty Years of Penal Servitude'.

What had he done? According to his own admission, certain eternal and effectual laws that govern success in life had decreed that he should be a complete washout; and the frustration that was the outcome of this misplaced confidence in parapsychology drove him to seek consolation by deceiving his wife with another woman and then taking to drink. His mistress apparently never stopped nagging him about his drinking, while his wife threatened to divorce him, her endless refrain being that he should give up either the mistress and the drink or herself. Driven to distraction by the two women, he decided one night to do away with both of them, which he did, and then gave himself up to the police.

Then there was Djossou, a black who had been a clerk in a small firm and was now serving a ten-year sentence;

when he had been in charge of the cash he had falsified the books and so managed to divert large sums of money which he had used to build himself an imposing double-storey house. Now he occupied one of the larger cells reserved for prisoners of his kind. He often chatted with Boullin and listened to the case-histories told by his 'out-of-the-ordinary criminals'. They spent much time in each other's company and had even become friends. Manthonier, who had noticed them frequently exchanging smiles, called them 'the inseparables', with a mixture of irony and sympathy.

The lights went out in Boullin's cell about ten o'clock. The quiet of the prison precincts was broken only by the squeaking of bats as they hung upside down from the telegraph wires, flitted from wire to wire with widespread wings or rustled in the foliage of the fruit trees, shaking down the fruit before it was completely ripe. The aromatic scent of mangoes, pawpaws and naseberries pervaded the air, wafting above the outer wall of the prison and hovering high above the rooftops.

Ahouna remained squatting in the middle of the cell where the guards had thrown him, until Toupilly sent him flying into one corner with a well-aimed boot into which he concentrated as much force as animosity. The tiny cell was unlit except for the faint gleam that filtered day and night through a minute skylight.

He groaned with pain and then lay motionless as a corpse for many hours. Some time later he raised himself but was unable to remain on his feet and collapsed again in the corner of his cell, resting his wounded back against the rolled-up reed mat which had served as a bed for the murderers who had successively occupied number 59 in Ganmê prison.

He folded his arms over his bent legs and hugged them tightly to his chest as if they were a treasure he was protecting; resting his chin on his grazed knees that oozed like a burst abcess, Ahouna gazed into space, his mind a blank. The faint light that entered through the tiny aperture high up in the wall against which he was leaning scarcely lit up the wall opposite.

Ahouna had no idea where this light came from and made no attempt to find out; he considered it an optical illusion, to be compared to all the fine ideas he had had about life and which had vanished like so many mirages. But by dint of staring tirelessly at this gleam he finally experienced a feeling of relaxation and physical well-being; then he began to be aware of his surroundings, although he had still no idea of the cell's size, feeling himself to be in some unconfined space.

He opened his eyes wide and stared at this pale, milky line of light, like the reflection of the first faint gleams of the rising sun or of a fading twilight. He felt the cool comfort of this false twilight; he even felt at ease in his squatting position, perhaps because he had been in the habit of remaining thus on the top of Mount Kinibaya from where, as an adolescent, he had guarded his father's cattle and sheep which he drove out to graze on the sweet fresh grass of the valley.

As Ahouna concentrated his gaze on this gleam of light a waking dream was sketched before his eyes; the vision became clearer and he felt suffused with happiness. Kinibaya rose up before him in all its splendour, under a strangely blue and sunlit sky; fissured and lined with crevasses from its exposure to the elements, the mountain raised its sharp peak none the less proudly into the air.

The source of the river Kiniba gushed forth from the mountain that gave it its name, cascading down its sides to reach the channel through the pasturelands where it flowed majestically without ever overflowing its banks. Bakari's cattle quenched their thirst along the edge of the water; little green and reddish birds alighted delicately on the animals' backs, pecked at their black coats, flecked with white or rust; the beasts flicked their tails like fly-whisks and the birds flew away, cheeping and chirping merrily.

Assani, the best pedlar in Founkilla, stood surrounded by his wares in his little canoe, which had been hollowed out of a long tree-trunk, and paddled with sensuous delight along the river. He dipped his long pole with casual regularity into the deep green water, leaned on it with seeming lack of effort and drew it out dripping with a glistening mixture of water and sunlight that looked like liquid gold; then he began the operation all over again.

Ahouna could hear the soft murmur of the water as it lapped at the side of the boat, the regular faint tap of the pole against the edge of the canoe; as Assani's pole dipped into the stream, each widening ripple was echoed in his heart, suffusing him with a feeling of sensuous well-being, and his features broke into a smile. His perception became more acute and his smile grew stronger. He felt that strangely sweet sensation that comes over a man when he quenches a great thirst with a tiny glass of cool water. Under the spell of this delightful vision, conjured up by his imagination which he had thought to be crushed out of existence, he raised his hand towards the tableau that was passing before his eyes, smiled and even called out jokingly as of old, 'Hey there, Assani! pleasant journey! I hope the water stays calm. Don't make too much profit: Allah doesn't like thieves! And beware of the women!'

His hand fell back at his side on the damp ground of the dungeon and sleep overtook him. He sat back or rather crumpled into a heap.

As he drooped from his squatting position he was conscious of a peculiar sensation: it was as if he had dived into a deep still pool, descending easily, without hindrance, in search of something precious, some unknown happiness; but he was amused by the feeling of diving down ever deeper and deeper and a last smile, the smile of a happy child, spread over his countenance and he fell into a sound sleep.

His head fell forward on his chest and he began to slaver; his legs stretched out in front of him, his arms lay lifeless at his sides as his head and shoulders rested against the wall. A slimy stream of transparent saliva ran slowly from his half-open mouth on to his narrow almost hairless chest.

Reality? Dream? Intuition about the future which is shrouded in mystery? In his heavy slumber, Ahouna heard the shouts of an argument.

'Drown him!'

'No, burn him alive!'

'Rather let's bury him alive!'

'There must be no trace of him left on the face of the earth or under the earth; so let's burn him to cinders!'

'Look out! the huts are on fire ...'

What terrible premonitions these unknown voices carried! But why should Ahouna worry about them? Willy-nilly, he had no more choice, his fate was in too many hands, and none of these cries from his subconscious could snatch him from his slumbers.

Ahouna slept; but Affognon's eyes were still wide open. It was one o'clock in the morning; he got up, struck the wall of his cell with his clenched left fist in a gesture of impotent defiance and murmured sadly, 'Ah, you resist, the ceiling resists and the ground beneath my feet resists too. I also have resisted. I have struggled effectively against many things, but what has been the good? Everything in life is futile; now it is enough; we must make an end; I refuse to go on being a slave. I am a child of the earth, and the earth seems the only place in the world where existence should ... ought to mean being a free man and feeling free. Alas! I deluded myself, but now I have no more illusions. Now, I will be free or else cease to exist; I will not continue to be a slave; that is incompatible with living; I will be invulnerable.'

He felt in his heart the cruel pointlessness of the enveloping darkness; suddenly the impenetrable blackness of his cell awoke an irresistible echo in his heart. Affognon removed his hand from the wall, unclenched his fist. Coolly, unhurriedly, he took a few steps across his cell as if inspecting it. He stopped, unfastened his belt and took it off; then he took out of his pocket a penknife he always carried with him; he had not been searched on his admission to prison, as he had been considered trustworthy and unlikely to have the idea of doing anything foolish.

Affognon sat down, held the buckle of the belt between his toes, pulled on the other end of the leather and used it as a strop to sharpen his knife. Then he put the belt back

Snares without End

on, stood up, looked coolly at the weapon and offered up this sublime prayer to the god of blacksmiths:

> Gou, my father was a smith in your service.
> I have never believed in you nor in any god,
>   but my thoughts go out to you alone now,
>   at this moment of my life.
> Dogs are normally sacrificed to you.
> I am less than a dog, I am lower than a
>   beast, as I am not a free man.
> Yes, I offer up my whole being in sacrifice to
>   you:
> You are a god like other gods, a stranger
>   and invisible.
> You have asked nothing of me, but I know
>   that you love blood.
> It has always seemed to be more important
>   to serve the unknown from whom I never
>   expect anything, than man who pretends
>   to be my neighbour.

At the end of his prayer he calmly opened his veins and watched his blood seep out; but it seemed to him to flow too slowly; he wanted it all to be over as quickly as possible. So he sank the knife just above his left clavicle; the blood spurted out suddenly as if under strong pressure. Affognon had the courage to bury the weapon deep in his flesh, till nothing was visible except a little cut, a sort of incision.

He made an effort to remain on his feet, to stand firmly upright, but he could not prevent himself falling heavily; he uttered a stifled groan, like a pig that is muzzled before its throat is cut. Blood flowed from his mouth, as from a gargoyle, and he muttered through the choking mass of haemoglobin, '... Tomorrow ... tomorrow ... it will be light ... then ... life ... will ... continue ... Affognon ... or ... someone else, it isn't ...'

He tried to clench his teeth, but his mouth fell open in spite of himself. And so he lay, with staring glassy eyes, sprawling in a pool of blood like a slaughtered satyr, till the following day.

Snares without End

Outside dawn was breaking, the stars paled and a velvety mauve moon began to climb the sky. At the presbytery Father Dandou slept fitfully, dreaming that he was saying the funeral mass again, and murmuring half aloud, '*Tu autem eruisti animam meam ut non periret.*'

Inside the prison walls the bats squeaked more faintly than the previous evening, but they rustled more noisily in the foliage of the fruit trees, as if their number had miraculously increased in the course of the night. Ripe mangoes and naseberries lay scattered on the ground, giving off a powerful aroma. Rats and mice squeaked in amorous encounters, while the air rang with the distant crowing of cocks.

Soon the whole prison was afoot and the prisoners began to sweep out the yard, while Hounnoukpo, the most feared of any of the sergeants, went round opening up the cells. The sky gradually lightened, the moon grew pale and wan and the sun announced its imminent appearance by a red glow, low in the sky, beyond the town.

Hounnoukpo opened Affognon's cell and stood dumbstruck. He closed the door again and went to inform Toupilly and Mauthonier, who came a few minutes later.

'Oh, the bastard! these lousy niggers are all alike; when they're not bumping other people off, they're doing themselves in. Sociologists would do well to bring their nonsense up to date about the niggers, always telling us that suicide is unknown among these great apes!' Toupilly shouted, striding up and down in a state of great agitation.

'Suicide is much more frequent with us than with the Negroes,' said Mauthonier, reflectively.

'To hell with all these comparisons, you're always dinning them into my ears and siding with these creatures. You've got far too high an opinion of them.'

'They're human like us, men just the same as us ...'

'That's where you're wrong, Mauthonier! Blacks aren't men, they're apes. Nature's created them as a riddle, a cruel disturbing riddle for European logic to wrestle with constantly, and they're all the more terrifying as you never know where you are with them. Our world and our civilisation is on the road to ruin, Mauthonier ... Look at this goat, for example, who's just done away with himself, and we've not the slightest clue to the weapon he used.'

'As usual, you're getting excited over nothing. Anyway, what man is not a riddle for other people? We're a problem and a perplexity to the blacks too.'

'Oh, spare me any more of your arguments. Holy shit! What a hell of a country, where the sun grills a man's cranium as soon as it's light!' grumbled Toupilly.

Mauthonier looked at him with a smile that indicated, 'Poor fool! No one asked you to come to work in Africa. You've been in this country for ten years and you've only been back to France once. Photographs taken of you ten years ago show you a tall, slim young fellow with plenty of hair on your head; now you're a bald little man, with the beginning of a corporation and your nerves very much on edge. What are you complaining about? I've worked with you for seven years and I know that we have an easier time than our counterparts in France ...' He added aloud, 'Tossou, take your motorbike and go to Houinta and tell Affognon's family that the prisoner killed himself in his cell last night.'

'We'd better go and see if that other crazy idiot, Ahouna, hasn't hanged himself!' Toupilly said, fidgeting nervously with his fingers.

They reached the open door of Ahouna's cell, where he lay curled up like a hunted animal against the reed mat which he had not troubled to unroll.

'Look at him! ... Black as pitch, dry as a pumice-stone, and he found the strength to murder a woman! Really, if he's got a soul, it must be even blacker than his skin!'

'A murderer is a man, just like other men; the colour of his skin and his physique neither add to his crime, nor make it any less.'

'For Chrissake! you'll die of lockjaw, you will!'

'Rather of lockjaw than of bawling-matches, and all the better for me.'

Toupilly shrugged his shoulders and went off to the

offices, from where the clicking of typewriters could be heard.

In Ganmê, as everywhere in Africa, corpses are buried quickly; any delay and the heat is responsible for turning the deceased into an object of revulsion.

It was not yet eleven o'clock and Affognon's body was already taking on extravagant proportions. A few flies had surreptitiously entered the cell when Hounnoukpo opened it. When it was reopened for the burial, the flies were hard at it. Then Boullin and Toupilly began a discussion on the relative interest of Phoridae – 'the commonest type of fly' according to Boullin – Lucilae, horseflies and Calliphorae, for, by a strange coincidence, the respective fathers of the convict and the commissioner of police had both been insect collectors, with a special interest in flies.

Mauthonier looked at them half reproachfully, half contemptuously, for he considered it both indecent and immoral to dare to hold this type of discussion before a man's mortal remains, even if it was only Affognon's, though he was far from being the worst, nor his crime the most serious of all the prisoners in Ganmê; but the two Europeans continued their inept exchanges.

'I don't much care for horseflies,' said Toupilly. 'They look so clumsy when they settle on a piece of meat.'

'What about flesh-flies, commissioner? What do you think of them?' Boullin asked enthusiastically.

'Flesh-flies? Now there's a fly for you! They're the most intelligent of all; they can breed very fast without the usual conventions. That's what attracted me to them in the first place, when I had a chance to see them in action, the way they reduce procreation to its simplest form.'

'I've also seen them in action, but I prefer Stomoxys; they're like little surgeons ... one jab with their sting and you've had it! My father wrote a very authoritative article on the Stomoxys fly ...'

'For God's sake, shut up! A man's a man and your corpses won't be any better than Affognon's when you're dead!'

And, looking Boullin straight in the face, Mauthonier

added angrily: 'Don't forget that Affognon was a better man than you; you're a double murderer and he wasn't a real criminal. And now please note that as from today you'll lose most of your privileges and you'll go and work regularly in the quarries like all the rest of the murderers in this prison.'

Boullin made himself scarce. Toupilly said nothing. Mauthonier lit his pipe and continued to chew on his anger until the policeman sent to Affognon's home returned with the dead man's uncle, a tall, upright emaciated sixty-year-old, as thin as a lath. The man declared that he had come to announce an ancestral decree and to supervise the funeral arrangements closely.

'Our family, indeed our whole clan, has no pity on murderers and suicides. He who kills must be killed in his turn: either burnt at the stake or buried alive; the man who takes his own life is considered unworthy of burial and must be thrown to the vultures ...'

'Affognon took his own life, that's a fact,' Mauthonier interrupted. 'But it's also a fact that your ancestral decrees are fast disappearing and you're now living under French law, the same as us. As it happens this law does not decree that any French subject or any people who live under France's protection should be thrown to the vultures, even if they do kill themselves in a fit of despair, to escape from their condition in revolt against existence.'

'White man, you seem to like great haste. It is true that I speak too slowly and you are impatient to be rid of my nephew's corpse; but try to let me finish my words. I am simply expounding on our traditions, under which we lived before the arrival of your fathers in our lands. We accept your laws, but you must respect our customs and traditions, for to admit the one does not necessarily imply renouncing the others. So we throw suicides to the vultures, if the gods, whose decision we request by means of the "voice of the cola nuts", decree that they shall not be buried, not even without a coffin, but the gods sometimes order them to be buried in a mat. As it happens, Affognon has the benefit of this privilege.'

'The gods are very kind, and I am the first to express my

gratitude to them. The manner of burial that they permit will save us the waste of several square yards of birch wood!' said Toupilly, adding immediately to Dégonnon, the interpreter, 'Dégonnon, will you send a guard to tell the carpenters to stop making the coffin; the gods are against it.'

Norbert Dégonnon was a man in his forties, still youthful and fresh, whose actual age it would be difficult to guess. He had negroid features. His adult face still retained that severe expression that he had trained himself to adopt when as a young teacher, fresh out of the William Ponty Normal School, he had been obliged to look severe in order to get respect and enforce discipline in class.

When Dégonnon returned Mauthonier said, 'Will you tell Monsieur Djékou that we accept the will of the gods. Tell him that although I am a Catholic, I am first and foremost a human being who understands and respects the customs of the natives of the country in which I am a guest and which I am beginning to think of as my own country too. Tell him that we are all Frenchmen here, including this poor Affognon, his uncle Monsieur Djékou and yourself. But tell him also that the Commissioner and I are anxious to know whether the gods have not changed their minds about the dead man since they were consulted, so we would like them to be consulted again.'

Toupilly smiled. Dégonnon translated. The old man looked surprised, but he dipped his hand into a sort of whitish nightcap, made locally, which served both as a cap, a purse and a depository for nuts. He took out a cola nut that had already been divided into four, broke it and held it in his closed hands. He then gave some explanations; the two Europeans as well as Dégonnon watched him attentively. Djékou murmured some incantations and held out the pieces of nut to the ground, to the sky and to the four points of the compass, then to the gods and to the shades of his ancestors, finally to the body of Affognon, which was now covered with a pagne. After this ceremony he opened his hands, which he kept closed till then, and dropped the four quarters of the cola nut which he had been holding ...

If two of the pieces fell face up and the other two reverse side up, or if they all fell face up or all reverse side up, then the shades of the ancestors, Affognon's spirit, the gods and the whole cosmos accepted that the dead man could be buried, but without a coffin, that is with the body simply wrapped in a mat. But if on the other hand only one or three pieces of the cola fell face up or reverse side up, the corpse must be burnt ... The gods had not changed their minds.

Amused by the ease with which Djékou made the gods speak, Toupilly asked him to repeat the process two more times. The man obeyed but the gods maintained their decree.

A few minutes later Affognon left his cell in the shape of a parcel solidly tied up in the mat on which he had spent every night since his arrival in prison. The body was placed on a litter carried by six prisoners. The sun was high in the sky; it was nearly noon. A host of flies buzzed round the sinister parcel, which was accompanied by Mauthonier, old Djékou, a dozen constables and poor Ahouna, completely at a loss; Toupilly had ordered him to take his place in the procession on the grounds that it was his fault that 'that idiot Affognon had committed suicide' and that 'nothing like this would have happened if that idiot of a Father Dandou hadn't thought it his duty to be so zealous in his service to God and men.'

Ahouna, handcuffs on his wrists, walked as if treading on cacti the one and a half miles from the prison to the burial place.

It was a vast open space surrounded by a low wall and overgrown with tall casuarinas that at night rustled loudly in the slightest breeze.

Affognon's body was thrown into a grave that a small group of prisoners had dug two hours previously. Uncle Djékou dropped the pieces of cola nut in, that he had used to consult the gods. The grave was closed and the old man returned home, sick at heart.

Chapter 13

Ahouna's skin clung to his bones; his body was covered with cuts and weals and bruises from the stones and lashes that had rained upon him; he had to receive medical attention for fear he would die before he could stand trial. He had spent a month in one of the wards of the little infirmary at the back of the prison. Now he walked slowly around the prison yard that vibrated in the sun, trying to breathe deeply but gasping for air in spite of himself, as if he had been deprived of it from birth.

Beneath his bushy hair, Ahouna's large bony forehead seemed to be ever peering after something in the distance; his small black eyes were almost invisible in his contorted face; his temples projected above his sunken cheeks; his scanty beard made his face appear longer than it was and accentuated its terrible emaciation. The bones of his scraggy neck, his ribs and shoulder-blades were visible through his desiccated skin, which was stretched tight as a drum long exposed to the sun. His one and only boubou hung about him like a rag, exposing the chest of a consumptive.

Ahouna Bakari walked up and down, indifferent to his fellow-prisoners, indifferent to the ripe mangoes and naseberries that fell from time to time, indifferent to the afternoon sun which, for the first time since he had entered the prison, showed him his shadow, spread out before him on the ground.

But he suddenly stopped short and gazed at this shadow. He placed his hands on his hips and noticed that the shadow copied him, taking on exaggerated dimensions and looking like a winged monster.

'A monster, that is what I have become. Is that what I really was?' he said to himself as he dropped his hands to his sides.

His shadow resumed the shape it had been before: long, oddly thin, a real walking scarecrow. He started at

---

Snares without End

it, with dilated eyes, not letting it out of his sight, giving the impression of a hunter stalking his prey. With taut nerves, his bony feet poised in a firm stance, he looked as if he were about to leap after his shadow. Then he seemed to think better of it, remembering that he had given up pursuing anything; nothing in life interested him any more.

Ahouna sighed. He suddenly felt that he had not sighed once since he had entered prison. This air, or rather this breath that came out of his nostrils, reassured him: there was still something living inside his chest, under those wisps of hair, and in his belly that seemed to adhere to his spine; he existed. He was not free, but he existed and seemed to be satisfied with this existence, although it too was a matter of indifference to him. A melancholy smile passed over his cadaverous face; as he thought of his wife and their children he started talking to himself like a man who has lost his wits.

'Anatou, Anatou, I always thought of you as half of myself, as my second self; what have you done to me? What have you done to my soul? What have you done to my life? In one moment you burnt everything up inside me so that I could turn into my true self. You showed me what my true self was; but did you need to do this? What did I do to you, Anatou, that you had to treat me so badly and cast me into this bottomless pit, where my soul is eroded by the dizziness of imminent death? Oh, what a fall, Anatou, what a fall ...!'

'Cheers you up no end, this sun, eh, Ahouna!' said Boullin, coming up to him.

'Oh, yes, very,' replied Ahouna without turning his head to see who addressed him.

'You look very thoughtful, as if you're sorry to be here.'

'If you say so. Everything is indifferent to me, but I am searching for my being,' Ahouna answered, still not looking at the speaker.

'Your being?' said Boullin in astonishment.

He had never heard a criminal talk this way before. Ahouna then turned his face to him and he noticed that the new inmate's eyes, though black and strangely deep, seemed to have paled and become almost transparent.

'Yes, my being. I know it's lost, burnt up. I'll never find it again, but I am looking for it just the same,' Ahouna replied slowly.

'Come now, old chap, don't lose your wits! What have you done that hasn't been done before and will be done again?'

'You tell me not to lose my wits, but that is what inevitably happens as soon as you lose your being.'

'You've lost what you call your "being"; you said it had been burnt up, and that's certainly why you are here, in the cooler, the only place in the world where anyone can find what he's lost, if he wants to.'

'Don't joke, white man. You should rather pity me. It's a hard thing to lose one's being, the way mine disappeared for ever, just when I'd realised what it really was,' Ahouna said sadly.

'You've got my admiration and my pity, the way you worry your head about such a trifle. But how many people did you bump off, to make your conscience give you so much trouble?'

'Only one, just one woman, and she was completely innocent; she'd done nothing to me, white man. Wasn't that enough …?'

'Call me Boullin. We're a democratic lot here … You say you only killed one woman and that was enough; whichever way you take it, it must have been enough for you, since I heard you were caught three days after your crime. You were wrong to run away. *I* gave myself up of my own free will,' said Boullin with an imperturbability that startled Ahouna.

'Of your own free will?'

'Exactly. After having twice lost my being, to use your expression.'

'You're joking again, Boullin; you can only lose your being once!' retorted Ahouna.

'You ought to be able to lose it every time you commit a crime, if you could be separated from it. As it happens I killed two women.'

'Two women? Two human beings? You must be a monster!'

'Yes, two women. My wife and my mistress.'

Ahouna stopped short, taken aback. Ferdinand Boullin told him his story rapidly and added, smiling ironically, 'That's why I'm here, in the cooler, blessing French justice for quite often replacing capital punishment – if you've got a clever lawyer who can make nice long speeches – by deportation, with the added privilege of several years' hard labour.'

'So you are doubly a criminal and they won't kill you?' cried Ahouna in astonishment.

'But, my poor fellow, the world is a wilderness full of criminals! If they had to kill the lot of us, every time our crimes happened to be found out, there'd be no one left to inhabit the wilderness and work it! It's better for them to put up with us than to have the world depopulated. Here, just look at those two white women picking up fruit at the other end of the yard: the one with the light golden hair, like corn-silk, is Madame Nicéphore; she killed her husband, a jealous fool who made her life a misery. She got eighteen years and still has seven to go; after that, she'll be free and she can start her life over again. Her neighbour, the red-headed beauty, is Mademoiselle Couvrant; she liquidated a lover who was pestering the life out of her; she's still got nine years here, but she isn't wasting her time. She's expecting a kid – Foublard's handiwork. It's a bloody bind; because of their carryings-on, we seven Europeans – there are seven of us, including three women – haven't got the right to meet any more in the evenings for a bit of chit-chat sometimes far into the night, as we used to just before your arrival ... So you see, life isn't so bad here and you might even be able to find your "being" again!'

'It's surprising that there are so many white people here,' said Ahouna, as if from the depths of a dream.

Boullin smiled, looked down, stroked his abundant beard, ran his fingers through his dark brown hair that looked like a dishevelled wig, since they didn't shave the heads of any of the white men any more, contrary to prison regulations.

'There are fewer white men than blacks, but the fact that we are here at all is proof that we are all men. What is a bit unjust is the fact that the blacks sleep in dark dungeon-like cells and we have the right to special huts. Foublard and the others are housed at the other end of the cells; my hut is over there behind the naseberry tree.'

'It's not a serious matter, but it is a proof that what you call democracy is an empty word perhaps,' Ahouna remarked in an expressionless voice.

'This Ahouna is no fool,' murmured Boullin, and then asked him, as he had asked so many other newcomers, whose confessions filled his notebooks, 'If it doesn't upset you, tell me how you came to kill a woman, now I've told you about myself.'

'I'll tell you one day how I came to lose my being,' Ahouna replied, suddenly thoughtful.

'You'll give me great pleasure. I like to hear my fellow-prisoners talk about their lives, and I hope it won't be long before you tell me all about yourself, preferably before your trial, because after that your real life as a convict will begin, and I'm afraid we won't have as much time for chatting as we do now.'

'Do you think ... that ... they'll make me suffer very much?' asked Ahouna. His melancholy voice made Boullin smile, but he did not hide the bitter truth from him.

'But of course, old fellow, that's the way it has to be! They'll begin by shaving your head.'

Ahouna looked down, fingered his beard and his greasy hair. He said to himself with some optimism that they might possibly let him live, since Madame Nicéphore, Mademoiselle Couvrant, Foublard and Boullin, who was a double murderer, and plenty of other criminals had been there for years. But he was terribly distressed not to know what the future had in store for him, now that he had talked to a European who, in spite of seeming quite likeable, appeared to have a terribly black soul, and he murmured, 'Yes, that's the way it has to be. Why torture myself any more, since that's the way it has to be? I've already given up everything; from now on I might as well think of myself as dead, truly burnt up. Oh, that too means nothing to me!'

He clasped his skeletal arms about his emaciated body and suddenly began to shudder involuntarily, like a man suffering from tetanus. Boullin noticed this and turned to look at him.

'You're wrong to get worked up like this; it doesn't help.'

Ahouna hugged his tatters about his bones; he was really cold in spite of the still burning sun. At this moment Toupilly and Mauthonier crossed the yard and stopped near them.

'Boullin, you will go on working in the quarries, that's understood?' said Mauthonier.

'Yes, sir!' replied Ferdinand Boullin, standing to attention like a soldier.

'Don't take advantage of the permission we gave you to question your fellow-prisoners, to get information from them for this report you're supposed to be preparing. And don't badger Ahouna with questions; he's still very weak.'

'Right, sir.'

'Ahouna, you'll go with the other prisoners to the quarries tomorrow, to get some idea of the place and the work,' Toupilly said.

Ahouna did not reply. Mauthonier had it on the tip of his tongue to protest that the new inmate ought not to leave the prison, firstly because he had not yet stood trial, and then because he was still too weak; but he said nothing, and they walked over to Mademoiselle Couvrant to tell her that she was to be relieved from hard work because of her condition.

'You heard that?' Boullin asked Ahouna, as soon as they were alone.

'Yes, but what's it all about?'

'You'll see tomorrow.'

'Is it hard?'

'Everything's hard in a prison like this; it's to be

expected. But I prefer not to talk about the quarries, especially when Hounnoukpo is one of the guards on duty.'

'Who is Hounnoukpo?'

'You don't know him? You'll see him tomorrow. He's the most advanced of the guards. He's a lance-sergeant; in the war he killed a lot of Germans and won some medals. He boasts about having been to France and he can't stand anyone who got his name into the papers at home on account of having committed a murder. He couldn't get a job in a prison in France, so he takes it out on us here.'

'He's lucky he's not a convict himself; there's nothing to prove that he wouldn't be the worst murderer if the opportunity ... no, if circumstances forced him to it,' said Ahouna, thoughtfully.

'You know, Hounnoukpo doesn't think so.'

'Allah have mercy on him, but what is he up to?'

'I don't know; I only know he doesn't understand that one can be driven to crime, that's why I'm terribly afraid of him. Hounnoukpo is the only man I'm really afraid of in this prison, as he's equally ruthless with white and black alike,' Boullin said, his terror appearing clearly in his expression.

Ahouna perceived this and was himself smitten with fear.

Chapter 14

Four o'clock in the morning. The prison awoke and the activity of its unchanging ritual began: the ordinary prisoners swept up the leaves and fruit that had fallen in the yard during the night, while those who were condemned to hard labour left the gates of the penal settlement. The bats still rustled in the foliage, uttering little sharp cries; rats and mice trotted about, sitting up now and then for a few minutes on their little grey haunches, scratching and squeaking with delight before trotting off again.

The gang of thirty convicts shuffled off between the casuarinas, carrying their lamps which gave off a reddish glow. Sixteen guards, armed to the teeth, rifles slung across their shoulders, revolvers and sword-bayonets stuck in their belts, whips in their hands, walked solemnly on each side of the two columns of prisoners with Hounnoukpo in charge. Each convict was manacled by the right wrist and attached to a long steel chain whose ends were padlocked to the right hands of the two men at the head of the columns. A loud clanging of metal mingled with the sonorous rustle of the wind in the casuarinas.

There was Boullin; and Foublard, the artist who, in Mauthonier's words, 'made no bones about getting a screw even in jail'; there was Gerbette, a former policeman, Madame Nicéphore and three black women. Ahouna stumbled along in the rear of one of the columns. Except for him and Boullin, most of the convicts harboured an unreasonable animosity against their fellow-prisoners; it was as if the presence of the others in this gang was responsible for their own presence ...

Owls fluttered screeching among the trees and the black women huddled closer together, cursing these 'sorcerers' birds'.

The convoy advanced flanked by the row of lanterns held in their left hands. Seen from afar, it looked like a fabulous monster.

After an exhausting two hours' march the gang plunged into a tunnel of dense, tall grass overgrowing a footpath just wide enough to allow the convicts and their guards to pass. The carnivorous grasses lashed the legs of the prisoners as they passed, drawing blood; they gritted their teeth so as not to cry out, stiffening themselves to bear the onslaughts of these ruthless plants, placed there by an ironic fate. Sica, one of the black women, unable to bear the pain, suddenly screamed. A guard silenced her with, 'We've had enough from you!'

Sica had never been able to stand up to the stinging attacks of these plants; attractive, sensitive, abhorring suffering, she had been cast into jail by a stupid murder for eight years, and for the last three years, six times a week, she had had to submit to the minor torture, weeping and protesting her innocence, saying how little she deserved this ... Ahouna too grumbled, but one of the prisoners remarked, 'Today, you're only an onlooker, out for the walk; don't make a fuss because a few plants are stroking your legs!'

'These people are hardened; they're not men any more, although not one of them has told me that he has lost his being. What! to talk about "stroking" when you're being bitten deep into your flesh? There ought to be some way of avoiding such useless suffering. Death is better than that. Boullin told me that Affognon killed himself to escape from suffering. He doesn't really know anything about it, but that's what he thinks. Well, since that's the way it is, I'll do the same, as soon as I get the chance ...' So Ahouna was thinking, when finally the convoy emerged from the green tunnel and began to climb down into a huge granite abyss which stretched for more than a mile in circumference.

'The quarries!' murmured Boullin, fetching a deep sigh of despair.

They had arrived at the centre of a huge granite amphitheatre, surrounded by a high massive natural wall ending in gigantic jagged crags, which seemed from afar to be veritable mountain peaks. More than two hundred steps cut out of the rock led down to the heart of this abyss, that Madame Nicéphore had christened Hell. The column continued its march for a further five minutes, then came to a halt in front of a cave where their tools were stored: pickaxes, heavy hammers with long handles, known as stonebreakers, shovels, hoes and baskets.

Dawn had broken in a bright blue sky, full of a promise of life and happiness. Wood-pigeons cooed; countless, nameless wild birds sang merrily. The lanterns were extinguished. The sun rose dazzling in the sky, clothing mountain peaks and foliage with its golden radiance. But as always, the abyss was filled with misery and suffering. Here and there lay the corpses of convicts, with their skulls horribly crushed, the pelvis swarming with flies, vultures, worms and beetles competing for the organs from a thorax. At the first glimpse of this awful sight, Ahouna fainted dead away. Boullin raised him to his feet.

'Hey, there, you're worse than a kid of a girl; this is only the introduction to what's waiting for you in a few days when you're really one of us.'

'Don't scare the wits out of him, Boullin,' said Roubert, a tall, dark fellow, very thin and weak-looking.

'He's a likeable character, much too sensitive; I don't want him to have any illusions when he joins our *corps de ballet*,' Boullin replied with the smile of a man who knows best.

'Of course, you're making him cough up the whys and wherefores of his crime. I'm wondering what use this sociology course will ever be to you,' remarked Gerbette, the former policeman, whose crop of red hair had been turned a pinkish mauve by exposure to the African sun and the hardships of the penal settlement.

'I can put everything to some use,' retorted Boullin, putting some distance between them as he saw a guard approaching.

Ganmê baked in the sun. A powerful stench rose from the depths of the gorge, spreading everywhere,

Snares without End

enveloping guards and prisoners alike, hovering persistently above their heads. The guards lit their pipes or their cigarettes and began to smoke. At mealtimes, they went off to eat in groups of four at a time in a distant corner, where the stench was hardly perceptible, while the other twelve, heavily armed, watched over the convicts. The latter ate their midday meal on the spot, where it was distributed to them – breakfast did not enter into their routine as long as they worked in the quarries.

Each one of the prisoners had grabbed a tool. The women's job was to pick up the chips of crushed granite; they had collected their baskets and work had begun.

The rock began to give beneath the blows of pick and stonecrusher; sparks flew where the hard granite resisted. Wherever there was a crack, a fissure, they drove the pick in, battering harder, ever harder, still harder. The gorge resounded like a forge manned by frantic monsters, hammering chaotically against their anvils. The cracks began to gape wider, the rock shuddered, vibrated, gave here and there. Tools were hurriedly thrust into the widening cracks, groping around for a hold, biting furiously into the rock, with all the cruelty and hatred that would be shown against a flesh-and-blood enemy. The mountain gaped open, tumbling boulders and blocks of granite which flew off like missiles.

Beads of sweat covered the convicts' faces, blinding their eyes, streaming down their backs. The women filled their baskets with crushed granite, carried them on their heads protected by a pad to where they piled their contents up in their individual heaps.

Madame Nicéphore stopped and fetched a deep sigh; she turned her weatherbeaten face, eroded with suffering, towards the guard who was standing over them. The man understood her mute question and did not shout as duty required, 'Come on now, get on with it; we're not in a rest-home!' Then she knew that she could rest for a brief moment ...

She was tall and fair-haired and must have been quite a beauty, in a slightly depraved way; this depravity could still be seen in her jade-green eyes. Ahouna gazed at her, bewildered that such a good-looking woman could kill her husband.

Boullin was struggling against a solid granite wall, humming *La Madelon*. Foublard was singing a popular song just under his breath. Roubert was a bit needled with them for singing, but said nothing and went on sweating away. A native of the Mina tribe was intoning the song of the heavy workers; a Nago was droning a dismal tune; a native of Martinique was singing of his distant island home; he was a young man of thirty-two who had committed a crime the day that he had gone from the theoretical study of 'gratuitous acts', which he must have only half digested, to put the theory into practice, killing his fiancée for no other reason than the desire to perform 'a gratuitous act'.

The rock yielded in showers of sparks; chips of stone scattered; blocks of granite crumbled. A Fon softly chanted a funeral dirge; a sharp flint – so sharp that it might have been chamfered – flew out from the rock and pierced his eye. The man dropped his pick, stood speechless for a second and then let out a howl of pain, like a dog in the presence of death. Everyone quickly gathered round him.

Cossi raised his head and the chip of granite could be seen planted in his left eye, from which a frightful jelly-like mess oozed, like the liquid from a broken egg.

After his fainting attack, Ahouna had been walking up and down as if he too were on guard duty. At the sight of the accident, he sank to the ground, buried his face in his skeletal hands and groaned.

Djossou was used to scenes of this kind and removed the chip from his countryman's eye.

Adjaï, a black woman who was doing seven years' hard labour, wept, protesting that it was better to die than be mutilated like this.

Cossi himself stopped his wailing but, as in a daze, he asked his fellow-prisoners if he had really lost his eye; the fact had taken him so much by surprise that he could not believe that it had happened ... He had been coming to this inferno for ten years; his legs, like those of all the other prisoners, were a mass of scars and sores. He had seen more than one of his fellows die, but he had never thought for one moment that he would leave the penal settlement with any physical disability. 'Just let me finish my time here in one piece,' he thought. 'The years of imprisonment will leave their mark on me, I'm sure, but I'll get out with my body and mind intact, with enough strength and reason to start life all over again.' Such was the strange optimism of this man.

Unable to bear this painful sight any longer, Madame Nicéphore suddenly stripped off her coarse homespun smock and took off her cotton undervest, revealing her well-formed body and her still firm breasts for everyone to see.

'Here now! What's going on? No scandal here!' shouted Hounnoukpo fiercely, brandishing his whip, ready to lash out at Madame Nicéphore who, naked as a slug, seized the whip, declaring coolly, 'I'm not out to attract admirers, nor to shock anyone here. I've given up trying to please a long time ago. Flog me if you feel inclined!' she finished, letting go of the whip.

She tore up her vest and used it to bandage the black hole from which the jelly still oozed, and which made Cossi unrecognisable.

The threatening arm of Hounnoukpo fell powerless beside his burly form. Madame Nicéphore put on her smock again and took up her basket.

The gang, more dead than alive, prey to exhaustion, sunstroke and terror, was beginning to disperse when a huge viper shot out from behind a sunbaked rock and made for a black convict, who struck it dead with his pick. Surprisingly enough, Boullin broke into sudden, regrettable rage. He threw down his pick, shouting, 'Bugger all this! Bugger! bugger! bugger! I'm fed to the teeth with this helluva life!'

'Now then, pick up your tools and get back to work!' a guard shouted.

'Shit!' was the answer he got.

'Who're you calling a shit?' enquired Hounnoukpo.

'You! Lance-Sergeant Hounnoukpo, all of you here,

Snares without End

myself and God himself into the bargain!' he shouted, quivering with fury.

All his fellow-prisoners, caught up in his reaction, of which they understood neither the cause nor the meaning, began to tremble for him. Hounnoukpo leapt towards the rebel and slashed his whip across his back.

'Yes, kill me if you like ... aah! shit again; that's all I think!' he shouted.

Hounnoukpo struck him hard across the face in a vain attempt to subdue him, yelling, 'Cut it out, you understand! Belt up, I'm telling you!'

'No, I won't. I'm a man, and if I'm not free at least I've the right to kick up a row.'

'Kick up a row? What about? Who're you bawling about, you poor fool?'

'I'm bawling about my life, about life in general, about men, about you in particular.'

Hounnoukpo only caught one word. 'About *me*?'

'Yes, about you, Hounnoukpo, you poor sod, you!'

The whip whistled across his face, the blood spurted from his ears, the blows rained furiously down on his back which also streamed with blood, but the miserable wretch would not be silent.

'Kill me, and to hell with it! ... What a joke! You know what? ... I can't help it. ... I like all men, I don't care what colour their skin is; I knew lots of blacks at school in Montpellier, I was friends with them in Bordeaux, but I can't stand a nigger giving me orders, still less for him to lay his hands on m ...'

His words were lost as blows from the heavy horse-hide whip rained down on him, forcing him to swallow the rest of his bluster. Hounnoukpo, blacker than ever in his fury, vaunted his threefold claim to fame.

'What! you dirty half-wit, you damned jailbird! As long as you're here, even a mule will have the right to put you in your place, you low-down murderer; and you'll do as a mule tells you, if he's put in charge of you, because he'll have *deserved* the right to order you about ... And I'll have you know this: in the first place, I know France and I fought in the war there, I did; in the second place, I saw

Marshal Lyautey and I've got a great respect for him; *he shook my hand,* and he gave me his photograph, with his signature on it; in the third place, Sergeant-Major Kofi Hounnoukpo never disobeyed orders from his chiefs, whether they were black or white. And I'll see that you obey me, and I'll put the fear of God into you. You're the lowest of the low; you're nothing but a butcher, and I loathe you and I loathe all your kind. Got it?' he concluded, as he laid into Boullin.

'Yes, I've got it, but you won't stop me loathing you too, and yelling that I can't stand being bossed over by a nigger!'

Hounnoukpo flared up again, but immediately managed to control himself, with the thought that all the prisoners in his charge were more or less mad.

'Even if I beat him till he gives up the ghost, he'll never change his tune, the jailbird!' he said to himself, then shouted, 'Go on! Back to work!'

Once more pickaxes and stonecrushers bit furiously into the rock. Ahouna, terribly distressed by the heart-rending sight he had just witnessed, wept silently into his bony hands.

'Boullin, my friend, how could you bring down so much suffering on yourself? You are such a good sort, you who've got no more illusions and have recognised the seriousness of your crime and accepted the consequences. Why did you let your tongue run away with you like that? You must be on your guard against everything, Boullin, even against what is inside yourself,' he moaned softly.

To be sure, rebellion was smouldering in Ahouna's heart too, but he was very much on his guard against it and kept it under control. 'What is the use? What can such an outburst lead to? It can't help; the only act of rebellion that I must commit henceforward will be to renounce life in favour of death; for whichever way I turn in this world, I shall always fall into the hands of men,' he continually repeated to himself.

Ferdinand Boullin did not think likewise. He could not: his conception of man's life was profoundly different from the simple wisdom of Ahouna who, despite his

_____

Snares without End

decision to remain indifferent to everything since he entered the prison, nevertheless recoiled as strongly as before from the slightest suffering. Boullin, for his part, accepted this suffering with stoicism. He was convinced that this was the price he had to pay for his crime.

For all that, there was a resurgence of rebellion in him, and he manifested it as a legitimate action. He had experienced these feelings today because man, the only animal who understands the meaning of liberty, and who can feel it vibrating within him at every moment of his existence, had given voice within his heart and sunk teeth into his flesh. Absurd as it was, a whole past which he had thought for ever annihilated had been reborn, and he had felt the urge to rebel.

All these convicts experienced the same sensation, the same feeling, the same gnawing pain; the men betrayed their rebellion in their walk and their tense faces; it was apparent in the way the women filled their baskets and loaded them on to their heads. Rebellion commanded the movements of these hands armed with pickaxes, stonecrushers, shovels; it was rebellion which attacked the rock before the tools ... the useless rebellion of convicts.

The sun burned down mercilessly; the incandescent, suffocating heat of Africa spread a vibrating, diaphanous shimmer above the shaven heads of the black convicts. Their sweating bodies gave off a powerful, nauseating smell of rotting leather under their ridiculous, thick, ash-grey, sack-like uniforms, which would have made it impossible to distinguish one prisoner from another, if they had all been black or all white.

A pickaxe struck furiously at the rock, bit into it and remained fixed. An enormous block of granite gave way suddenly, fell to the ground, and blood spurted out from under it as if it were gushing out of the ground. A man was dead, flattened like an insect, buried without a cry; not because he had not had time to cry out, or indeed to escape from this terrible death, but because he had preferred to end it all thus. This had always been the greatest desire of Favidé. The man who was apparently the least troublesome of all the convicts had just died, and

Hounnoukpo coldly took out his register, opened it and crossed his name off the list.

'He's better off dead,' Boullin muttered. 'It's really ridiculous to suffer for a crime that you haven't committed. He was simple-minded, one of those idiots that very rarely appear on this earth; he didn't kill anyone but he became one of us because he couldn't prove his innocence. A man's got no right to behave like that; the world doesn't belong to the innocent or to fools, and Favidé was just as wrong to be born at all as to have been unable to defend himself against all the scum and all those stronger than him, who made him into a jailbird.'

About four o'clock they put the tools away in the cave and their right hands were once more shackled to the chain. They picked up their lanterns and the loud clatter of the chain was heard once more. Exhausted, near to collapse, the gang once more climbed the granite steps without looking back down the gorge.

Behind them a flock of vultures screeched angrily around Favidé's body, which they could not devour because it was literally buried beneath the block of granite, while those which had alighted first tore savagely at the victim's feet and hands.

The convoy plunged into the green tunnel, emerged again, crossed once more the realm of the carnivorous plants; Sica wept and moaned softly. Cossi, the man who had lost his eye and who was chained behind her, murmured by way of consolation that she should try to bear up as at least she hadn't been disabled.

When the gang got back to the prison, and were no longer strung along a chain like the bead necklace of some fabulous monster, Boullin went up to Ahouna, saying, 'So, now you have seen what the quarries are like.'

'You were stupid. Why did you defy him like that? You disappointed me,' said Ahouna, without answering his friend's question.

'You're right, but you can't understand me ... Anyway, you've seen what happens there.'

'Yes, and I pray to Allah, even though I know he's now against me, to see that I never have to work in that abyss where I felt I was the other side of death.'

'But death itself begins here on earth. I'd even say that death's realm is on earth and not anywhere else and you will have to submit to your ordeal, Ahouna. You will go and work in the quarries. You will sweat there until you feel yourself turning into a rock like that collection of granite that your pickaxe will break furiously, with a loathing that is nameless because it is unreasonable.'

'Never!' cried Ahouna in terror.

'You're here to suffer, I've told you that already. Perhaps in a week, in a month or two, you'll be taken to Ouidah, to Cotonou, then to Porto-Novo. In Ouidah, people will come and abuse you, Christians, Mohammedans and Fetishists will curse you and spit on you; in Cotonou, a cosmopolitan town, the crowd that is usually indifferent, always in a hurry, will suddenly become a host of idle onlookers who will descend on you like a colony of bluebottles on a piece of meat. Blacks, whites, crooks, honest men – if there are any – will stare at you like a rare animal. In Porto-Novo, Ahouna, people of every tribe, Goons, Nagos, Yorubas, will gape at you stupidly and curse you till they kill your poor soul; perhaps you'll be stoned again there, like you were the day you arrived in Ganmê ... And you'll have no redress against it all, because your life as a convict will be beginning. I've told you this already, but listen to me again: *you will lose what you call your "being" again.* You will realise this when you've stood trial and been condemned to several years' hard labour and you come back to Ganmê to sweat it out in the quarries.'

'Never, never, never!' Ahouna replied in a strangled voice, his heart suddenly gripped in an atrocious anguish.

He darted wild glances around, and then let his eyes, shining with a distant gleam, rest on Boullin. He reflected for a moment and then said, 'Will you do something for me?'

Boullin gave a faint smile: 'What? ... lend you a penknife, a razor-blade, something you can kill yourself with?'

'Yes, yes, that's right; help me,' whispered Ahouna.

'I've got nothing; look at my beard ... besides, they took everything away from us after Affognon's suicide. Listen: even if I had the wherewithal to help you, I wouldn't lend it to you; you've got to suffer; you've got to learn what a penal settlement really is, and give a meaning to it, and to your own existence as a man who has lost his being,' said Boullin.

'But my life is dead, it's got no more meaning for me, and the prison has got no meaning either!' whispered Ahouna angrily.

'Just because your life has no meaning and prison has no meaning, it's up to you to give them a meaning. "Seek and ye shall find", as the man says, and he was right; I can see now how sublime that man was.'

'I don't want to seek for anything; or rather, yes, what I'm seeking for now is death; whatever form it takes, wherever it may be, I want to find it and the sooner the better. I want the hour of my departure for Ouidah, Cotonou and Porto-Novo to come quickly or never to come at all. You understand me, Boullin, my friend.'

'So be it! Amen.' Boullin commented ambiguously.

When two days later the chain-gang returned to the quarries, as they did every third day, an incident occurred which seemed to drive Ahouna quite out of his wits. Scarcely had the work begun than a rock face, the height of a double-storey house, that had long been unsteady, crashed down, completely burying Boullin and a black prisoner.

Ahouna cried out in terror, burst into tears and walked like an automaton towards the granite steps, shouting that he wouldn't remain a moment longer in this inferno. He was seized and handcuffed.

He sat staring wild-eyed at this crude and monstrous tombstone, from under which came streams of blood on which a swarm of flies had already settled. Ahouna sobbed with grief. Madame Nicéphore looked at him thoughtfully, deeply moved because she tried in vain to understand his sorrow. Then she looked down and wept silently.

'Poor Boullin! he wasn't a bad fellow,' said Foublard.

Snares without End

'No, he wasn't a bad fellow; cynical, sometimes rebellious, but decent!' said Gerbette.

Hounnoukpo opened the register, and for the first time in the fifteen years that he had been coming to this inferno, his hand trembled as he struck off the names of Boullin and Goudjanou, the second victim.

Chapter 15

Ahouna was inconsolable; he could not prevent himself from silently mourning Boullin's death. The dead man now seemed as dear to him, as indispensable as this thing he called his 'being'. The vacuum which had appeared in his soul immediately after his crime became even more perceptible. And, considering himself as already a dead man in the midst of his fellow-prisoners, he had not concerned himself unduly with the intimations of tragedy that haunted him; but now these corresponded to a reality and a certainty.

In Zounmin, where Ahouna had killed Madame Kinhou some months previously, several family palavers had been held; these had given rise to lively arguments which had degenerated into a bitter quarrel among the children and relatives of the victim; some of them wanted to forgive the murderer and to try to forget his existence, while the others opted for an uncompromising vengeance. One last meeting was to take place this evening, and old Dâko emerged from his hut, whose high, conical roof came nearly down to ground level, leaving only a small part of the mud wall visible.

Now in his nineties, wasted and hirsute, he must once have been tall, muscular, well-built, in short a fine figure of a man. He was now bent nearly double and walked leaning on an exaggeratedly long ironwood stick that overtopped his stooping form, so that the top of it could be seen before old Dâko himself came into view.

The older he grew, the more his shrivelled, desiccated muscles adhered to his bones, dropping away from his dull black skin. This outer covering, that must once have been smooth and supple, now fell in wrinkled folds from the old man's pendulous chops, increased the length of his huge ears that were as full of hair as an artichoke heart and hung loosely from his chin and forearms like the dewlap of an old stag.

Snares without End

The patriarch of Zounmin was also Madame Kinhou's father-in-law. As the peace-loving old man crossed the ancestral courtyard, rapt in thought, his gait had something of the sober majesty of a heron. He went to sit on a little stool carved out of a solid piece of iroko wood. When seated he looked rather as if he were squatting with his knees touching his freshly shaven chin, and his arms folded across his thighs. He wore his loose pagne, woven in Kana, like a peplum, exposing his broad chest that was covered with white frizzy hairs, like the hair on his head. A large reed mat was spread at his feet, which were wide as a duck's and looked as if they were too big and possibly even too heavy for his thin, skeletal ankles. Before his arrival five young men had emerged from the huts constructed here and there around the circular courtyard and had settled themselves on this mat.

They sat facing the old man under a wild fig tree which scattered its thick shade over the courtyard; a full moon had already climbed high in the cloudless sky.

'Since the death of my son Gbênoumin,' Dâko began, 'the atmosphere of our little farm has been heavy with a certain curse, and we must come to an agreement so that we can drive out, or try to drive out – for this is not an easy thing – the evil spirits. As you know, Gbênoumin's soul cannot rest as long as there is disagreement among us, his family. His soul is calling out for rest, so it is our duty to unite, so that we can in all sincerity set up his *legbà* and his *asen* to ensure the protection of the spirits and his continued presence in our midst. We should also be thinking of doing the same for Kinhou, my daughter-in-law. The dissension that descended on Zounmin shortly after her murder has caused inordinate delay in arranging her *Jonu* and the other ceremonies that we should have organised in her honour within two or three months of her burial. For these reasons I wish to call on you once again with my most earnest prayers, to forgive – nay, to forget even – those melancholy, unhappy and painful events of the past, which I am sure the gods themselves will take upon themselves to avenge. I wish, my children, to bring back to Zounmin your uncles and aunts, our

Snares without End

cousins, nieces and nephews who have been driven away
by your intransigence and forced to wander in the bush
and try to build another farm for themselves elsewhere.
You must not leave them time to accomplish this
undertaking. If you let them finish, it will be certain to
perpetuate this dissension. Now, I am convinced that you
are sorry to see the family divided in this way. I am sure
that it is only your obstinacy that makes you insist on
avenging Kinhou's death; and I do not speak idly, for I
know that my daughter-in-law's soul is opposed to your
intrigues ... My children, believe the words of an old man,
although they may seem to you to be unreasonable and
too peace-loving; Zounmin is the home of our ancestors;
their spirits are there, as you all know, in the hut behind
the fig tree, where we pay tribute to them every *zogbodogbé*,
the fair-day when we make our sacrifices to the fetishes;
they are everywhere on this farm and take part in all our
activities; they watch over our lives and our well-being.
Beware lest they turn their backs on us, my children, and
join with the evil spirits to contribute savagely to our
perdition and to the annihilation of the whole of
Zounmin. Zounmin, to the best of my knowledge, has
never heard the sound of quarrels, or trembled with
misfortune. And now, misfortune and wretchedness
hover in the air, they are over our compound; I feel their
imminent presence over our heads, as they are about to
descend on us, if we do not calm ourselves, if we do not
unite so as to make the spirits of the dead and the gods
favourable to us and give us their blessing and help.
Cease, I beseech you, my children, this headlong race
towards destruction, before it is too late. Prudence is
worth more than regret and remorse!'

Houinsou, the dead woman's eldest son, a tall, strong
man of thirty-three, replied first.

'If the destruction of Zounmin must indeed take place,
as you predict, it will not be until we have carried out our
plan, grandfather,' he said firmly, 'however unreasonable
this plan may seem to those who have broken away from
us, and can no longer be considered members of our
family, and to you yourself, who have stayed with us.'

'No! This vengeance is the height of folly and shall not take place in Zounmin!' the old man replied.

'You have lived your life, grandfather; at your age, you can allow yourself to forgive any crime; but for our part, we are young and need to act. We must prove that the deeply felt demands of our generation are completely different from yours, which is moribund. That's what you don't seem to understand!' said Tôvignon, with an arrogance that the old man found hard to bear.

'What is the use of an activity that is founded solely on vengeance? Should you act even if it were only to do evil?' old Dâko asked anxiously.

'Certainly, grandfather,' replied Houéfa.

'No! not unless you are mad, crazed with madness, mad enough to be sent to the asylum in Cotonou!' retorted Agossou, the youngest of the Gbênoumin brothers.

'Hold your tongue, you little wretch. You've been to school and learnt a lot of stupid nonsense that stops you thinking and feeling like everyone else!' objected his uncle Houngbé, Kinhou's only brother, who had been living in Zounmin since the disagreement had arisen over the punishment to inflict on Ahouna.

'Dâgbo (grandfather) never went to school, he's never known any school, but he doesn't think or feel the same as you for all that!' retorted Agossou again.

'Dâgbo is dâgbo, and that's sufficient,' said Houinsou. 'As for you, you've lost your roots, you're a traitor and argue the way you do because you don't know any better.'

'Better to have lost one's roots, to be a traitor, a slave even, and remain a sensible reasonable man,' said the old man.

'If to love your own mother and want to avenge her death at any price means that you're mad, then I prefer my madness to what you call good sense and reason,' Houinsou declared angrily.

'French justice has made itself responsible for punishing our mother's murderer, and I loved her as much or even more than you did, for all your thirst for vengeance and bloodshed.'

'It's all your fault that we had to take the murderer to

Ganmê,' snarled Tôvignon. 'And it's also the fault of all the people who hide themselves away in the bush,' he went on, getting more and more worked up. 'If it weren't for dâgbo and you and all the other idiots, everything would have been all right, even in spite of the police. Oh! French justice, French justice ... I'd like to know what our mother's murderer will suffer in the name of this justice that you keep dinning into our ears. You can't impress us just because you've got what you call your *settifika*. You think you're very clever but you're not, and you know nothing about French justice!'

'Prison, penal settlement, forced labour, floggings, all kinds of ill-treatment by the warders,' muttered Agossou, trying to recall some of the things he had learnt at school.

'May the gods of leprosy and of the plague carry you off with all that nonsense they stuffed you with in school! If a mosquito stung you, you'd want to send it to prison, to penal settlement, condemn it to forced labour and flogging!' said Houéfa.

'Such punishment is nevertheless worse than death!' said old Dâko, thinking of what he had heard about the Ganmê quarries.

'You know nothing about it; but that's not the point,' declared Houngbé. 'Whether it's in Ganmê or anywhere else, in prison or penal settlements, people eat, they're alive. They're deprived of what they are accustomed to, they haven't got their liberty, but they are alive all the same. Well, what we have to do is to see that our mother's murderer no longer lives: he has killed and he must die!'

'No one lives for ever, and this man from the northern regions will die one day or another,' observed Agossou.

'He will die, that's a fact, but that's not what interests us,' Tôvignon replied. 'He took a life and his life must be forfeit. We must cut short his existence by killing him as soon as possible.'

'What you are planning will be *dé-votchi*, a vain and futile enterprise, a nice ripe nut whose kernel you will never find, however much you search, because it will be hollow and empty,' said Agossou, in a voice of imprecation.

'What is that to you, you damn smart Aleck?' shouted his uncle.

'If you carry out this lunatic enterprise, you will be driven to eat Dead Sea fruits for the rest of your lives. Your uncle Houngbé put you up to this, I know; he has you all under his thumb; this boy that I've never thought of as a man, is the incarnation of evil. If you knew, my poor children, into what a maze he is leading you, you would immediately give up your foolish plans!' cried the old man tragically, as he rose to his feet.

'*Tôvi dô: zankou! Nonvi dô: aniwêdo zanmê?* Blood is thicker than water; would you sing the same song if your own blood was involved?' sneered Houngbé in the tone of he who has the last word.

At this crude insult old Dâko resumed his seat. He had never considered his late daughter-in-law as a stranger to Zounmin. Ever since that now distant time when Gbênoumin and Kinhou had got to know each other and begun their courtship, the old man had always thought of his future daughter-in-law as one of his own kith and kin. From that time onward the image of Kinhou was inseparable in his mind's eye from that of the young man. After their marriage, as he watched her going about her domestic activities, his image of her was always the same. The older he grew, the more Gbênoumin and Kinhou seemed to him like sister and brother. He had never addressed his daughter-in-law otherwise than as 'my daughter' and he used the same intimacy in conversation with her as with his own children. And now a whipper-snapper young enough to be his grandson remarked disrespectfully, with an insolence only equalled by his arrogance, that he was against their plans for avenging this same daughter-in-law's death, because she was not his own daughter!

The moon no longer hung directly over the courtyard, which was now completely shaded by the wild fig tree. The ghostly shadows of the densely packed huts with their conical roofs stretched out as far as the bushes that surrounded the compound. A couple of owls flew majestically across the sky and perched on the iroko tree that stood high above the surrounding bush, and from there they rent the silence and the tranquillity with their sinister hooting. Houngbé started slightly, then regained his control, muttering some cabalistic incantations which had the power of countering, or better still, of cancelling out the ill omens that these birds of prey are supposed to announce, in Africa as well as in every country where superstition has a hold on men's minds.

Young Agossou noticed his uncle's mutterings and said to himself, 'The fool! he thinks he's going to kill my mother's murderer; he thinks he's strong enough to succeed in his abominable plan, but he trembles like a dead leaf and mutters incantations because some night birds screech!'

Old Dâko sighed, 'I swallow all that you have vomited, Houngbé; I have not waited till I am an old man to forgive my neighbour the hurt that he does me, but retribution will come.'

He had scarcely finished his sentence than the peremptory screech of the owl was heard again three times, answering through the night air. Then Houngbé and the three nephews who were on the side of vengeance murmured their cabalistic ritual in chorus. The old man seized the opportunity to state, 'These birds of ill omen never used to fly over Zounmin; but they have been flocking here in great numbers ever since we have been torn asunder and divided by these dissensions which persist because of you, Houngbé, Houinsou, Tôvignon and Houéfa. I repeat you, senile and useless as I may appear to you, a terrible misfortune is brewing, is threatening Zounmin and may well, I fear, descend on us here very shortly. The proof, that you must also have observed for yourselves, is that for the past two weeks *agaê*, the screeching owl, has been perching every night on the iroko tree, and hooting his single note that foretells misfortune ... So danger is imminent, my children, and it is up to you to drive it away, while there is still time.'

'Too bad!' declared Houinsou.

'The gods themselves are on our side!' added Houngbé, clinching the argument.

'That is not true! Curses upon all those of you who seek to dishonour the gods!' cried the old man, pathetically now.

For one long moment there was silence. The venerable old man shivered. He wrapped his loose pagne, one fold of which dragged on the ground, more tightly around his emaciated form. The night had grown colder. The earth gave off a damp smell, as after a storm. Old Dâko felt vanquished, overcome, beaten in the task he had set himself of cleaning out this filthy pigsty; he decided to abandon his fruitless arguments and leave these four fools to their senseless undertaking. He knew exactly what they planned to do and might have told them he would denounce them to the authorities in Ganmê; but he knew he would never do this. One does not reach the age of ninety and more to play such a ridiculous role; and was it not to avoid being traitors to their own family that the others had left Zounmin for good, to go and live in the bush?

'So I too must leave!' the old man said to himself, but he quickly changed his mind. He thought that perhaps he could speak once more before deciding on his action.

'I am going to tell you a story.'

'I've never heard anyone tell stories in Zounmin; it seems to me that such primitive customs are forbidden here by an ancestral decree,' objected Houinsou, putting into the expression of his voice all the pride and conceit he felt, that he wasn't completely ignorant of the customs of this family farm that went back three hundred years.

'That is true, but in circumstances like these – and such things have never before occurred in Zounmin – our fathers, when they were at the end of their tether, as I am, had recourse to moral tales and their symbolic meaning,' said the old man, who then began one of those Dahomean tales that are well known in the land of the Fon people:

'One day, three men took a wager. The first one said, "When my mother dies, I shall not bury her until I have been to the home of the nymph who lives at the bottom of Lake Nohoué, and asked her for a stone from her bed." The second one said: "If my mother dies, I wager that I

shall not put her in the ground until I have obtained a
shroud from the hands of Thunder." The third one said:
"_I_ shall bury my mother with the tail of a live lion!"

'The first man lost his mother.He ran to the edge of
Lake Nohoué and threw himself into the water. At the
bottom he found himself in the presence of the water-
nymph. "Do you not know," said the spirit, "that my
dwelling is forbidden to people of your kind, and those
who venture here never return?"

' "Yes," replied the man, "but I beg you, great spirit, to
save me! I maintained before my friends that I would not
put my mother in the ground until I had first asked you
for a stone from your bed. And my mother has just died!"

'The spirit took pity on him and gave him a stone from
her bed. Shortly after this, the second man lost his
mother. He went off to the realm of Thunder.

' "What are you seeking here?" asked the god.

' "All-powerful god!" he replied, "pardon my
presumption; my mother has just died and unless you
take pity on me I cannot bury her, for I have wagered that
I shall only bury her wrapped in a shroud from the god
Thunder."

'Thunder took pity on him and gave him a shroud. The
third man lost his mother.

' "Shall I be the only one not to honour my promise?"
he lamented. Then, after a moment's thought, he said to
his wife, "I am going to look for a live lion. Watch over
the corpse of my mother, and if tomorrow I have not
returned, then lift the lid of the calabash behind my hut. If
the blood that you see in it is boiling, then give a stew
made from tortoise flesh to my dogs and unchain them."

'He walked straight on, and arrived at nightfall at an
isolated cave. An old woman came out and reprimanded
him sharply: "Don't you know that you are here in the
dwelling of the lions and no human being ventures into
these regions with impunity?"

' "Yes," sobbed the man, "I know all the risks I am
taking in coming into these regions; but I beg you to save
me. I have sworn to bury my mother only with a lion's
tail. If you do not come to my rescue, I expose the author

of my days to being deprived of burial honours."

'The old woman – the lion-keeper – reflected and said, "I will hide you beneath a pitcher. When the lions return, you must not move. When you hear 'Hitô! Hitô!', they will be asleep; come out then and cut off a tail and be off."

'At sunset, the lions returned from hunting and began to pester the keeper. "We can smell flesh to eat!" they roared loud and long, raising their heads and sniffing the air. But the old woman did not give anything away. Exhausted, the lions lay down to rest. Soon "Honou! Hounou! Gben!" could be heard, then "Hitô! Hitô!" and the lions slept.

'The man came out from his hiding-place, cut off the tail of one of the lions and was about to flee. A shrill roar set the whole cave in excitement. The lions set off in pursuit of the rash individual. When they were just upon him, he recited an incantation and immediately an enormous fire flared up between him and the furious felines. The lions also said their incantation and the fire was extinguished. The man caused a river to flow and the lions dried it up. Then there came bottomless precipices, an impenetrable forest etc. And each time the lions surmounted the obstacles.

'When the adventurer had no more incantations left he climbed to the top of a tall bombax tree. The lions surrounded the tree. The man was done for ... unless his dogs ...

'In fact he had been gone for three days, and the dogs had not been let loose. His wife, overwhelmed by sorrow beside the body of her mother-in-law that she watched over day and night, had forgotten to watch the mysterious calabash. As chance would have it, a horsefly settled on her leg; she crushed it with a swift, well-timed blow. At the sight of the blood that spurted from it, she remembered what her husband had told her. She ran to the calabash and when she reached it, the contents had boiled over onto the ground. She swiftly prepared a turtle stew, fed the dogs with it and let them loose. The dogs raced off to rescue their master in distress. It was about time. To hasten their revenge the lions were going at it with tooth and claw, and in ten winks of an eye would have been masters of the situation when the dogs arrived on the scene. They were no ordinary dogs. They had been ritually immunised and could fight against the lions without fear. The struggle lasted "the time it takes to go from Agbômê to Kanan" – about three hours – and no lion was left alive.

'The hero of this tale owed his life to his dogs, or rather to the fortunate chance that led a horsefly to sting his wife. But before that happened he had almost fallen a prey to his terrible adversaries.

'You can guess the moral of this tale, which in case you know already: "Do not gamble with danger; you may well pay with your life." '

The old man was sublime; he told his tale with emotion and a sense of tragedy. He stopped, as if to get his breath back, but resumed immediately, while his audience listened intently. 'What dog will come to rescue you from the danger that you are in? And then, we are no longer living in a world which attaches importance to fairytales. All the fantasies are dead, destroyed, and man is no sooner born than he faces life with a spirit of realism ... I repeat to you for the last time: even if you know where you are going, you have no knowledge of what awaits you. Come now! who has not been young once? I too used to love to take risks, I still do, but not when they are based on such folly, such idiocy as this project that you are embarked upon. Do now what you will; I wash my hands and my feet of it and I leave Zounmin for Oussa. I live here because this is my ancestral farm; Oussa is my personal domain, built with my own hands. I abandon Zounmin to your hands, which already smell of the crime you are about to commit, but I take with me the soul of my father and of our ancestors; they had a horror of crime and even detested the country of Abadahoué Djéssou, the abode of the dead. And so I leave you with my curse, *Hélou mi!* may calamities be upon your heads!'

He rose rapidly to his feet and draped his voluminous pagne around his old bones.

Young Agossou sprang to his feet, asserting vehemently, 'I'm going with you, dâgbo! I've already said that one doesn't have to go to school to learn not to behave like a brute or a savage, and you've just given us proof of this!' he declared as he set out behind the old man stooping over his stick.

They left the four accomplices who were bent on avenging Kinhou's death, crossed the courtyard which was now in darkness as the moon was setting, and returned to their own huts. A little later they emerged, old Dâko carrying a basket of woven reeds, too heavy for his frail hands that for ten years had leant on his ironwood stick. If Agossou had not chosen to accompany him to Oussa, he would have loaded the heavy pack on his bent back, ready to give up the ghost in the course of his journey.

With Agossou were Zinsou and Zinhoué, his twin brother and sister, aged twelve. They were too young to take part in the discussions, but they were aware of the decision of the four rebels and disapproved of it. Zinsou, the boy, had expressed his point of view also: 'For my part, I'd be only too happy for my brothers and my uncle to kill my mother's murderer, if the death of this bad man could bring our mother back to life. But if that is impossible, then it would be better to leave the murderer alone, for he too will die one day.'

So when Agossou woke them from their deep sleep and suggested that they leave with him and dâgbo for Oussa, they hurried to fetch their little wicker baskets, for they immediately understood that the dissension that reigned between the grown-ups had grown more bitter.

They all took up their baskets, or rather Agossou put the others inside with his own, making one single pack containing the belongings of the three of them, which he hoisted on to Zinsou's head. He then took charge of their grandfather's pack which he placed on his own head. He opened the march, followed closely in single file by the twins and old Dâko, leaning heavily on his stick, and holding in his left hand a little closed calabash soaked in palm-oil and containing, if the old man was to be believed, the fingernails and toenails, as well as a few locks of hair, from all the ancestors and members of the family who had died in Zounmin, together with some minute cowries, dried chicken blood and tiny quantities of numerous other bits and pieces.

As the little group reached the far side of the courtyard, in which the other members of the family who were thirsty for vengeance were still talking softly beneath the fig tree, the old man stopped, grasped the calabash tightly to his chest, placed it on the ground, took it up again, and felt his heart vibrate. He felt a deep emotion stirring the depths of his soul, but he tried to speak firmly: 'I am leaving with the young people. We are going away with the souls of the ancestors and of all our dead, including Gbênoumin and Kinhou. The spirits of the dead ancestors which used to wander here and have protected this compound for three centuries will accompany us too. From now on, the asens which are still there in the little hut behind you are nothing but useless constructions of iron and copper. Zounmin is empty. Farewell!'

No one answered him, and the venerable non-agenarian, still preceded by the trio of grandchildren, left the ancestral home.

Then they plunged into a narrow, twisting path, half hidden beneath the high grass that was drenched with dew, which would lead them to Oussa in five hours' march. But half an hour after they had set out, the old man looked back; he stopped for a second, guessed, rather than saw in reality, a vast circle of clay pots which protected the conical roofs of his ancestral home against the infiltrations of the rain. Once more he felt his heart vibrate; the very depths of his soul stirred as with a physical ache; his whole past rose up within him, as if in revolt, but he set out again, weeping silently.

In Zounmin, the great disc of the full moon disappeared behind the iroko tree. The four accomplices continued their discussion.

'Well! that old thorn-in-the-flesh and his brats have gone; good riddance! Now we are free, absolutely free, the gods be praised!' said Houinsou with a sigh of relief.

'So it's agreed, isn't it, uncle Houngbé, that you'll be the one to give yourself up to the police, so that we can carry out our plan successfully?' asked Tôvignon, who would have liked to have had this honour himself if the oracle, Fâ Aïdégoun, had not designated his uncle.

'Yes, and we must hurry, for day is breaking and it is getting light. We should be out of here before the last cockcrow, according to the indications given by Fâ Aïdégoun,' said Houngbé impatiently.

The four conspirators got up and two went to the henhouse, and the others to the shed, from where they returned a few minutes later with two black cockerels and a black kid. They also had some cola nuts, a pod of Guinea peas, a calabash full of palm-oil, a pint of palm-wine brandy and a little calabash filled with fresh water.

They left the farm, crossed through the bush and made their way to the foot of the iroko tree, the fetish tree that was the haunt of other gods named 'Tolêgbâ, Aïzan ...' there they lit a little wood fire, sprinkled most of the oil, the alcohol and the water over the foot of the tree and the other gods. They knelt down and Houinsou prayed:

'All-powerful gods, the other members of our family are in disagreement with us and have abandoned us. But you are completely of our opinion that we must avenge the death of our mother, your daughter. You are with us, and you yourselves will guide our footsteps. Fâ Aïdégoun himself has chosen our uncle Houngbé and has said, "Houngbé will give himself up to the police; he will spend one moon in that place so that all will take place for the best. He also said that the last day that Houngbé spends in the prison in Ganmê will be the one when he escapes with the murderer whom we shall punish in our own fashion. But how will he get out of that prison? Fâ Aïdégon has explained, "Anger will bring the best counsel." But he has also composed the strangest of allegories:

' "A great serpent shall rise up on its tail and reach to the height of the prison wall. Houngbé and Kinhou's murderer shall use this serpent as the sole means of their escape! And then, some time after their departure from prison, vengeance will be satisfied, whilst light shall shine over Zounmin."

'If you all agree with this decision, all-powerful gods, then let this be known by the voice of the cola nut.'

Then he broke the nuts, put the pieces in his hands, sent up a prayer, invoked the gods and the spirits of the ancestors, even those that Dâko had taken with him, spread the quarters of the cola nuts on the ground in front of the gods, and it turned out that they all agreed with Fâ Aïdégoun!

The conspirators were pleased ... happy. They offered up a libation, followed by a sacrifice: the blood of the two cocks and the kid was sprinkled around the foot of the trees and the other fetishes; the cocks were plucked, drawn and then roasted on hot ashes; the feathers, the viscera and the entrails were offered to the gods with the heads and the claws; they themselves ate the best portions.

As for the kid, the gods only got the blood; they wrapped the entrails and the viscera in banana leaves which they hastily cut from the plantation that extended behind Zounmin. Then, steeped as they were in their religion, upheld by their belief in the over-subtle allegories of Fâ Aïdégoun, the rebels tied the heavy young goat, still dripping with blood, on to Houngbé's back. Houngbé suddenly had the vague impression of being a corpse that was about to be consigned to the sea. His three nephews then tied his hands with a rope long enough for one of them to lead him like an animal on a leash.

When they had finished they set out. After a good three hours' walk this macabre convoy reached the police station in Ganmê, accompanied by a host of flies and curious onlookers.

Toupilly greeted Houngbé with a hail of blows, which took the pretended thief greatly by surprise; he had not at all expected this treatment and he suddenly saw thousands of golden stars in a sky where the sun already blazed, although it was not yet ten o'clock, and still pursued its tranquil course towards the zenith.

Snares without End

'You dirty nigger! Aren't you ashamed to steal a kid?
... You old bastard. If I wanted to steal, I'd do better than
that! Look at him! He hasn't even had time to make the
most of his booty! Take the blockhead away. Shove him in
jail!' said the commissioner, and turning towards the
three brothers, but speaking to Monsieur Dégonnon, who
translated for them, 'You really have bad luck,
gentlemen. I'm very sorry about this; after the murder of
your mother, now someone's got it in for your flock. It's
true the crime might be more serious, but don't worry;
French justice will see you right.'

Chapter 16

When Ahouna got to know Houngbé he told him he ought not to have stolen from Zounmin.

'I had to!' Houngbé replied with feigned sadness.

'That's a pity; but I hope that if you had known of the great sorrow that descended on Zounmin because of me, you would have directed your steps to some other property.'

'What's done is done ... and in any case, I had no choice,' Houngbé said. 'But now my main business is to set about escaping as soon as I get the chance.'

Ahouna went several times to the quarries, but always as a spectator. The scenes in this inferno, after Boullin's death, made him literally ill; his delicate health was upset and he spent another two weeks in the little prison infirmary.

Houngbé had secretly confided to Ahouna his wish to escape as soon as he could; he spoke of this again the day Ahouna was discharged from the hospital.

'What is the use? You stole a kid and probably some other rubbish as well, and you've been put in jail, which is right and proper. You must pay the penalty, as Boullin used to say, a friend of mine who died in the quarries. After you've done your penance you can go home, stronger and wiser for your experience in prison,' Ahouna commented.

'Never will I spend six months in this place!' retorted Houngbé firmly. 'I'm quite determined to escape.'

'Your energy amuses me; you don't seem to realise either the height or the strength of the walls which surround us.'

'My heart scorns these high walls, crowned with broken glass, as it scorns all the difficulties in life, when my wife and children call. You would understand my feelings if you had a family too,' Houngbé said, speaking softly as he always did when they met.

'When his children call! So he has children,' thought Ahouna, 'and that is one of the reasons why he swears to escape from this place. My children, what has become of my children? How are they living? What have they been told about me? What do they think of me? Think? Can they really think? Except for my little Bakari, and perhaps Fatou, none of them will have really known me ...

' "Your father left me one night, for no reason; he abandoned you all, and I have done my best to bring you up," Anatou will have told them.

'And when she sees Pylla, the Poullo who will have started courting her again, she will tell him how sorry she is she didn't marry him; she'll say her husband landed her with four kids and then left the lot of them ... No, I won't let them think of me as such an unnatural father, such a foolish husband. I must have the courage to be a worse criminal than I am. I killed out of anger; I will kill now for a much better reason. That may contradict everything I said, but it's proof that I am a man: a bundle of senseless contradictions. I must find a way of killing Anatou. After this crime I shall open my heart to all those near to me; and then, like Boullin, I shall give myself up to justice, if necessary. But my children, my poor old mother, Mariatou, Séitou and Camara will know how I came to kill a woman of Zounmin and why I was revenged on Anatou. Anatou must die. And so I must speak seriously with this man!' So Ahouna thought to himself. And once he had made this decision, he asked with an expression of pity and interest, 'You have children?'

'Yes, two toddlers.'

'I have four. The oldest will soon be twelve and the youngest two,' Ahouna said sadly and, as his tear-filled eyes gazed into the distance, he added, 'I would like to escape too, on account of my children and my poor mother ... but I have no illusions; such an attempt seems useless, doomed to failure.'

'Don't talk such nonsense. Despair has never saved anyone; on the contrary, anyone who gives way to despair is lost beyond redemption!' Houngbé replied firmly.

'You have not lived as I have lived. You have possibly

not loved as I have loved. And so, you have not been deceived by life and by Allah as I have been. When one has reached this point, one prefers indifference and complete emptiness to all the hopes of continuing existence that spring from certain people's talk.'

'There is no such thing as complete emptiness ... And besides, you dwell too much upon your past. What misfortune has befallen you that no one else has ever endured before you?'

'Take me with you, if you can!' declared Ahouna passionately.

'Be prepared to leave at all times. I will warn you as soon as I am sure of myself.'

At these words Ahouna was shaken with a violent fit of trembling; he lowered his head sadly and wept silently, from pity and grief, as if he had only just lost what he held most dear in the world. He gazed at Houngbé again, then they separated, having caught sight of Toupilly who did not like seeing them together ...

Houngbé was happy, convinced that he would be able to escape with Ahouna, if Fâ Aïdégoun's predictions were correct. Ahouna was happy too, at least at the idea that he would go and confess to his family before killing Anatou.

Mauthonier had been to visit me in Zado, and told me that the Zounmin people were out of luck, explaining about Houngbé's theft.

'Be on your guard! I know my countryfolk,' I had replied.

After I had told him at length of Ahouna's life, Mauthonier expressed the desire to write to Camara, simply to let him know that an unfortunate accident had befallen his brother-in-law, who was at that time still in Ganmê prison.

Camara informed Fanikata, and the two men set out for the south under the pretext that Ahouna had been found, wounded and ill. Ahouna's brother-in-law had read in three Cotonou newspapers, the *Dahomey Star*, the *Dahomey Lighthouse* and the *Dahomey Voice*, that an unidentified man from the northern regions, a savage, had murdered a woman, the mother of several children, who had been widowed for two years. Camara had paid no attention to this item of news. He never imagined that his brother-in-law, who had disappeared more than four months ago, had found his way to the south, where everyone was supposed to be clever and witty. He had never for one moment suspected Ahouna of getting involved in a brawl. Neither could Fanikata. He knew what his son-in-law had suffered because of Anatou's folly; his disappearance had caused him much sorrow and anxiety, and he had never given up looking for him in their own region ...

Houraï'nda had been dead for ten years, but one of his lorries took them as far as Bohicon where they caught the train. This journey with Camara was Fanikata's opportunity to tell Ahouna's brother-in-law of the moral climate in which Anatou and her husband had been living a few months previously.

'But that is madness! Ahouna is not the sort of man to be unfaithful to his wife!' exclaimed Camara indignantly.

'That's just what I couldn't make my daughter understand.'

'We could also have tried to convince her, if he had opened his heart to us.'

'Ahouna told me he didn't want to cause anyone any trouble. He even forbade me to speak to you about this, with the excuse that you had had enough sorrow in your own country and for nothing in the world would he have you regret your decision to come and live in his father's compound ... His mother would also have been very upset if he had told her about his troubles.'

'It's extremely sad,' murmured Camara.

'The harm is done, and we can do nothing more about it ... But what has happened to Ahouna? What can he have done that a police inspector writes to us about him? He's in prison and my daughter is responsible for all this!' said Fanikata dejectedly.

The two men hid their faces in their hands and remained so for the rest of their journey.

When they arrived about six o'clock that evening at

Ganmê station, they asked the first policeman they saw if he would take them to see Monsieur Mauthonier.

'Have you got a summons or an appointment to see him?' asked the man on duty.

'Yes, a letter inviting me to come and see my brother-in-law who has had an accident, it appears,' Camara replied in more correct French than the policeman. He was about to introduce Fanikata, but the latter intervened, declaring, 'I am an ex-soldier, Warrant-Officer Fanikata, father-in-law of the man who is in prison for reasons that we do not yet know,' he said, placing his hand on the military medals that he wore on his chest.

They set out for the prison and the constable, Houssou, asked them, 'What is the name of the man you are going to see?'

'Ahouna Bakari,' Camara replied.

Houssou started slightly and looked searchingly at the two men from the north, astonishment writ large in his deepset eyes.

They passed people who seemed in an extraordinary hurry, agitated, talking volubly. No one looked at the strangers; no one took any notice of his neighbour, nor of anything that was happening around them as they walked along Glélé street. Cars and bicycles overtook them at full speed, trios of young bare-headed European girls passed them whistling, or wriggling their bottoms in their printed cotton dresses. Fanikata darted a sly glance at them, remembering his escapades as a soldier in France, and smiled discreetly to himself. African youths and girls, in native dress or European clothes, walked hand in hand along the pavements, laughing.

'This is in truth the south, a typical southern town. Nothing has changed since I visited these turbulent southern regions several years ago. On the contrary, everything has got worse,' thought Fanikata. At this moment Houssou asked again if they really knew nothing of what had happened to Ahouna.

'Nothing at all,' Camara declared firmly.

'Then I'm sorry to tell you Ahouna Bakari is a

murderer,' he said coldly.

The two men from the north stopped dead, terror-struck. Houssou, too, was forced to stop.

'It's not true! He must have been falsely accused!' Camara said, suddenly haggard.

'Indeed, it can't be true! it's impossible!' declared Fanikata in great distress. 'My son-in-law has not the soul of a murderer, he isn't the type to do anything like that.'

'Nevertheless that's what he did. He killed a poor woman, a widow, and for reasons no one can find out. He's had a hard time since he came to Ganmê; he's been seriously ill. It's a good thing you've come to see him, for in two or three days at the latest he'll be taken to Ouidah, then to Cotonou and Porto-Novo, so that the people can see him, after which ...'

Houssou did not finish his sentence. Camara and Fanikata were no longer listening to him. The three men walked on. Suddenly Camara recalled the item he had read in the three Cotonou newspapers about a man from the north who had killed a woman, the mother of several children, for unknown reasons. The epithets 'barbarous', 'monstrous', employed by the *Dahomey Voice*, and which came from the pen of M. Santos, to describe the criminal, came back to Camara's mind. But he still wondered if this could really refer to Ahouna.

They reached the west gate of the prison, which led to the quarters occupied by Toupilly, Mauthonier and the prison chaplain, Father Dandou, as well as the iron-roofed building that housed the twenty-five policemen permanently employed as prison warders.

The three men crossed the courtyard with its beds of flowers and walked down a path covered with little white pebbles of equal size. Houssou rang at Mauthonier's door. The inspector's wife opened it; she was a handsome Neapolitan, with a head of very black, rebellious hair, that was continually escaping from the bun into which it was caught back. Houssou saluted and asked, 'Is Inspector Mauthonier at home, please, madam?'

'He is with the chaplain,' she replied with a pleasant little smile.

They walked over to Father Dandou's lodge; Houssou rang again and the priest himself answered the door. The policeman saluted.

'Good evening, Father; these two men are looking for Inspector Mauthonier.'

'Thank you, Houssou. Monsieur Mauthonier is with me.'

The two visitors entered and the policeman left.

Mauthonier rose from his armchair where he had been sitting discussing with Father Dandou and me the article 'The Meaning of Death' that I had given them to read in the course of the week. He gazed at the two men from the north, after shaking hands with them cordially; he then said, identifying each of them correctly, 'I'm very glad you have come. You must be Monsieur Camara; and you, Monsieur Fanikata, poor Ahouna's father-in-law.'

The two men looked at him in astonishment.

'I too am very pleased to make your acquaintance,' I said. 'Don't be surprised that the inspector recognised you so easily. Ahouna loves you both dearly. He adores his mother and his children, his sister Madame Camara and her children; he told me so much about you all. I'm not sure that he doesn't still love Anatou, in spite of all the harm she has done him. Ahouna talked to me about you at such length and in such detail that we feel we have already met you,' I explained in a voice which betrayed my sadness, in spite of myself.

Fanikata looked down; Camara tried to control the tears which misted over his eyes.

'It seems that he committed a murder,' murmured Fanikata in a trembling voice.

'Yes, alas! ... He killed a woman, a widow. Oh! it was not a premeditated crime: Ahouna was driven past endurance by the crisis that his wife unleashed in his heart, hypersensitive man that he is,' Mauthonier said.

'It's not possible, it's quite impossible for Ahouna to have killed anyone!' declared Camara, rebelling at the thought.

'Alas! my poor Monsieur Camara, I understand your feeling only too well, but this is unfortunately exactly what he did do,' Mauthonier replied thoughtfully.

'I find it hard to believe. My son-in-law doesn't look like a bad man; he hasn't got the soul of a criminal,' Fanikata repeated.

'That's true; nothing about him would have led one to suppose that he would ever turn into the man he is today,' I said. Meanwhile Father Dandou, who had asked them to take a seat, repeated his invitation.

'It's not worth sitting down. We know no one in this town and we don't yet know where we are going to spend the night,' Camara said.

I would have liked to invite them, but where could I put them up in a town where I was staying with friends? Father Dandou offered them his hospitality.

'Don't worry, you can sleep at my place,' he said; adding immediately, 'You know there is no such thing as a criminal soul. He whom you call Allah and we call God created all men with good souls, and I refuse to believe that Ahouna's soul is wicked.'

'Could we see Ahouna?' Camara asked.

'It's seven o'clock, too late to visit the prisoners, but you'll see him tomorrow,' Mauthonier answered. He immediately telephoned Toupilly, who arrived five minutes later.

'He's a peculiar creature, your Ahouna, a potential monster. We've got criminals here who've committed murders for what one might call justifiable reasons. But your miserable Ahouna – he's a mystery. He opened what he calls his heart to Monsieur Houénou, who told Inspector Mauthonier and Father Dandou about him. They've all let me know what they've gathered and from this I deduce, as one would say in France, that this sublimely sensitive man, this hypersensitive person, is a psychological monster. He doesn't want a lawyer to defend him, but I've found one for him. But it's useless to hold out false hopes: Ahouna is a lost cause. Either he'll be executed, or he'll be condemned to penal servitude here for life,' declared Toupilly, gesticulating like a voodoo priest in a trance.

This heartless volubility shocked us all, and deeply upset

Camara and Fanikata, who lowered their eyes.

'Goodbye, gentlemen. I'm on duty. The weather is damned stormy and I must do my rounds,' he added.

Mauthonier shook hands with Father Dandou, with me and with the two northerners, muttering angrily to himself as he thought of Toupilly, 'Barbarian!', then he joined his wife and children who were waiting for him for dinner.

'That man may be sincere, but he's insulting,' murmured Fanikata, ruminating on the commissioner's words as I left the lodge.

Chapter 17

There was not a star to be seen. The sky was black as if painted with pitch. It was deep into the night and, as far as I can recall, it was impossible to see anything, even two yards ahead. It was extraordinarily sultry, with not a breath of air stirring the leaves of the trees in the prison yard. Dead silence reigned, broken only by the squeaking of the excited bats.

As usual, the warders had taken all the prisoners back to their cells after the evening meal and had stayed with them until Hounnoukpo and the police sergeants came to lock up.

Toupilly was now doing his rounds, a dazzling torch in one hand and a revolver in the other. Like the bats, he seemed excited, nervy; so, contrary to his habit, he went hurriedly from door to door. Stout, heavy-jowled, prematurely bald, he was hurrying because Solange, his secretary, who was also his mistress, had been waiting for him for the last half hour in his quarters.

He leaned against each door to make sure that it was closed, and gave it a good kick; then the occupant of each cell shouted 'present' and Commissioner Toupilly went off to repeat these stupid operations at the next cell. When he finally finished, out of breath, he stopped for a moment, breathed deeply, hitched up his trousers and went off to inspect the corridor, about six feet wide, which ran between the outer wall and the back of the long dormitory which was divided into cubicles. This inspection was also ridiculous, as there was never anything in this corridor. But as Toupilly walked through it that evening his foot struck against a long pole with a little sickle at the end. It was one of the instruments used to pick ripe fruit in the prison yard, before the birds and the bats could get at it.

This pole had no right to be in this place. Who had left it there? This was never discovered. Toupilly was annoyed; he seized the pole and hung it angrily against the wall, instead of taking it to the toolshed or calling a warder. He rapidly finished his round and joined Solange.

The gods would not exercise over men's fates more power than they actually possess if men did not do their bit towards making them powerful. Houngbé believed in the gods of Zounmin and counted the days. Before giving himself up to the police he had had a master-key made locally and had hidden it in a little pocket sewn to the crotch of his trousers. For the last three nights he had left his cell between midnight and one o'clock, crawled to number 59, opened the door with extreme precaution and whispered a few words to Ahouna to prove that he could get access to any cell and that he would escape when the opportune day came.

That night Houngbé left his cell. He was surprised by the thick darkness, but he was pleased, for this favoured his project. He crawled to number 59, opened the door and indicated to Ahouna to wait for him, to be ready to follow him if all went well. Although he was mortally afraid at the sudden thought that perhaps he would not see the serpent, he continued to crawl towards the outer wall and entered the corridor. But once there, he wondered for the first time – so great his faith in the oracle's predictions had been – 'How shall I be able to make use of a serpent to climb a wall this height? A serpent? It's ridiculous!'

His hand brushed against the end of the pole; he pulled it away hastily, and drew back slightly; his heart was beating wildly and he was sweating like a cauldron. If he had stopped to think for a moment, he would have realised that the object he had touched did not move and so could not be alive. His only preoccupation was to discover whether or not the oracle's prediction would be fulfilled that night, which, according to Fâ Aïdégoun, was the last one that he would spend in this prison. If he did not get out, he would have to sit out his ridiculous sentence as a pretended thief.

Houngbé, all a-tremble, most carefully stretched out his hand again towards the object, touched it again and it did not move. He felt it all over, realised its hardness, its solidity, its efficacity for the operation he was now going to undertake. He was ashamed of his panic, of his anxiety, of his trembling, of the sweat that continued to stream down his body, and he nearly burst out laughing.

He quickly made his way back to Ahouna and told him to follow him. Ahouna obeyed. He would see his children again, he would see his old mother Mariatou again; he would see Camara, Séitou and their children. He would kill Anatou.

At that moment a distant gleam of light filtered between the foliage of the trees. The two men sensed rather than saw it. They huddled rapidly against the wall alongside which they were crawling, but they soon realised it was only the light of the rising moon. It announced the dawn of a new day. Far away, the crowing of a cock re-echoed through the air. Ahouna thought it must be one or two in the morning.

They reached the place where the pole hung. Houngbé made a sign to Ahouna to climb up, and he did as he was bid. At the top of the wall he tore his hands on the broken glass, but he took no notice of the gashes. He felt so pleased at the thought that he would soon be out of prison. He sat for a moment and then jumped, cruelly tearing the flesh of his buttocks. His blood flowed along the wall, but he still took no notice. He was happy; he was free; he would go and kill Anatou. Houngbé was already beside him, after also shedding his blood, but less seriously, on the wicked prison wall.

They were now free of the prison grounds, in a teak wood that bordered the northeast side of the prison. They walked quickly, side by side, like two good friends. Suddenly three fellows wheeling a bicycle emerged from a corner of the wood and surrounded them. Houngbé recognised his three nephews and ranged himself on their side.

For the last five nights they had been coming, between midnight and half past three, to wander in the precincts of the prison, wondering what they would do if the oracle's predictions were not fulfilled.

Snares without End

Then the four rebels from Zounmin seized hold of Ahouna.

'But they are your friends?' he asked Houngbé in terror.

'Silence, murderer!' Houngbé whispered to him.

One of them started to stuff a bunch of straw in his mouth. All his hopes suddenly vanished and he was again seized with despair, overwhelmed once more with the conviction that there was no possible thing to live for. He spoke to them in a curiously gentle voice, in which there was no trace of sadness, nor regret, nor any intention of arousing their pity.

'You don't have to worry. I surrender completely. I'll not make a sound.'

These words greatly surprised them. They even thought them an impertinence, and each one of them in turn hit out at him. But they did not gag him.

They threw him on the ground and bound him from head to foot; then they tied him securely inside a sort of wicker cradle big enough to hold a grown man. These huge baskets, that the Fons call *akôkô*, are used to carry pigs to market for sale.

They then hoisted him, bundled up like this, on to the carrier of the bicycle that belonged to Houinsou, Kinhou's eldest son, covered him with an old sack and went on.

They took a path across the bush, and then other short cuts through the long grass that was drenched with dew, which got them back to Zounmin about two hours after they left the teak wood.

They put down their sinister bundle. They rapidly shaved each other's heads, as if for the ceremony marking the end of a period of mourning, as Fâ Aïdégoun had ordered. Without wasting a second they erected a stake, unfastened the bundle containing Ahouna and immediately bound him to the stake with a long chain, which must have cost them a pretty penny. Then they piled faggots high around the funeral pyre that it fell to Houngbé to light, so setting the seal on his part in the exploit.

The fire began to burn; the wood crackled; the flames

rose up, now red, now a bright blue, licking round Ahouna's feet. But he did not move, did not speak. Was he already dead, or did he still live? The flames rose higher and he saw his children, terrified, in tears, with his nephews and nieces, his old mother Mariatou, Séitou, Camara, Ibayâ and Fanikata, all weeping. He was sad, unhappy that they had to witness this terrible, inhuman, monstrous sight. Soon his tattered boubou was devoured in the flames which burnt his eyebrows and his hair. At this moment he saw Anatou in the midst of their children and he murmured in great distress, 'Anatou!'

Then, like a photographic negative, the image of his wife was printed on his strangely dilated pupils, and anyone who could have got near to him would have verified the truth of this phenomenon.

'He's speaking!' said Tôvignon.

'He's a tough type,' said Houéfa.

'You mean a monster?' asked Houinsou.

'Well, we're free at last; our vengeance is satisfied!' said Houngbé, as they sat round in a circle, where a few weeks ago they had had their last argument with old Dâko, and now they watched the body of Ahouna Bakari consumed by the flames.

At four in the morning, when the convicts were wakened to be taken to the quarries, confusion broke out among the prison officers. Sergeant Hounnoukpo crossed the courtyard, littered with the damaged fruit dropped there during the night by the bats. As he made his way towards the cells, with his heavy bunch of keys, he noticed that two of them were wide open ... Terribly surprised, he hurried to ring at Toupilly's door. The commissioner shouted and swore angrily, 'What the hell's the matter?'

He was furious at being interrupted so early, when he was just making love to Solange, a very pretty, slender Dahomean girl, well bred and sufficiently well educated to be both his secretary and one of his mistresses. Hounnoukpo hurried to one of the windows of the residence, that he knew was near Toupilly's bed. In great agitation he apologised for bothering his superior, but he had just found Houngbé's and Ahouna's cells wide open.

'What? What the hell are you talking about?' yelled Toupilly, by no means in a hurry to get out of bed.

'Yes sir, number 33 and number 59 are open and there's no one there!' the sergeant insisted.

'You must have left them open last night then,' retorted Toupilly, still in Solange's arms.

'No, I locked them, sir. Otherwise you would have found them open, as you must have done your rounds after I locked up,' Hounnoukpo replied, unanswerably.

He then went and rang at Mauthonier's door. The inspector himself opened and was told the news. Mystified at the turn of events, he dressed hastily, took a torch and his revolver and followed the sergeant. Meanwhile Toupilly was simmering with anger at having to leave Solange.

'Damn and blast! To bloody hell with this rotten country! Forgive me, Solange my pet! I'm very fond of you, but you do live in a helluva god-forsaken country!'

He joined Mauthonier and Hounnoukpo who had already discovered the pole hanging on the wall.

'They'll drive us all mad, these damn niggers!' he yelled.

'We don't know yet how they managed to unlock the two doors, but this is what they used to scale the wall.'

Toupilly looked closer and pointed out the blood stains on the wall.

'The bastards! Can you just imagine!' he shouted. Then he suddenly remembered how he had stumbled against the pole and how, in his irritation and hurry to join Solange, he had hung it on the wall where it now confronted him. Should he admit that he was partly responsible for Ahouna's and Houngbé's escape? He turned sharply away; if the fugitives were capable of opening their cells, they could also manage to do the same for the toolshed and get this pole out.

'We haven't a moment to waste,' he said. 'Hounnoukpo, call ten of your men; take your revolvers and follow me on your motorbikes. Mauthonier, you stay here. It's a pity Inspector Gantché is still ill and can't come with me. In any case, none of the other cells must be opened.' Then he suddenly had a sort of revelation, but as he was not a genius, and even less a saint, it was the kind of revelation that occasionally occurs to fools, and he added, 'Where are the two northerners?'

'They stayed the night at Father Dandou's!' Mauthonier said.

'I daren't make any definite accusation, but the fact that Ahouna escaped the very night they arrived seems most suspicious to me and extremely worrying.'

'They haven't seen Ahouna yet.'

'I know, I know ... but arrest them just the same!'

'Really, Toupilly. That's quite unreasonable.'

'Oh, you always take the niggers' part. You don't know them. I'm telling you, your belief in God won't help you to understand them and their black hearts, neither will all your psychology.'

'Don't let's stand here arguing. The main thing is to find the fugitives!' replied Mauthonier curtly.

'All right! keep your hair on. Please go and tell those two men to come over to us, with the chaplain. Oh! that man! Everything's gone wrong since that Dandou started interfering in our business. It's because of him that Affognon committed suicide. Who knows if he didn't have a hand in Ahouna's escape? And then there's that other idiot of a sociologist or archaeologist, another buggering nuisance!'

'I'll bring them all to you straight away. But please don't slander anyone. You go off to Zounmin; I'll look after everything here.'

Father Dandou came with his guests. Camara was carrying a little bundle which contained a boubou for Ahouna, as well as his kpété and his tôba.

Warned by Mauthonier of what had occurred, I turned up too. We were all dumbfounded at the news of Ahouna's escape, but no one had time to ask any questions.

'Follow me!' the commissioner ordered.

Outside the policemen were waiting with their motorcycles. The priest, the two northerners and myself were taken by four of them on their pillions and the procession moved off with Hounnoukpo in the lead and Toupilly last but one.

The beams from the headlamps cut through the darkness, which was no longer so dense now that the moon had climbed high in the sky. When we had done about twenty miles at full speed along a high road, we branched off on to a narrow path which led to Zounmin, about a mile and a half away. Half way to the farm we could see flames rising up in the air.

'The bastards! They've set fire to the farm! Go faster!' said Toupilly.

We quickly reached Zounmin and were astonished to find four men busy trying to put out the fire.

Hounnoukpo immediately recognised one of them in spite of his recently shaven head; he seized hold of him and ordered his mates to grab hold of the other three, who were promptly handcuffed.

'Are you sure this is Houngbé?' asked Toupilly.

'Yes, sir!' replied Hounnoukpo, who then asked the fugitive where Ahouna was.

Houngbé, expressionless, knowing the game was up, turned his head towards the stake, now reduced to ashes, from which a penetrating, sickening, indefinable smell arose.

'You've burnt him! cried the sergeant.

'Yes.'

'What have they done with him?' asked Toupilly.

'They've burnt him,' I answered, rooted to the spot, a prey to emotions to which I am still at a loss to give a name.

At first Toupilly could not believe his ears. He approached the pile of ashes, still red and smoking, and saw the pitiful truth. Horrified, completely bowled over, he seemed to be thrown into a sort of terrible nightmare, not knowing what to do with the murderers. He walked round and round, muttering, 'Good God! Good God! They've burnt him, the bastards! Bastards! What a set of bastards!'

'Our last hut's on fire!' shouted Houéfa, gesticulating with his handcuffed hands.

'Let it burn!' retorted Hounnoukpo.

The flames rose into the air, blazing furiously, to rival the day which was dawning brighter. And so the meaning of the last of Fâ Aïdégoun's cryptic prophecies became clear: 'Then, a short time after their departure from prison, vengeance will be satisfied, as the day breaks over Zounmin.'

Motionless before the pile of ashes, Father Dandou wept silently like a child in disgrace.

Camara and Fanikata, as soon as they were capable of movement, took two long sticks that lay at the foot of the wild fig tree, and with heavy hearts they began to scrape out of the embers, with pious, scrupulous care, the bones of their brother-in-law and son-in-law. When they had finished this operation, they made a little heap of the bones, on to which Fanikata poured the remainder of the water that the rebels had used to shave their heads and which they found in a calabash at the foot of the fig tree.

Camara untied the little bundle that he was carrying, took out the boubou and spread it on the ground. Then, his eyes blinded by tears that he could no longer control, he placed the bones with trembling hands on the garment, together with the kpété and the tôba, tied up the bundle again and picked it up.

When he got back to the police station, Toupilly told Mauthonier what had occurred and ended his account with a rain of blows about Houngbé's ears.

'Who would have believed it, Mauthonier? This bastard got himself into prison to avenge Madame Kinhou's death and he had a master-key fixed to his penis! It's incredible! Oh! the monster! I'll have you all hanged!'

Mauthonier said I had been right when I had told him not to trust Houngbé and, turning to Toupilly, he added, 'Let's rather try to turn them to some use. We've been at war for the last eight months and France needs soldiers. You'll see this as soon as you read your mail,' he said, looking at the four murderers, still aghast.

'Good idea! We'll inform the Ministry of Justice and the Ministry of Defence. They will manage to get some advantage out of this gang of monsters.'

'Papgunaïkopoulos came back from Cotonou yesterday. Gamard is still with his regiment. We can talk to them today so that we can be rid as soon as possible of these folk with their inscrutable souls,' Mauthonier said.

'Quite right!' approved Toupilly, then, turning to Camara and Fanikata, asked, 'What are you going to do with these bones?'

'Is there a train for Bohicon?' Camara asked as if in a dream.

'Yes, there's a train at eleven, in an hour's time,' I replied.

'We are going back to Kiniba,' said Camara, 'where we shall bury Ahouna's bones and his musical instruments at the foot of Mount Kinibaya.'

Caraf Books
Caribbean and African Literature
Translated from French

Serious writing in French in the Caribbean and Africa has developed unique characteristics in this century. Colonialism was its crucible; African independence in the 1960s its liberating force. The struggles of nation-building and even the constraints of neocolonialism have marked the coming of age of literatures that now gradually distance themselves from the common matrix.

CARAF BOOKS is a collection of novels, plays, poetry, and essays from the regions of the Caribbean and the African continent that have shared this linguistic, cultural, and political heritage while working out their new identity against a background of conflict.

An original feature of the CARAF BOOKS collection is the substantial critical introduction in which a scholar who knows the literature well sets each book in its cultural context and makes it accessible to the student and the general reader.

Most of the books selected for the CARAF collection are being published in English for the first time; some are important books that have been out of print in English or were first issued in editions with a limited distribution. In all cases CARAF BOOKS offers the discerning reader new wine in new bottles!

The Editorial Board of CARAF BOOKS consists of A. James Arnold, University of Virginia, General Editor; Kandioura Dramé, University of Virginia, Associate Editor; and two Consulting Editors, Abiola Irele of the University of Ibadan, Nigeria, and J. Michael Dash of the University of the West Indies in Mona, Jamaica.

Guillaume Oyônô-Mbia and Seydou Badian, *Faces of African
    Independence: Three Plays*
Olympe Bhêly-Quénum, *Snares without End*